The Legends of King Arthur : Book 1

THE FIRST ROUND TABLE

Inspired by Arthurian Legend

By Ben Gillman

Editor: Nick Bowman

Cover Credit: Fiona Jayde Media

For Vered

who makes me feel like a king everyday

FOREWORD

"This is the oath of a Knight of King Arther's Round Table and should be for all of us to take to heart. I will develop my life for the greater good. I will place character above riches, and concern for others above personal wealth, I will never boast, but cherish humility instead, I will speak the truth at all times, and forever keep my word, I will defend those who cannot defend themselves, I will honor and respect women, and refute sexism in all its guises, I will uphold justice by being fair to all, I will be faithful in love and loyal in friendship, I will abhor scandals and gossip-neither partake nor delight in them, I will be generous to the poor and to those who need help, I will forgive when asked, that my own mistakes will be forgiven, I will live my life with courtesy and honor from this day forward."
-Sir Thomas Malory,

Le Morte d'Arthur: King Arthur and the Legends of the Round Table

TABLE OF CONTENTS

PROLOGUE
Of Myths and Legends

For over two hundred years, the mighty castle Tintagel stood strong, regal and majestic for it was able to withstand any attack by man or army.

But not by a dragon.

To be fair, dragons hadn't been seen in the lands of Briton for nearly a century. Not a single one had been spotted in the skies. There hadn't been any rumors of sleeping dragons beneath murky swamps or sodden quagmires. Nary a goat had been swooped off under mysterious circumstances that could only be attributed to the behavior of a hungry dragon. The danger of dragons seemed to have passed, and a collective sigh of relief had been shared amongst all the people throughout the lands. Contrary to popular belief, however, the reptilian beasts weren't defeated by crusading knights, for even the bravest of warrior had trouble slaying a full-grown dragon. The monsters had no points of weakness other than their eyes, and it was nearly impossible to get past their teeth in order to reach that small point of frailty. More than a few knights had lost limbs or their very lives in various schemes to strike a dragon at its point of ocular weakness. Dealings with dragons simply never ended well.

To give knights their due credit, however, they had successfully driven out the sphinxes so that those beasts now mostly took up residence in the deserts far to the east. Similarly, the chimeras, who once were quite a menace, had been cast out and forced to return to their original homes in Greece. The brave chivalrous knights of the land had, despite terrible dangers, successfully managed to whittle down the numbers of ogres, trolls, and giants. Some of those daunting creatures still popped up from time to time, but it was much less often than during the darkest of days, and on the odd occasion that one of those monsters did appear, knights had become fairly adept at dealing with the menace.

Nonetheless, the knights' aptitude for conquering beasts and monsters had never fully extended to the realm of dragons. Towering over fifty feet high, with fangs as long as a man's arm, razor-sharp talons and a powerful barbed tail, dragons were a foe that no one had adequately found a way of dealing with. Which is why the people who resided in those lands were most relieved when a curious bit of luck saved them.

The knights had recently set their attentions to conquering the mammoths after a particularly nasty incident where a stampede of an entire herd had left a small town in ruins. These gargantuan beasts had a nasty habit of stomping on pigs with their massive feet, and skewering bulls with their long twisty tusks, not to mention the devastating effects of the icy blasts that erupted from their hairy trunks whenever they sneezed. It had all become such a problem that a boisterous band of knavish knights led by the all-mighty and alliterative Ambrosius Aurelianus created a great mammoth drive that urged the entire herd up to the last vestiges of an ancient land bridge across the Atlantic. Ambrosius and his knights spooked the thundering herd enough so that they charged across the land bridge, causing it to collapse beneath their massive weight with every thundering step they took. The herd was last seen vanishing into the distance as they headed west and became the problem of whatever people happened to be living in the Americas at the time.

What no one had realized then was that the mammoth, with its generous bulk and expansive stores of fat, had become a preferred meal for a fully-mature dragon. It took a lot to sustain a reptile that weighed nearly a hundred tons and expended massive amounts of energy with flying and breathing fire and general rampaging. Of course, the dragons tried to find other food sources, but after having developed a taste for mammoth, they found sheep to be too hairy, and cows not hairy enough.

As a natural consequence of its chief source of food being gone, and waning support from the other beasts and monsters that were being steadily dispersed, the number of dragons slowly dwindled. It had now been nearly a hundred years since anyone had seen one of the scaly, yellow-eyed creatures. It was supposed that there weren't more than a dozen dragons still alive, and many people suspected they were gone altogether. Sure, there had been persistent rumors that King Uther Pendragon kept one as a pet, but most sensible people ignored that as simply clever propaganda. In fact, over the past several decades more and more people were beginning to doubt whether dragons had ever existed at all. It's a funny thing how what was once considered fact can drift so quickly into the territory of mere rumor and eventually fade into the realm of murky legend. Dragons rapidly became nothing more than common characters in children's stories. The truth was melded with the fiction until no one was really able to distinguish which was which anymore. Nor did it really matter. Dragons could be used as convenient nighttime story villains to cajole tiny children to stay in their beds until sunrise. Or they could be cast as noble, misunderstood beasts of legend used by allegorically-inclined poets to inspire the masses. They could even be portrayed as frolicking whimsical creatures used by folk singers to metaphorically represent something different altogether, even though that was generally considered to be downright silly. It honestly didn't matter if the stories were true or not, because the question of whether or not dragons truly existed, or if they were being properly portrayed as they actually were, became unimportant. It was the stories themselves that had become important now, and the lessons and themes that they sought to evoke. The fact was, in the hearts and minds of the common folk, the threat of dragons was gone. And it made absolutely no difference whether or not dragons were as dangerous as the old stories said, or in fact whether dragons were even real at all.

Except they were real.

And they were extremely dangerous.

And one was now laying waste to the once impenetrable Tintagel Castle.

This Red Dragon seemed particularly fierce. Who could say where it was getting its food source, because it looked fully grown, robust, and ferocious. Its leathery wings spread out to their fullest span and were nearly wide enough to wrap around an entire wall of the expansive castle. Its powerful barbed tail was spiked with ten-foot-long spears, and it was strong enough to crush entire towers with a single flick. And the dragon seemed to have no end to its fire.

The poor bowmen who had been stationed on the castle's defensive walls didn't stand a chance. Their arrows, which were made to pierce armor, bounced uselessly off of the thick hide of the Red Dragon. Even the best of them didn't have the skill to successfully avoid the twisting bull horns that protruded from this particular dragon's head and so hit it in the eye. All that their volleys of arrows served to do was make the dragon aware of their presence, and that was singularly bad for them. The massive beast would twist in the air, turn its great head at them, draw its breath and let loose a flood of fire. Most of the bowmen were able to survive behind their shields, but it confirmed their worst fears that this was a hopeless losing battle. It wasn't long before even the bravest men dropped their bows and shields, abandoned their posts, and ran for their lives. Up until that dark night, some of the men had wholeheartedly believed that dragons were simply imaginary creatures. Some had thought that dragons still existed but would never show their ugly heads again. Some had been convinced that dragons couldn't have possibly been as bad as the old stories claimed. But now, as they all fled their stations from the onslaught of the terrible beast, there was one thing they all agreed upon:

This was very different from the legend they thought they knew.

~   ~   ~

CHAPTER 1

The Siege of Tintagel

Inside the grand throne room, the dragon's fire flickered through the multicolored glass of a towering window and illuminated the face of a beautiful young man with pale blue eyes and golden hair. Arthur was seventeen years old, and although he stood within an arm's reach of the throne, he was quickly coming to the painful realization that he wouldn't be sitting on that majestic golden chair anytime soon. Just outside, the sounds of chaos rang clearly through the night. There were the shrieks from the Red Dragon itself, but also the war cries of the invading army of Saxons who were insistently pounding at the gates and scaling the mighty castle walls. There was the rumble of thunder and the crashing of lightning in the tumultuous storm. And there were screams of terror from the many thousands of people who had called Tintagel their home. Arthur knew that most of those people, like himself, were in very real danger of losing their place in the world tonight.

Despite the tumult and destruction outside, Arthur couldn't bring himself to think that all was lost. The simple reason for his stubborn hope was the beautiful girl who stood steadfast at his side. Guinevere had been born just a few short months after Arthur, and they had been nearly inseparable ever since. She was slim and lovely with pale skin and a crown of elaborate braids woven around her oval-shaped head. Whenever they were inside the castle, and she was in the midst of her many handmaidens, Guinevere had her hair perfectly attended to, and pulled and prodded into a dizzying assortment of careful knots and twists that gave her an air of absolute composure and grace. But Arthur vastly preferred to see her with her hair down. He loved seeing that long, shiny brown hair tumbling free and flying in unpredictable directions. From the time when they were children, they would steal horses and ride out across the plains, or they would sneak up to the highest towers where the wind blew strongest, and Arthur loved to gaze upon Guinevere's hair shaking wild and unfettered. He was unlikely to get a glimpse of it again anytime soon.

The hideous profile of the Red Dragon sailed past one of the ornate stain-glassed windows, and Arthur saw the fear that crept over Guinevere's face. The boy-who-was-meant-to-be-king took the lady-who-was-to-be-his-queen's hand and laced their fingers together. He wanted to tell her that everything would be all right. He wanted to tell her that he'd always keep her safe. He wanted to tell her that very soon the world would be at peace again and everything would make sense.

Instead, Arthur said weakly, "This isn't how I imagined finally getting you alone."

Almost instantly, his face flushed scarlet and he was secretly glad that the throne room was dark and empty so that it was possible that Guinevere wouldn't notice. He had been taught by the greatest swordsmen in the land on how to wield a blade. He had

15

been instructed by the most expert riders on how to mount a steed. He had been tutored on military tactics, and international politics, and even the mystical workings of the magical arts. Yet somehow, no one ever managed to teach him how to talk to the girl he liked without sounding like a complete fool.

"Don't worry yourself," said Guinevere as she squeezed Arthur's hand. "At least there's a roaring fire."

Arthur laughed. Even though the world as they knew it might be ending, she could still make him laugh. God, he wanted to kiss her. The thought leapt into his mind, and refused to yield. Arthur suddenly found his breath had become husky and his throat became dry as he imagined leaning forward and brushing her soft red lips with his own. He resisted the urge, however. There was a way that things were done; he'd been instructed about it for all of his seventeen worldly years. One day he would be king, and she would be his queen, and then he could kiss her and feast upon her beauty to his heart's delight. That day was still far off, though, and he'd have to wait for the proper time. Arthur knew that it was the right thing to do. Definitely the right thing to do. Absolutely the right thing to do...

But that didn't make things any easier.

After all, he was still seventeen, and young people do have certain, undeniable urges.

"We'll be all right, won't we?" asked Guinevere, and her voice came out small and trembling.

Arthur turned to her, took her hands into his and gazed into her warm, brown eyes as he said, "Through fire or storm, I will always be there for you."

He may not have been taught how to talk to women, but sometimes Arthur excelled on his own. Guinevere could've melted right then and there.

Arthur knew that now was his moment. Damn his royal training. Damn the rules of lords and ladies. Damn the proper moment. He leaned in. His warm breath caressed her soft lips, and he could smell the sweet scent of lilacs as he inched toward her.

Closer. Closer. Closer...

But it was not to be.

The mighty oak doors of the throne room crashed open and three older men rushed in. Arthur's father, King Uther Pendragon, dressed for battle in his armor flecked with gold and adorned with the twisting family crest that depicted a majestic white dragon, led the way. At his heels were old Leodegrance, Guinevere's silver-haired father who shuffled along as quickly as his stiff bones would carry him, and Sir Aggravaine, a massive, hulking, beast of a knight.

Arthur wished they could have waited a few more moments.

The King looked to his son and boomed, "Arthur, thank God. We've got to get you out of here."

"Father, I won't leave Guinevere," Arthur said. "I want to keep her by my side. We can protect her, and we—"

But Guinevere stepped up beside him and silenced him immediately with a simple, soft touch of his shoulder. He didn't want to hear what she had to say even though he already knew that she was right. She would be safer if she left him. He was the son of the king, and the rightful heir to the throne, which meant he was a target, and she would be a target as long as she was with him. As much as Arthur hated to admit it, Guinevere was in more danger with him than away from him.

"Arthur, it will be all right," she said. "Sir Aggravaine has always protected me. My father and I will be safe."

She motioned to the towering, bald-headed form of Sir Aggravaine, who curled a lip in the closest thing he could muster to a smile. Then Guinevere took Arthur's hand, and she gently placed something into it. Arthur felt the soft lump and opened his palm to see a lovely embroidered handkerchief bearing Guinevere's family crest with an exquisite "G" nestled in the center.

"Come for me just as quickly as you can," she said, "And when you do, you can return this."

"I promise," said Arthur.

The young lovers touched hands one last time. Then old Leodegrance took Guinevere's shoulder and led her away. The old man and his daughter followed the imposing form of Sir Aggravaine. They quickly crossed the throne room, opened a small door off of the chamber's wall, and were gone. Arthur watched them go with a heavy pit in his stomach. But his father stepped up beside him and placed a heavy hand on Arthur's shoulder. It was meant to be a reassuring gesture, but Arthur couldn't seem to muster that particular feeling at the moment.

"You'll get her back," said King Uther as he patted his son's shoulder, "just as you left her."

~ ~ ~

As the rain poured down and turned Tintagel's central courtyard to mud, a small contingent of knights stood at the ready and faced the twenty-foot-tall wooden gate that was the primary access point into the castle at large.

Boom. Boom! BOOM!

The wooden gate rattled and cracked but didn't give way. And yet secretly, Sir Lancelot was hoping that it soon would. Despite being one of the younger knights at only twenty-four years of age, Lancelot had already built himself quite the impressive resume. He had won dozens of tournaments, he had slain countless monsters, and his skills with a sword were unparalleled. Without a doubt, Lancelot was the one knight who was always ready for a skirmish, and even more than that, he was always convinced that he would emerge victorious. And victorious he always seemed to be, whether it was against his enemies, or with the ladies. As prodigious as he had become in battle, his reputation with women was quickly becoming just as legendary. It helped that he was impossibly handsome. He had a broad powerful chest, and thick muscular arms. His jaw was square, and it housed a collection of perfect teeth that defied the medieval times with their shocking whiteness. All in all, things had been going just right for Lancelot for quite a while now, and he had no reason to believe they were going to change anytime soon. Nonetheless, despite all of Lancelot's varied accolades, there was one glaring omission that was currently staring him in the face.

He had never defeated a conquering army.

But he was now ready to add that to his list of accomplishments.

Lancelot stood at the front of the contingent of several dozen knights who had been assigned to defend the castle's main gate. At his side was Sir Percival, and the differences between the two men couldn't be more apparent. Lancelot was tall and strong, while Percival was on the smaller side and not exactly imposing. To his credit, Percival had always been quite good as a tactician, but now that they were bound for battle, it was Lancelot who was in his element.

"L-Lancelot, it's hopeless!" stammered Percival. "Vortigern's men are pouring in from all sides. And they've got a d-d-dragon!"

But Lancelot laughed as he said, "I know, I know, I want to slay the dragon too. But first things first, we do our duty to the King—" and now his voice erupted into a roaring bellow, "AND CUT DOWN EVERY MAN THAT COMES THROUGH THIS GATE!"

For a moment, the pounding on the gate actually stopped.

But only for a moment.

Boom. Boom! BOOM!

"Well, you can't say I didn't warn them," said Lancelot with a shrug.

Suddenly, with a crash, the gate was ripped to splinters. Lancelot grinned as he moved his feet into fighting position, lifted his sword, and prepared to add a new verse to the inevitable song that would one day be written about him.

Lancelot was doomed to disappointment.

Although he was prepared to put his life on the line, and battle for fame and glory, his brothers in arms didn't share in his enthusiasm. As the invading Saxons ripped and tore their way through the gate, it quickly became clear that the small contingent of knights was going to be easily outnumbered. Add to that the terror of the Red Dragon that soared above them, and it was Percival's bravery that gave out first, quickly followed by all of his fellow knights. The slim, nervous Percival dropped his sword, and the other knights quickly did likewise. Lancelot could barely believe his eyes as he watched these once courageous men turn tail and run.

With barely a backward glance, Percival cried, "I'm s-s-sorry, Lancelot. I'm sorry..."

Lancelot, alone, stood fast. His face dropped into a frown for the briefest moment, but then he reminded himself that he was the mighty Sir Lancelot. He was the greatest knight in the land. Probably in the world. There was nothing that he couldn't overcome. As he took a deep breath and filled his massive chest, he was warmed by the fact that if there was anyone who could single-handedly take on an entire army, it was he.

"Right then," he said, "I'll do it myself."

And with that, he raised his sword and braced himself for the oncoming horde.

~   ~   ~

Uther Pendragon charged along the high battlements that ran atop the castle walls. He knew it was a terrible risk, that this path was exposed to attack, not to mention the fact that there was currently a dragon soaring overhead. However, it was a risk that Uther felt he must take considering that this was the most direct route to a series of secret tunnels that snaked through the castle and led to a hidden exit. Uther's greatest concern now was for the small band of people that followed at his heels. Chief among them was his own son, Arthur. As he ran, Uther scanned the castle's perimeter and saw that the Saxon army had breached the front gates and were beginning their steady invasion of the courtyard. The beleaguered king hoped that his knights were able to hold them off, but he secretly worried they couldn't possibly prevail. He also saw Saxon warriors scaling the castle walls and prowling the perimeters, looking for other points of weakness. They seemed to be everywhere, and the cover afforded them by the Red Dragon's fiery onslaught gave the invaders a distinct advantage. In a fair fight, Uther was sure that he could've defended his keep and driven the Saxons away, but any fight that involved a dragon was no longer fair. What bothered him most of all was that he just couldn't understand how they had gotten control of a dragon in the first place. Dragons were all but extinct. Uther himself had never seen one, and had never known anyone else who had either. He had cultivated an image that his family had secretly kept one as a pet for hundreds of years, but that was really just playful nonsense. Dragons couldn't be kept as pets. They were immensely powerful and dangerous creatures, and it would take someone equally powerful to control one. The thought of it all made Uther very uneasy.

The small group raced along the castle's walls, and they passed a heavy oak door that looked like it was on the verge of giving way. On the other side, the invading army pounded over and over again, and it was clear that once they broke through there was every chance that they would overtake Uther and his followers. The king made a split-second decision, and halted.

"The rest of you push ahead," commanded Uther. "I'll stay here and cover your escape."

As Uther expected, his son had something to say about that.

"Father, no!" said Arthur. "Let me stay with you. Let me fight. We can defend the castle. We can win."

A flush of pride swelled in Uther's breast at his son's strong words. For the past seventeen years, Uther had done his best to prepare Arthur for the great destiny that lay before him. He had teachers and advisors and mentors and even a wizard as a tutor. It seemed as though all of that had paid off as Arthur's bravery now shone through. Nonetheless, Uther raised his mighty hand and waved away his son's suggestion.

"No," said Uther, "it is imperative that you escape here, my son. I am the king, and I have a duty to stay and fight with my people. But you are the future of this kingdom. If anything should happen to me, I need you out amongst our subjects, rallying them, and preparing to continue the fight."

Uther could see the anguish upon his son's face as Arthur struggled to take in the words. It was clear that the boy understood that he should leave for the greater good, but that didn't make it any more palatable. Uther would've liked to explain many things to his son, but the pounding upon the door was louder now, and there was no time. It was crucial that Arthur get to safety.

"Arthur, you must go with Kay," said Uther as he gestured to a young man with a wild mane of long red hair. "Go to his father, Sir Ector. You'll be safe there. He'll raise you as his own son."

Kay was only a year older than Arthur, but he was courageous and bold with a knack for causing trouble and miraculously getting himself back out of it.

The red-haired young man stepped up next to Arthur and placed a hand upon his shoulder, but Arthur impatiently shook himself free of it.

"Father, I can help you! We can beat them!" And then suddenly the words were tumbling out of his mouth: "We can raise the White Dragon!"

Uther stared at his son with shocked, wide eyes. After a moment, a bemused smirk glanced across his lips. He couldn't help but admire Arthur's optimism, and his ability to retain hope against all odds.

"The White Dragon that gave our family its name hasn't been seen in a hundred years," said Uther. "Those are just myths and legends. But of no help to us now, I'm afraid."

Uther crouched slightly, though, and came to the height of his son, who at seventeen was nearly his father's equal in height, but not nearly his match in wisdom. Uther locked eyes with his son.

"But there is another legend, my son. Of a sword driven into a stone," said Uther, and he could tell by the fire in his son's eyes that he had captured the boy's attention. "Its name is Klærent the Stonebourne. And it is meant only for the king. For me. And for you. Find it. And it will guide you."

"But—" Arthur's protestations were quickly cut short as the oak door splintered nearby. There simply was no time.

"Go!" shouted Uther. "I'll hold them off, but if I fall, they must not take you. You must return. You must be King. Go!"

Kay grabbed Arthur again, but more forcefully this time, and King Uther Pendragon watched as his son was dragged way. Once Arthur had disappeared, carried away by faithful advisors, Uther took a deep breath and stilled himself. His face hardened into a battle-ready grimace as he looked across the battlements to see the large oak door burst open.

A tall man with armor that had been painted black emerged with several scowling Saxons just behind him. The warriors looked ready to charge at Uther, but their leader, Vortigern, raised a hand and his men fell back. Vortigern's black hair and beard hung long and tangled, a mess of grease and madness. He wasn't as broad-shouldered as Uther, but he was taller despite his slight slouch, and Uther couldn't help but acknowledge that the man struck an oddly impressive and intimidating figure.

The Saxons at his side seemed ready to rush upon Uther, and the king brought his hand down upon the pommel of his great sword, preparing for battle. But Vortigern clearly wanted to do the honors himself, and Uther was happy to let him try.

"Hello, Vortigern," growled Uther.

But the man in the black painted armor slyly retorted, "I'd prefer to be called '*King*.'"

"You're not a king yet."

And with that, Uther drew his broadsword. Vortigern did the same, unsheathing a hideous sword with a hilt of black obsidian. And the two men, the two who wished to be king, charged at each other and their swords clashed with a rattle like thunder.

~   ~   ~

Deep within the maze-like corridors of the castle, young Guinevere and her silver-haired father, Leodegrance, raced down hallway after hallway after hallway. They were close on the heels of the massive knight, Sir Aggravaine, who urged them forward ever faster. Despite his determination, Leodegrance stumbled as his old body betrayed him, and Guinevere caught him under the shoulder. Once upon a time her father had been a dashing, capable knight in his own right. Those days were long gone as he clutched the wall and gasped in long, rattling breaths. Guinevere tried to prop herself under her father's shoulder, and wished that she could give him some of her strength. She had never been at a loss for energy and enthusiasm, and it had served her well. All through her studies as a lady she had succeeded at everything that she tried. Horseback riding, needlepoint, the study of human behavior, Guinevere had excelled at them all. On the days when she had snuck out of the castle with Arthur to spend the sunny afternoons climbing trees or swimming in the lake, she never had any problem keeping up with him. Her natural athleticism and quick coordination never failed her. Even now her legs felt fresh and strong and ready to race to heaven and back. She only wished she could share some of that vigor with her failing father.

"We're almost there, Father," Guinevere said, doing her best to force an airy tone, "We'll soon be free of all this madness."

She hoped she wasn't lying. Despite her misadventures with Arthur, she had never been to these levels of the castle. Her bedchambers were on the uppermost floors. As were her study rooms, and the halls where she took her meals. Now she was being forced down into the darker, more uncertain depths of the world, and it frightened her. She hoped that soon they would emerge out into the fresh air and seek out the morning's sunshine and forget all of this forever.

But as her father drew in ragged gasps, Leodegrance reached down to his belt and lifted a long golden dagger. He placed it into Guinevere's shaking hands, and forced her fingers to close around the thin blade. Guinevere flushed, and was embarrassed as she blinked back unexpected tears. Just the feel of this alien weapon was a shock to the young lady in training.

"I'm sorry, my darling," said Leodegrance, "but in these dark times, only the strong survive."

Suddenly, Sir Aggravaine was back at their side and his gruff voice barked at them, "I've promised to protect you both. I can't do it here."

Leodegrance took a deep breath, steeling himself as best as he could, and with Guinevere at his side, the three of them continued running into the uncertainty of the night.

~   ~   ~

As the rain poured down and the dragon roared and spit overhead, Lancelot stood strong and fast in the central courtyard as if he were the lord of all creation. The brash, handsome, unbelievably skilled knight was single-handedly battling the entirety of Vortigern's conquering army. Fifty men at once with the promise of many more clamoring to get at him. He spun, blocked, and struck with brutal accuracy, supreme confidence, deadly skill, and amazingly —

He seemed to be winning.

"Is this all you've got?!" he shouted at his attackers.

Another spin. Another swing. Another kill.

"This is your conquering army?!"

Spin. Swing. Death.

"Long live the king!!"

~   ~   ~

Yet high upon the battlements, Lancelot's war cry was far from becoming a prophecy. King Uther Pendragon continued his deathmatch with his dark challenger, Vortigern, and neither seemed to be on the verge of yielding. The two men were evenly matched, exchanging one powerful blow after another. There was a volley of thrusts, parries, and feints. Even the most trained among the onlookers was unable to tell who held the advantage as the two men circled one another.

"I offered you a hand of friendship," said Uther, "and this is how you repay me?"

"You offered to rule me," said Vortigern. "You had a grand desire to be the king over all kings. Did you really think that I would simply fall under your banner?"

"I wanted to unite all the lands of Briton," Uther said.

"But with yourself at the head. Now see where your pride has gotten you," sneered Vortigern. "Your castle has fallen, Uther Pendragon. And now it's time for a new king."

Vortigern struck with surprising ferocity, and the strength of his blow forced Uther down to one knee. But Uther was not a man to bow.

"I'll eat that dragon of yours before I call you king, Vortigern," said Uther as he sprung at Vortigern once more, forcing him into a defensive crouch. Then Uther added, "And I'm far from beaten. I have allies that you could not compre—"

But before Uther could finish, a crack of lightning split the skies. Out of the black, swirling clouds overhead, a blinding bolt of light shot forth and charged the night air with its wild electricity.

When it withdrew an old, bearded man with a crooked wooden staff stood at the spot.

"Merlin...?" Uther said, his voice barely a whisper as he tried to control his dismay.

But Vortigern's face had twisted into a wry smile as he spoke. "Come, come, Uther. You should've realized... Only one with immense power can control a dragon."

Merlin raised his long wooden staff and pointed it at the Red Dragon, which immediately circled in the black skies. At the wizard's silent command, the Red Dragon spun and dove toward one of the castle's towers. It opened its jaws, and spit out a roar of fire.

Vortigern jeered triumphantly at Uther, "Your wizard betrays you. Your knights abandon you. And I will find your son wherever he hides. You've lost."

But with a mighty roar, Uther struck at Vortigern and their battle raged on.

~ ~ ~

The massive, hulking knight, Sir Aggravaine, continued to lumber forward, with Guinevere and Leodegrance struggling to keep up as they rushed further into the lower corridors of the castle. Turn after turn after turn they had raced, and more than once Guinevere had completely lost her sense of direction. They were now deeper into the castle than she had ever imagined she would go. Nonetheless, Guinevere's mind worked at a furious pace so that she could retain some idea of their present location. A deep feeling of unease had settled in the pit of her stomach as she began to suspect they were going in the wrong direction. She had tried to dismiss this apprehension, but it clung to her like a spiderweb that couldn't be flung aside.

Aggravaine led them to an old wooden door with rusted hinges, but as he reached for the handle, Guinevere's intuition screamed in protest.

"Wait! This doesn't lead —" But before she could cry out her warning, Aggravaine had wrenched open the door and revealed a room full of Saxon warriors. Their dirty faces were curled into leering smiles of broken, yellowing teeth.

In a flash, much quicker than his advancing age would've suggested, old Leodegrance drew his sword, but just as quickly he was grabbed from behind by Aggravaine. The hulking behemoth seemed to take pleasure in unsheathing his long knife and pressing it against the old man's throat.

Blinded by anger and betrayal, Guinevere gripped the golden dagger that had been in her possession for only a few short minutes. She cursed herself for ignoring her instincts and putting her blind faith in Sir Aggravaine as she took a stab at the beastly knight. From now on, she swore that she would trust only herself. Despite her best efforts, Aggravaine was a much more experienced warrior than she, not to mention over twice her size. It was all too easy for him to bat the attack away with his free hand, and then, with his massive strength, he grabbed Guinevere by the front of her dress and lifted her into the air.

Guinevere's blood flared as she spat at him, "We trusted you!"

"Don't worry, m'lady," was his growling reply. "My orders aren't to kill you. Yet. My advice: find a way to be useful."

With that, he shoved her into the hands of the waiting Saxons.

~ ~ ~

In the castle courtyard, things weren't going as well for the Saxons. In an amazing display of swordplay, Lancelot continued to fight dozens of oncoming warriors at once, and he was more than up to the task. With a speed and ferocity that could only be matched by the storm that raged overhead, the mighty knight cut, slashed, and conquered anyone who dared to come within arm's reach of him. The rain poured down, and he was covered in streaks of blood, mud and sweat, yet he wouldn't have wanted it any other way.

With a roar of triumph, he taunted his attackers, "I must say, I'm a little disappointed. I've heard so many stories of the strength and viciousness of the Saxons. And yet I feel like I could go on all day. Vortigern's mighty army beaten by—aaaahhh!!!"

In the space of a single, almost unimpressive moment, everything changed.

A blade cut through the air and silenced Lancelot. His once joyful face quickly dropped into a pained grimace, and as he drew in a rasping breath, he looked to his right arm and saw—

His right hand had been cut off at the forearm.

The horde of Saxons paused for a moment as they too took in the terrible sight, and it was almost impossible to tell who was more stunned. In the heat of the battle, none of the Saxons were even sure which one of them had landed this crippling blow. However, Lancelot's surprise only lasted an instant, and he composed himself as he said through gritted teeth,

"A... lucky... swing..."

And, with a supreme effort, he snatched up his sword into his left hand and valiantly fought on.

~ ~ ~

Atop the battlements, the mighty clash ensued between Uther and Vortigern. Uther's strength was failing him as he swung his broadsword again and again. Vortigern feinted a thrust, and Uther deflected clumsily, giving Vortigern enough momentum to twist their locked swords and flick Uther's away. Disarmed, Uther dropped to his knees. As he gasped for breath, his eyes rose and sought the wise, old face of the wizard, Merlin. There had been a time when Uther would've considered Merlin his most trusted advisor. But now Merlin stood aside and watched without making a move to help. His eyes were impassive and detached, not the friendly eyes that Uther would have hoped for as he began his desperate plea.

"Merlin... You swore me an oath..."

A twinge of annoyance flashed across Merlin's face, but then the wizard raised his staff and as he spoke, his words came out musically as if they were supernaturally carried on the whipping winds that tore at his cloak. They seemed to come from everywhere as he said,

"The Mighty King,

The King of All,

For He Who Rose,

It's Time to Fall."

And, with the booming finality of his words, Merlin pointed his staff at Uther. A terrifying roar ripped through the skies, infecting Uther and all who heard it, and the Red Dragon curved through the air and soared toward the defeated king at the bidding of the wizard who had betrayed him.

~ ~ ~

In the courtyard, Lancelot was completely surrounded by Saxons. He held out his sword defensively with his left arm, and spun quickly like a feral tiger surrounded by hunters. However, there was no doubt that he was wounded terribly.

Bloody.

Broken.

Beaten...

And yet he snarled, "I give you this one last chance... Leave now, and you may live. Stay and I, the mighty Lancelot, will slay every last one of you."

For a moment, the Saxons hesitated. Fear on their faces. But only for a moment. And then, all at once, they charged.

And Lancelot was overtaken.

~ ~ ~

Cutting through the black, stormy skies, the Red Dragon flew toward the battlements where King Uther awaited his doom. The fallen king heaved in exhaustion, but lifted himself to his feet, and

THE LEGENDS OF KING ARTHUR BOOK 1

stood as tall as he could muster. His eyes locked on Vortigern, then on Merlin, then passed along each of the onlooking warriors as he summoned every ounce of strength he had left so that his voice boomed with a last surge of confidence.

"My son will return."

The Red Dragon was very close now.

"He will reclaim my throne."

The beast was opening its monstrous jaws. It drew terrible breath through its reeking fangs.

"HE. WILL. BE. KING!"

Flames poured from the Dragon's mouth.

And King Uther Pendragon was engulfed.

~   ~   ~

At a distant, deserted corner of the castle, several rocks came tumbling out of a small portion of the wall that had remained untouched by the dragon's fury. One by one, a small stream of people poured out of the hole, survivors from the fallen castle who were now like rats fleeing from a burning building. They quickly darted away from the castle toward a nearby cluster of trees and the uncertain safety of the forest. Each of them knew that they had little hope of ever seeing their home again.

His wild, red hair whipping in the stormy winds, Kay pulled young Arthur along, but Arthur jerked himself free and spun to look back at the castle that was meant to one day be his. Distant screams still hung in the air, although they were becoming fainter and more spread out now. The Red Dragon beat its massive wings as it lowered itself to perch upon the highest walls, causing them to crack under its immense weight. Arthur gazed up at it, and saw the figures of Vortigern and Merlin silhouetted in the many fires that were still raging despite the pouring rain. The terrible truth that his father must have fallen settled upon Arthur, and he realized with a jolt of sadness that he was now a king.

A king whose burning, fallen kingdom was reflected in his eyes.

~ ~ ~

CHAPTER 2

Sir Ector's Farm

"I-I-I don't know if I can do this."

Arthur could barely believe the words that were coming out of
Percival's mouth. The man was a knight. He had been sworn to
protect loyal subjects of the kingdom. He was bound to the service
of Uther Pendragon, and it was irrelevant that Uther was dead: the
duty still stood. But now the slim, pale-faced knight was
stammering and sputtering and refusing to keep eye contact with
Arthur.

"I'm—I'm sorry, Arthur," continued Percival. "I f-f-failed you.
We all did, but I—"

"Sir Percival!" shouted Arthur, and it snapped the knight out of
his stupor. "Pull yourself together. That's an order."

Percival fell silent at Arthur's word, and it gave Arthur a
moment to take a deep breath and calm himself. His head was still
swimming from the events of the past twenty-four hours. Just a day
ago, Arthur had barely managed to escape Tintagel with his life.
The greater challenge laid ahead, however. Seemingly in the blink
of an eye, everyone had begun to look to Arthur as the new leader.
Now he was giving orders, and perhaps even more surprisingly,
people were following them without question. And Arthur couldn't
have felt less prepared. It was true that for all of his seventeen short

years, he had been trained for this day. He had taken lessons with teachers and tutors and a traitorous wizard, but that was all that it had been. Lessons. He had never actually had to give an order that had any weight, or that could mean the difference between life and death. Suddenly, that was now the case. As remarkable as it might've seemed, some of the very same men and women who had been his teachers just yesterday were now looking at him for guidance today.

Arthur felt very alone.

"Percival, I don't care about yesterday," said Arthur, doing his best to make himself believe it too. "All I care about is keeping these people alive today. And once we've gotten through today, then tomorrow and then the next day. You are a knight of Tintagel, and I need your help."

To Arthur's great relief, Percival stood a little taller and managed to look Arthur in the eyes.

"I'm—I'm at your command, sir," said Percival.

His acquiescence actually sent a fresh stab of fear through Arthur. It was one thing to get Percival and the others under control, but now he had to actually figure out what to tell them. The past day had been full of confusion, and it had taken all of Arthur's training to keep his small band of followers out of harm's way and undetected. They had journeyed into the nearby forests and immersed themselves in the concealment of the thick trees. Nonetheless, Vortigern's Saxons had pursued them with a vicious hunger. It didn't help that, upon escaping the castle, most of

Arthur's surviving followers were maids, children, and aged advisors. The group was well-equipped to cook hot meals, play silly games, or just read. They weren't prepared for a rough existence on the run. The lone able-bodied man among them was Kay, and he seemed to want to forget all about the others and just push on toward his father's farm. Arthur had struggled despite his exhaustion and fear to keep everyone moving while also keeping Kay under control, but it was a struggle that couldn't have gone on for long.

A few hours after daybreak, a great stroke of luck had arrived when Arthur stumbled upon Percival and a group of a dozen other knights who had also taken refuge in the woods. At first the men had begged for mercy for fleeing their posts during battle, but Arthur didn't have time to reprimand them. He needed help and he'd take any he could get.

"Vortigern's Saxons will continue to hunt me until they come back with my head," said Arthur. "And that means that as long as I'm with these people, they're in danger. Percival, I need you and the others to lead them away from here and to keep them safe."

"B-B-But I can't!"

"Yes, you can!" said Arthur with a flash of frustration. "You all failed to show your courage last night in battle. I expect better of you today. There's very little time, and these people need your help."

Percival and the other knights nodded. They were quickly falling into line. Arthur just wished he felt more certain that they he was giving them the right orders.

"I'll leave here immediately with Kay," said Arthur, and he noticed a burst of excitement on Kay's face. "We'll lay a trail to draw the Saxons after us and away from you and the others. Take the people deep into the forest. Find some refuge. Use all of your considerable ingenuity to keep them safe. You can do this."

Then, with a wordless glance, Arthur turned to Kay and his red-haired companion grinned. They were ready to go. Together they started to race deeper into the trees, but they had barely taken a few strides when Arthur heard—

"Wait!" called Percival. "Wh-where will you be?"

"It's better if you don't know," was Arthur's brisk reply, because he wasn't entirely certain himself.

And he was off.

Almost immediately, Arthur felt a certain weight lifting off of his chest. Without doubt, the safety of his followers continued to nag at him, and even deeper than that, Arthur's mind kept drifting back to Guinevere, and he was filled with anxiety about whether or not she had made it out of Tintagel alive. However, Kay was a marvellous distraction to all of that. Within in the hour, Arthur found himself racing to keep up with Kay, who had spent much more of his childhood exploring the forests that stretched out through the nearby countryside. Arthur's experiences had been much more structured as he was trained by royal hunters in formal tracking or orienteering, but Kay preferred to just charge boldly amongst the trees, and leave Arthur scrambling to keep up. On more than one occasion, Arthur nearly forgot that their lives were in peril, and he slipped into the fantasy that this was simply another enjoyable day of training in the wilderness. In no time it almost felt like this was just a friendly competition. Arthur and Kay would compete to see who could be quicker to clear a thick patch of brush, or who could devise the most clever snares to leave behind for the Saxon trackers, or even who could mimic the best bird call, as if that was in any way appropriate to the terrible danger they were now in. Several times, after a full-out sprint through the forest, Arthur would end up laughing, and smiling in spite of himself.

But before long his focus would drift back to Guinevere.

And the terrible weight of his duty would return again.

Arthur and Kay spent nearly a week in those woods, circling and doubling back so as to be sure that they weren't followed, and also making certain that the Saxons were led away from Percival and the others. On a few occasions they would dart into the villages that lay on the outer edges of the kingdom, but it was just to quickly grab some food or water. They were always surprised and disappointed to find Saxon sentries posted throughout. Vortigern had plotted his takeover well, and he had effectively seized control of all the many bordering towns and villages that relied on Tintagel for their safety and survival.

Which is why Arthur shouldn't have been so surprised at the scene that awaited them when they finally reached Sir Ector's farm.

The farm that Kay had grown up on lay on the furthest outskirts of the lands that could be claimed by Tintagel. Sir Ector was a tall, hard-working man who had always been a good and loyal subject. With his long sturdy limbs, he had carefully tended to his generous plot of land and quickly made it into one of the greatest providers of food for the entire kingdom. His farm was a bounty of golden grains, fresh vegetables, and healthy livestock.

Or, at least, it used to be.

As they came closer and closer to the farm, Arthur hadn't been able to ignore the smell of smoke that hung heavily on the air. When they emerged from the trees on the edge of the farm, it became clear why. The wheat fields had been burnt to the ground. The vegetable patches had been torn asunder. The livestock was scattered to the wild.

And in the distance, hanging lifelessly in front of the half-smoldering farmhouse, was the long sturdy body of Sir Ector.

Immediately, Kay tried to make a sprint for his father, but Arthur grabbed him and held him back. The young man with the wild mane of red hair struggled furiously to get free, but Arthur held him tight.

"Stop and think, Kay," said Arthur, doing his best to keep his voice low. "It's not safe here."

"That's my father up there!" shouted Kay, not bothering to keep his voice low in return. "I have to go to him! It's my father! Dead!"

"And my father's been dead for over a week now," reminded Arthur. "Their battles are over. But ours remain. And we need to be smart if we have any hope of avenging them."

This seemed to calm Kay at least for a moment. The furious thought of revenge settled in his mind, and Arthur could see a fire building inside of his friend who had been so playful just a day ago.

"What do we do now?" asked Kay.

"We need to get out of here," said Arthur, and before Kay could protest he continued, "We'll find some shelter somewhere else. We've got to plan our next move carefully."

"I won't leave my father hanging there," said Kay. "I have to at least give him a burial."

"It's too risky. Vortigern's men are probably waiting for us to show up here."

"Then bring on the fight!"

"Keep your voice down."

"I don't care who hears it! I'll kill the men responsible!"

"We have no idea what we're dealing with here."

"It doesn't matter who—"

"That's an order, Kay."

In the week that Arthur and Kay had been travelling together, Arthur had always thought of them as friends and equals. They were about the same age. They had approximately the same skills. They even had similar senses of humor and adventure. In the span of a few short days, Arthur had begun to rely on Kay, and hoped that this was someone he could trust. Yet now that Arthur had felt compelled to issue an order, he knew that an instant gap had opened between them.

A gap that might be impossible to close.

Before Kay had a chance to argue, the sound of hooves thundered upon the cracked, burnt ground. Arthur and Kay silently ducked back into the tree line and hid themselves amongst the heavy overgrowth as they watched the approach of several riders. A horse galloped into sight, straining under the load of its massive hulking beast of a rider. Aggravaine led the charge with four fully-armed Saxons right behind him.

"Who's there?!" bellowed Aggravaine. "We heard your voices! Come out and we'll make it quick!"

Once again, Arthur felt Kay tense, and it was clear that he was raring for a fight. Arthur knew, however, that they were completely outmatched. They were two teenaged boys with no weapons, who hadn't had a proper meal or a bit of sleep in days. In this condition, Arthur and Kay wouldn't have stood a chance against Aggravaine and the four Saxons. Luckily, Kay seemed to calm down simply by Arthur putting a hand on his shoulder.

Aggravaine turned to his Saxon comrades and barked, "Search the farms again. Feel free to make plenty of noise. And make it known that we have Guinevere. That should bring the boy king running."

Now it was Arthur's turn to nearly take leave of his senses and leap into a hopeless battle. Fortunately, Kay returned the favor and calmed Arthur with a raised hand. As Aggravaine and the others

44

rode away to begin their search, Arthur's brash desire for action quickly subsided. But as he glared at the towering, bald-headed Aggravaine, Arthur swore that the man would pay for his betrayal of Guinevere.

At his side, Arthur glimpsed Kay, who had locked eyes on the silently swinging body of his father. Once again, Arthur could sense the fury behind Kay's gaze, and he knew that the only thing that was holding Kay back was because Arthur had ordered him to.

"I swear to you, father," Kay vowed quietly to the distant body. "I will avenge you."

Arthur had never felt further apart from him.

~ ~ ~

CHAPTER 3

The Wildman of Orkney

The next several weeks were the most difficult in all of Arthur's young life. It didn't seem to matter where he and Kay went, they were always on the verge of capture and death. At first they tried to find refuge in some of the distant villages that were located on borderlands of Tintagel's kingdom. Vortigern had been too clever for that, however, and Arthur quickly discovered that there were rumors of Saxon spies placed in each and every town. That made staying there too risky for Arthur and for the simple villagers who sought to help him. Next they had tried the larger towns and cities that had sworn allegiance to Tintagel in exchange for protection. Arthur's hope was that they might be able to blend in with the hustle and bustle of the larger crowds. Once again, he was disappointed as he found calculating patrols and registries that made it impossible to slip into the anonymity of the city. More and more, Arthur and Kay simply found themselves traversing the forests. They would steal or forage whatever little bits of food they could get ahold of, but it was never enough. They would grab snatches of sleep when they could, but there was always the looming threat of Saxon trackers that made it impossible to truly rest. Little by little, as he edged closer toward collapse from hunger and fatigue, Arthur was losing hope that he would be able to come out of this alive. He was starting to doubt whether he'd ever be able to lay eyes on Guinevere again.

Then, starving, exhausted, and on the verge of losing it all, Arthur finally caught a break.

With no particular destination in mind, Arthur and Kay had been stumbling amongst the trees when a cracking sound broke the relative quiet of the forest. Panic seized Arthur as a wild, ragged man charged out from between the trees with his sword raised.

"Arthur! I've finally found you!"

For an instant, Arthur cursed his weary carelessness and thought that they'd finally been foolish enough to let a Saxon find them. But Arthur didn't have much time to worry. He'd stayed alive this long, and he had no intention of going down without a fight.

Besides, there was something familiar about this man.

As the wildman closed in, Arthur sprang into action. His tiredness and hunger disappeared as he prepared to tangle with the man. Arthur's legs tensed and he shifted into a defensive crouch to deal with whatever attack may come. Kay was more clumsy, but with his usual recklessness he leapt at the wildman. It was only too easy for their attacker to toss Kay aside, and the wildman caught him on the chin with a forceful elbow. Arthur watched as his friend careened backward and collapsed in a tangle of long red hair.

"I'm not here to fight you!"

But Arthur barely noticed the wildman's words as he snatched a fallen tree branch off of the ground and swung it at the strange

47

man. The wildman moved with impressive speed as he lunged out of the way of Arthur's blow. Then with a powerful swipe, the man knocked the branch out of Arthur's hands. Arthur tried to regroup, but in his weakened state, even this little effort had already taken a lot of out him. In an instant, the man seized Arthur by the throat and held him at arm's length.

For the first time, Arthur took in the wildman's strange appearance. He wore dented war-beaten armor that was decorated with faded paint depicting strange foreign symbols and runes. His hair and beard hung long and tangled, and were adorned with all manner of strange trophies and talismans. There were glittering precious stones, a copper Roman coin, an assortment of wooden pagan amulets, and even what appeared to be a shark's tooth. Arthur finally locked eyes with the man, and despite the hand on his throat, he was able to breathe easy at last.

"Sir Gawain!"

Gawain released Arthur and nodded. "I'm glad to see you're alive, Arthur."

Kay finally returned looking ready for another round of the fight as he shouted, "We're never surrendering to you. I'll send Vortigern your head before I let you take him!"

"It's all right, Kay," said Arthur. "We can trust him. Sir Gawain was one of my father's most loyal knights."

Almost mournfully, Gawain bowed his head at this honor.

"If he was so loyal, why wasn't he here during the siege of Tintagel?" demanded Kay with his usual lack of tact. "All of Uther's knights were supposed to be there. They were supposed to serve. Where was this brave warrior in his king's time of need?"

Gawain fell silent, so Arthur felt compelled to speak on his behalf.

"He's been away for nearly a year on my father's orders," explained Arthur with a dismissive wave of the hand. "And I'm very happy to see him now."

"I've been trying to track you for weeks," said Gawain. "I must say I'm impressed by what you've been able to accomplish. Vortigern's men have been pursuing you with everything they've got. And some of them are quite good at what they do. Some are very skilled trackers and hunters. It couldn't have been easy staying one step ahead of them. Well done, lads."

Kay beamed at the compliment, and he seemed to have forgotten that only moments ago he was prepared to fight Gawain to the death. However, Arthur heaved a great sigh.

"We're not sure how much longer we can keep it up," admitted Arthur. "We're in desperate need of rest. And food. And safety. Do you have any idea where we might be able to find any of that?"

"Oh yes," said Gawain, and a silver teardrop shaped amulet tinkled as he nodded his head. "We must set sail for Orkney."

~ ~ ~

The journey to Gawain's homeland of Orkney took them just over a month.

But what a month it was.

The trickiest part was simply escaping the kingdom of Tintagel undetected. It was one thing for Arthur and Kay to stay on the move amongst the forests, but now they needed supplies to hold them over for their long journey. Fortunately, Gawain had been well-stocked with food and was able to give Arthur and Kay their first decent meal in weeks. He had a few extra weapons and was also able to provide Arthur and Kay each with a sword, giving them an added sense of ease amongst the danger that might lie around any corner. Then they set about the difficult task of gathering what provisions they could before sneaking to the nearby harbors.

Once there, it was a matter of finding passage upon a friendly ship, preferably without letting the captain or the crew know who their passengers would be. This was easier said than done. Even here at the distant harbors there were rumors of spies placed by Vortigern to keep an eye out for Arthur in case he tried to escape. The idea of it nagged at Arthur. Was he trying to simply escape? Was he leaving his people behind and dooming them to the rule of the evil King Vortigern? Was he sentencing Guinevere to death by his absence?

Gawain had tried to assure Arthur that this was the best course of action, that Arthur was better off lying low for a while and then plotting a careful return to the throne. In addition, Gawain argued that a seventeen-year-old with little more than hypothetical training was ill-suited to lead a revolution. The wild lands of Orkney promised the opportunity for Arthur to put his skills into practice, and for Gawain to guide him to his full potential.

Kay was the persistent voice of dissent. He felt that they should gather whatever meager forces and weapons they could muster and take the fight to Vortigern immediately. He was itching for a fight, and he didn't seem to care if it only led to a quick demise in a blaze of glory. Kay wanted a battle, and he made it clear that, to him, it was worth dying to make a statement, and leaving was a cowardly course of action.

In the end it was Arthur's decision, and he trusted the measured plans of Gawain over the brash actions of Kay. So with some careful precautions they finally selected a ship and Arthur set sail for the distant lands of Orkney.

Yet his heart never left his homeland.

Those first few days, Arthur couldn't tear his mind away from Tintagel. Mostly he thought about Guinevere, and he would find himself gazing upon the embroidered handkerchief that she had given him, and that he had sworn to return. But he also thought about Percival and the other knights. Arthur wondered if they had found a safe place to hide, or if they had been captured and subjected to unnamed tortures for their loyalty to Uther Pendragon. Each night, Arthur lay down uneasily and was plagued with doubts about his choices and what lie ahead.

"Wake up, Arthur," said Gawain late one evening after Arthur had been tossing in his small cabin for a few hours. "It's time to begin your training."

"Whuh?" mumbled Arthur, trying to clear his muddled head. "What time is it?"

"What difference does that make?" asked the older grizzled knight. "When do you think you might come under attack? Always after breakfast? Maybe only when the sun is bright and full in the sky?"

"No, it's not that," stammered Arthur. "You're right, of course. But we're on a boat. How can we expect to get any training done here?"

"Can you tell me for certain where your battles will take place?" Gawain asked, once again brushing aside Arthur's confusion, although the knight didn't betray even a hint of annoyance. "You've been trained in classrooms. Or courtyards. Always with soft pads or wooden swords. You'll have no such luxury anymore. My job is to prepare you for anything. And I mean anything. You've already seen a dragon, but there could be much worse things awaiting you. I need you ready to fight in a hurricane. Against a dozen men. With a blindfold seared over your eyes. So the question is—"

And here Gawain extended a sword to Arthur.

"Are you ready?"

Arthur took the sword. And his training began.

Almost immediately, Arthur made his new mentor proud. He practiced at all hours no matter what the weather. While they were still at sea, Arthur practiced his footwork even amongst the rockiest waters. He dueled with Gawain while balancing high up upon the mast of the ship. He sparred with the crew mates even though many of them were over twice his size and had wrestled with giant squids in their past voyages. But Arthur was tireless. No matter how hard he got hit, he kept getting up. No matter how badly he failed at something, he practiced it over and over until it became like second nature to him.

Once they finally reached the land, Arthur threw himself into all of the challenges that his new surroundings provided. He had been given formal riding lessons almost since birth, but now he was learning how to tame wild horses without a saddle. His sword had almost become an extension of his hand, but he found himself tossing it aside to train with a spear. And once he had mastered that, he trained with a bow. Then a mace. And on and on and on.

The wild lands of Orkney proved to be the perfect training grounds as well. It wasn't nearly as civilized as Arthur was used to in Tintagel. The few small villages that existed there were separated by vast green frontiers. And all manner of lawless man and beast had taken up residence here. Under the tutelage of Gawain, Arthur learned how to track snow foxes through the moonlight of a winter's evening. Together they chased ghouls out of haunted churchyards and banished the spirits back into the afterlife. Gawain even allowed Arthur to take the lead in the slaying of a warlock who was trying to raise monsters to swim in the waters of Loch Ness. With a thrill of success, Arthur did manage to successfully vanquish the warlock, although he suspected that at least one of the monsters escaped and survived to continue swimming in the murky waters.

On his eighteenth birthday, Arthur became a man as he battled from sunrise to sunset against a band of pirates who had hoped to raid the ports of Orkney before setting sail for a journey that they claimed would take them over the edge of the map.

With each successful mission and each skill mastered, Arthur began to feel more and more at ease. He took pleasure in his victories and found himself reveling proudly as he vanquished beasts and freed small towns and villages from local warlords and villains. His body grew strong, and his mind became sharp. However, amongst all of his new adventures, the memory of his homeland began to grow dim.

It was Kay that finally brought Arthur back to his senses.

At first Kay had joined in Gawain's training with unbounded enthusiasm. After all, he and Arthur were fairly well-matched, and Kay made an excellent sparring partner. Very quickly, however, Arthur outstripped Kay and their little duels ceased to do Arthur any good. Arthur had advanced to practicing with Gawain or perhaps another nomadic warrior that they might stumble upon in the wilderness of Orkney. Yet Arthur couldn't help but notice that Kay was becoming more and more sullen and withdrawn. His temper had always flared on semi-regular intervals, but now it was a constant presence and his complaints eventually came back to the same refrain.

"We have to go back... We have to go back... We have to go back!"

Yet Gawain maintained that they needed more training. As the weeks and months stretched on, Gawain seemed less and less inclined to ever see an end in sight. It took a long time before Arthur realized that Gawain was haunted by something that the old knight seemed completely unwilling to discuss. This was a strange development since Gawain had always been so gregarious during Arthur's youth. When Arthur had been growing up, Gawain was one of his favorite knights. The grizzled warrior seemed to have an unending repertoire of fascinating stories from his many quests both in Briton and abroad. He had sailed with Vikings. He had wrestled with Roman gladiators. He had swum with pods of mermaids to Atlantis and back. If supplied with enough mead, Gawain could bellow on with story after story of crusades that would bring the grand feasting hall to complete silence before shaking it with peals of laughter.

But that Gawain was gone.

The Gawain who mentored Arthur now was a much more solemn and serious man. He seemed obsessed with training Arthur for the real world, and yet Arthur was beginning to doubt that Gawain was ever going to let them get back to it. It had become more and more clear that Gawain didn't want to return to Tintagel despite the fact that Arthur was quickly becoming the man that his homeland sorely needed.

Arthur found himself torn between his two friends. On the one hand, he agreed with Kay that they needed to go back. On the other hand, he knew that he needed Gawain at his side if they had any hope of success. More and more often, Arthur would wander off alone with his thoughts as he tried to plan his next steps.

One night he found himself in a grove of old gnarled elm trees. The moon was shining bright and beautiful. A gentle breeze rustled the heavy tree branches. It was cool and comfortable, and yet Arthur didn't notice any of it. He was so lost in his own thoughts that he barely recognized where he was as he muttered to himself and rehashed his many problems over and over. He was most surprised when a creaking voice responded.

"Yes, yes, that is quite the quandry..."

Drawing his sword quickly, Arthur spun at the sound of voice. Even absorbed as he was in his mind, he had been sure that he was alone. He scanned the area and didn't see anyone, so he called out warily, "Who's there? Show yourself!"

"Oh, pardon me!" cried the voice, and Arthur was astonished to see that it was coming from the trunk of a particularly old and twisted elm. "I thought you were talking to me."

"Um..." stammered Arthur, clearly caught off-guard. "No, I admit I thought I was alone."

"Oho! It surely seemed that you were talking to someone," said the tree.

With all of the strange things Arthur had seen over the past year, a talking tree wasn't all that unusual. And he had heard stories about spirits that were sometimes locked in ancient trees, and since that was bound to be boring for them, it seemed natural they might want to chat. Nonetheless, he wasn't exactly sure how to respond. Luckily, the tree seemed to notice the lull in the conversation and it spoke up.

"Well, now you know that you haven't been alone. You've been positively jabbering for weeks through these forests. None of us trees can get any sleep with all your babbling!"

"I'm sorry. I didn't realize I was bothering anyone," said Arthur, slightly abashed and then slightly more abashed at being abashed by a talking tree.

"Just like a human... So involved in your own problems that you can't possibly take the time to consider the wider implications on those whom you share this wide world with," said the tree, and then it added with a slight sway of its long branch which might have just been caused by a well-timed breeze, "Well, go on then."

"Excuse me?"

"Tell me your problem. You've woken me up now. I might as well hear it, and possibly I might be able to give you the solution, so that you don't wake up any of my fellow elms with your eternal, nocturnal prattle."

"I don't think you'd understand," said Arthur. "After all, you're just a tree."

"My, my, my, and you were so polite just a moment ago," scolded the tree.

"I just mean, you couldn't possibly understand my problems," said Arthur, and then he added quickly, "Not that you don't mean to be helpful! I just don't think you'll be of much use with all that I'm trying to deal with at the moment."

"I wouldn't be so certain," said the tree with a mild huff of indignation in its reedy voice. "I've been growing in this earth for longer than the lifetime of ten men. Since I sprouted from a seedling, I've seen the rise and fall of entire villages and kingdoms and empires. You might be surprised at the amount of wisdom that I've accumulated in these ancient branches. Go ahead, give me a try."

Arthur shrugged. *What could it hurt to ask?*

"I was born a prince, and I'm meant to be king," began Arthur, and soon the words were tumbling out. "But my kingdom was overthrown, and my father was killed by a power-mad dictator. Not to mention the castle, my former home, is being guarded by one of the last dragons on earth, as well as a wizard who I thought was my friend and teacher, but instead is just a murderer. On top of that, I'm not sure if the girl I was promised to marry is alive or dead. Also my best friend seems to have a death wish. And I can't figure out how to get my mentor to overcome whatever it is that's bothering him so that we can go and restart the fight. And if I'm being honest, sometimes I wonder whether I should just abandon the fight altogether. The long and the short of it is… I have no idea what to do next."

"Hmmm…" said the tree, and it seemed to carefully consider Arthur's words before it finally concluded, "In all my long centuries of existence, I'm not sure I've accumulated enough wisdom to crack that particular nut. Perhaps you should consult a stone."

Arthur chuckled. He hadn't honestly thought that the tree would give him any answers, but it felt good to get all of his worries off of his chest. For the first time in weeks, his mind felt a little easier and clearer as he said, "Absolutely. I'll be on the look-out for a stone to guide—"

Suddenly he fell silent. His mind raced as he remembered words that seemed to have been spoken a lifetime ago. Something stirred inside Arthur and he recalled something his father had said: "There is another legend, my son. Of a sword driven into a stone. It's name is Klærent the Stonebourne. And it is meant only for the king. For me. And for you. Find it. And it will guide you."

Amidst the chaos of the siege that night and then in his many struggles simply to survive, Arthur had all but forgotten about the legend that his father had spoken of. But now it seized hold of his imagination. There had always been rumors of ancient, mystical swords. They were each imbued with special powers. Powers of wisdom or strength. Some of them even had the power to make a man the king. Why couldn't this one be exactly what he was looking for?

"I know what I have to do!" said Arthur, spinning toward the tree, and beginning to feel excited for the first time in months.

But the tree had fallen silent. Apparently the ancient elm had had its say, and after a few short moments of silence, Arthur let it be and headed out.

As the morning sun rose and transformed the dark skies to shades of gray and rapidly blooming blue, Arthur strode back into his meager camp. He found that Gawain was already awake and Kay was beginning to stir as he rubbed sleep from his eyes. Arthur gazed at his two companions and uttered the simple words that he had become sure were the right command.

"We're going back."

~ ~ ~

CHAPTER 4

The Sword in the Stone

Over the centuries, there have been countless legends of magical swords cutting their way through history and into the murking realms of myth. Some were made by ancient swordsmiths who had stumbled upon the secrets of imbuing precious metals with strength and wisdom. Some were forged by powerful magicians who hoped that the swords would tip the scales between good and evil, although it was never certain which way they intended. And some were actually just convincing knock-offs being pawned by talented conmen, but they certainly looked impressive when mounted upon an impressionable nobleman's wall. Nonetheless, these swords had a way of creating incredible reputations. They might be used to inspire a downtrodden people to rise up against their oppressors. Or they might have been corrupted and used for murder and deceit. At least one of them simply ended up on the bottom of a lake for a century or so waiting for the right champion to finally come along and claim it. Yet throughout the annals of history, the great deeds of these swords were splashed upon the countless pages of books and children's stories.

That is, except for Klærent the Stonebourne.

He couldn't explain it, but Arthur was sure that this sword would be the key to completing his father's final wishes.

Gawain didn't agree.

In fact, he seemed to simply want to grumble about the whole matter.

"You have to understand, Gawain," implored Arthur, "this sword could be the guide that we've been looking for."

Gawain just grumbled.

"It's a legendary mystical sword."

Another grumble.

"This is what my father would've wanted."

A grumble that could've been a *hrrmph…*

"Sir Gawain, I need you!" cried Arthur as he finally lost his temper. "I can't turn my back on my people any longer. I'm going back to Tintagel and I'm going to rally those who are still loyal to Uther Pendragon. But I can't lead them. Not yet. My presence will simply call down Vortigern's full fury. They need someone who can lead the fight without being a distraction. They need you."

This time Gawain let out a long sigh, and then he finally spoke.

"Well, it seems as though you've inherited some of your father's wisdom," said Gawain. "All right, Arthur, I'm with you. We can go back."

Convincing Kay was a much simpler matter.

"Kay, I think it's time we returned to—"

Arthur barely had the words out before a maniacal glint flashed through Kay's eyes, and he all but shouted, "Finally! We can have our revenge!"

"No!" said Arthur quickly. "This isn't about revenge. And we can't just charge back in there and expect to do any good."

Now Kay was the one who was grumbling.

"We'll reunite with Percival and the others. Gawain will lead the rebellion, and in small increments we'll undermine Vortigern's regime. But slowly. One step at a time. Can I count on you?"

Another grumble. *What was it with Arthur's companions and grumbling?*

"Kay, you're my friend. Maybe my closest friend. But if we return to Tintagel, I'll be your king. And I'll need you to obey me. Can you do that?"

Arthur hated to have to put things in those terms, but Kay was too brash, too unpredictable, and Arthur felt that he had no choice. There was a long tense silence between them, but Kay finally nodded.

And just like that, they were off. The return journey seemed to pass in a blur. Arthur trusted the planning to Gawain, who procured them safe travel and made arrangements to slip back into the country unnoticed. But Arthur's mind was clouded with thoughts and calculations for how he might discover and take control of that mystical sword that so controlled his imagination. He found himself enthralled with the possibilities and he even managed to convince himself that his arrival would be met with a blaze of glory that might ignite a revolution.

But upon Arthur's return, things wouldn't be easy. Despite the warm welcome he received —

"He's back!"

"The king has returned! We're saved!"

"Thank goodness! Our nightmare is finally at an end!"

Arthur had been relieved to see that Percival had led what was left of his followers into safety. They'd even cobbled together enough food and shelter to survive. But it was a tough existence. The people were constantly in fear of being found out. They were never certain where their next meal would come from. They were tired and hungry and scared.

It was only natural that they saw Arthur as a returning savior.

And it made Arthur sick inside.

He had barely understood how much he had changed in the year that he was away. When he left he was just a boy, but now everyone saw him as a man. It was true that he was little taller, a fair bit stronger, and decidedly more handsome, but deep down he still felt confused and unprepared. He didn't feel at all like the hero that everyone seemed to think he would be. It didn't help when children would throw themselves at him and wrap him in tight hugs. Or when tired, over-worked mothers would burst into tears of hope at his approach. Or when men who had once advised his father now looked to Arthur for wisdom and guidance.

Arthur simply wanted to look for a sword.

Fortunately, Gawain took the lead with surprising speed and skill. The grizzled knight had seen his share of battles and strife, and he quickly set to work organizing the rebellion. He masterminded raids against Vortigern's strongholds and often came back with great stocks of food and drink. He utilized the talents at his disposal and smartly discovered Percival's gift for engineering which, with a little guidance, led to new shelters and tents that could provide more safety and comfort. Gawain even learned how to mobilize Kay's passions by allowing the red-haired young man more chances to take a free rein in the fight against Vortigern's loyalists. In fact, although it was unknown to any of them, Gawain's exploits would one day inspire future noble bandits when those same forests were known as Sherwood.

And Arthur took the opportunity to disconnect himself more and more. To Gawain's great frustration, Arthur began to slip away for longer and longer stretches as he sought out Klærent the Stonebourne. He ran down any leads he could find. No rumor or whisper was too insubstantial. He paid visits to old blacksmiths who might've kept track of impressive weaponry. He visited monasteries on rumors that the sword had ended up on some vaguely holy ground. He stole books and manuscripts that had even fleeting mentions of a sword that had spent a generation buried in a hunk of aged stone.

Finally, his persistence was rewarded when he caught word of an old churchyard that had been long since abandoned. Legend had it that a foolish old priest had decided to construct his church there without understanding that the land was prone to over-saturation even from the smallest of rains. Decades earlier, the ground had begun to soften and a thick fog rolled in until the entire plot of land slowly transformed into a murky swamp. Yet amongst the crumbling, faded tombstones there was rumored to be a large boulder with an old sword protruding from it. It took Arthur several tries to finally locate the old ruined cemetery, but once he finally arrived his heart leapt and he was sure that he'd finally found what he was looking for. His feet sunk ever so slightly with every step upon the soft wet earth.

But there in the center of the graveyard was the sword.

As Arthur approached he saw that its steel had faded and discolored. The blade was covered in moss, and the hilt seemed to have been at least partially inlaid with smooth granite stone. Upon closer inspection, he found the faded runes that roughly translated to, "This be Klærent the Stonebourne. The Sword of Peace."

With building elation, Arthur wrapped his fingers around the sword, and he immediately knew he had found what he had been looking for. From merely a touch, Arthur's mind flooded with images and ideas. He had impressions of his father and of a hundred generation of kings before. Arthur was inspired with thoughts of revolution and conquests in the pursuit of ultimate peace. But then with a shiver, Arthur was washed over by less pleasant flashes of bloody rebellions, violent overthrows, and murder.

Arthur caught his breath, and then with a mighty heave, he pulled and the sword slid smoothly and cleanly out of its resting place. Arthur had claimed the legendary Klærent the Stonebourne.

Then, with a tingle of exhilaration and fear, he looked down and saw a name blazing in red upon the misshapen hunk of rock:

PRINCE CATIGERN

~ ~ ~

Of course, no one said it would be easy.

The sword in the stone had given Arthur commands, and flooded his mind with premonitions, but now the difficult task of following them loomed before the young man. Suddenly, all of Arthur's training was being put to the test. Over the next few weeks, he found himself thrust into dangerous unpredictable dangers, battling with Vortigern's most cunning lieutenants, all the while trying to maintain an air of secrecy. More than once the demanding sword nearly got Arthur killed, but then each time, no matter how improbably, Arthur managed to emerge victorious. With the help of the legendary sword, he struck down some of Vortigern's most loyal allies, and time after time Arthur was rewarded with new followers of his own, or vital supplies for his hungry despairing people. Yet despite the gains the sword provided, Arthur couldn't help but worry that the costs were too great. He had never imagined that he would one day plot to retake the throne through his own mixture of violence and deception.

And the dangers kept growing.

Klærent the Stonebourne had once represented Arthur's great hope, but now it seemed to offer only a grim chance of redemption.

One cold moonless night, Arthur raced through the dark forest in the direction of the abandoned cemetery. He sprinted, pumping his legs desperately, as his breath came out in sharp rasps. His golden hair was longer and unkempt now, and his handsome young face was cut, bleeding and dirty as it was whipped by low-hanging branches. His clothes, which had once been so well-tailored and beautiful, were now little more than rags. He was a shadow of the carefree youth he had been just over a year ago.

Suddenly he emerged into the dark graveyard, thick with fog, and cluttered with its decrepit, moss-covered tombstones. The soft spongy earth sank unnaturally beneath his boots, giving him poor purchase on the earth. His eyes quickly raked the strange haunted surroundings, when—

A towering hulking beast of a knight, fully adorned in war-beaten armor, erupted out of the trees at nearly the same spot as Arthur had just seconds ago. Sir Aggravaine, as large and monstrous as ever, padded toward Arthur with a swagger and a grin. Arthur spun in surprise and panic at Aggravaine's arrival, and in his exhaustion he tripped and fell to the ground. Aggravaine sneered down upon the filthy young man at his feet.

"Well, well, well... the Boy King finally appears," growled Aggravaine.

Arthur scuttled backward, trying to put some distance between him and the oncoming brute. He didn't get far, however, before he ran into that massive hunk of rock.

With its moss-covered sword protruding out of it.

"Not very smart, boy," spat Aggravaine. "A cocky thief without any weapons, trapped in a deserted graveyard by one of the king's own knights…"

"Sir Aggravaine… Please…" pleaded Arthur.

"King Vortigern will be so pleased to receive the gift of your head," said Aggravaine as he closed in and his massive form filled Arthur's vision.

Arthur backed into the looming boulder, pushing himself up against it. He seemed to grope hopelessly for something, anything to defend himself with. And his hand closed on the hilt of the sword in the stone.

"You gonna pull that sword from the stone?!" laughed Aggravaine, as he watched Arthur's feeble desperate attempt to defend himself. "That's how you're gonna fight me? With some old sword that's been stuck in that rock for who knows how long?"

And, much to Aggravaine's astonishment, that's exactly what Arthur did.

With a mighty heave, the sword slid out of the stone. Sir Aggravaine's eyes went wide and his jaw dropped. But Arthur simply grinned. He'd been planning this all along.

"Good trick, huh?"

Despite Arthur's act, he had been in the graveyard over a dozen times now. It was true that the first time had filled him with fear and apprehension. After all, this was a graveyard, and a rather unsettling one at that, and Arthur was still a young man. Nonetheless, over time Arthur had come to rather appreciate this haunted place, and he now even considered it some of the friendliest territory for his varied and ambitious plans.

And it was all thanks to Klærent the Stonebourne, the trusty old moss-covered sword that Arthur now gripped by its smooth granite-encrusted hilt.

However, with a furious grinding of his teeth, Aggravaine rallied. The massive man drew his broadsword and took a tremendous swing at Arthur, a swing that could have cut a lesser man in half. But Arthur wasn't any man, and Klærent the Stonebourne wasn't any sword, and as he parried the blow —

Sir Aggravaine's sword shattered into a thousand pieces.

Now it was Aggravaine's turn to stumble in surprise. He collapsed in shock and fell to the ground, his generous bulk shaking inside his war-beaten armor.

"Not very smart, Aggravaine," Arthur said ironically. "One of the king's own knights, without any weapons, trapped in a deserted graveyard by a cocky thief...."

The disgraced knight furiously glared up into the eyes of Arthur, who seemed calm, possessed, and completely in charge.

"I want you to take a message to Vortigern for me."

Expertly, Arthur flourished his sword.

71

"Actually, the look on your face will say it all."

With one powerful arcing blow, Arthur struck. And Sir Aggravaine's head rolled off into the graveyard. Since his return to the kingdom of Tintagel, Arthur had heard story after story of Aggravaine's cruelty and viciousness. The hulking behemoth had risen to the point of being one of King Vortigern's most despicable and heartless mercenaries. As Aggravaine fell, Arthur couldn't help but flush with pride, and one thought stuck in his mind:

That one's for Guinevere.

After a moment, Arthur turned back to the stone. Written on the rock in bold red letters was the name:

SIR AGGRAVAINE

Arthur slid his sword back into the misshapen hunk of rock, and as he did so Sir Aggravaine's name burned brightly then vanished. Having completed his current task of dispatching Aggravaine, Arthur turned away and finally allowed himself a moment to sag from the effort of this feint. He took a deep breath when something caught his eye.

A new name was burning red on the stone, and Arthur knew that he was now being provided a new villain to track down and slay. By this time, Arthur had come to trust the stone and its suggestions, and he was sure that this next target would help move him ever closer to regaining the throne. With that in mind, Arthur approached the stone and read:

LADY GUINEVERE

His exhilaration gone, Arthur stared at this most unexpected name. It felt like a hand had gripped his heart and was squeezing mercilessly. This was impossible. Could the stone have made a mistake? Could it possibly be asking Arthur to commit this terrible sacrifice? His mind was reeling as absentmindedly his hand fell to his hip where, tucked into his belt, was a lovely handkerchief embroidered with the letter "G." His last gift from his lost love.

~ ~ ~

CHAPTER 5

How Guinevere Survived

Guinevere was doing her best to keep her perfect composure, but the rocky road ahead was making it decidedly difficult. She sat stock still in her luxurious carriage as it slowly cut its way through a thick wooded path. However, the carriage's large wooden wheels were poorly suited for the rough terrain of a little-used path despite the old driver's best efforts. Guinevere knew the kind old man in the tunic bearing King Vortigern's crest was trying to keep the carriage steady. Nonetheless he was failing miserably.

Glancing out the window, Guinevere spotted stray rays of sunlight breaking through the heavy overgrowth of branches and illuminating the path, but they did little to make it anymore accessible. The best Guinevere could hope for was to ride out this particularly tough bit of poorly-trodden road, and convince herself that something better had to lie ahead.

In point of fact, Lady Guinevere had never looked as good. Her appearance was carefully crafted with soft colors painstakingly applied to her face, and rich silken fabrics perfectly tailored to her slim curves. And, as always, her strong, shiny hair was arranged meticulously into thick, ornate braids that wrapped sumptuously around her head. Not a hair was out of place, and it was taking every ounce of strength and determination that Guinevere had to maintain that facade.

The carriage went over a particularly nasty bump, and Guinevere leapt in her seat and came crashing down with an "Oof!" She shot a glance at one of her ladies-in-waiting as she quickly recomposed and said, "Lovely ride, isn't it?"

The lady-in-waiting lowered her eyes and forced a smile. It was rare that Guinevere shared anything with any of them, and now that she had, they didn't know how to respond. That suited Guinevere just fine. She had learned to rely only on herself in the past year, and while she was sure that the ladies-in-waiting were perfectly nice people, Guinevere had no interest in digging deeper.

Guinevere's short moment of peaceful introspection was suddenly shattered as a rough voice from outside ripped through the air, and filled the young lady with alarm.

"Seize the carriage!"

Just outside came the sound of thundering hooves and cracking tree branches. Guinevere quickly looked out the carriage window to see four rebels on horseback emerging from the trees. Their horses charged, and at the lead was a young man with a wild mane of tangled red hair. Guinevere had vaguely known Kay back during the rule of Uther Pendragon, and she had never particularly liked him. He had always seemed a little too brash and had the habit of getting people hurt. Yet he had a funny way of talking his way out of any trouble, which somehow bothered Guinevere even more.

Now he was galloping after them, and that made Guinevere like him least of all.

There was a crack of the reins and the carriage leapt forward. Guinevere knew that the old driver wasn't going to give up without a fight, and she could hear him urging the horses onward. Unfortunately, Guinevere and her ladies-in-waiting were bearing the brunt of the damage. The carriage was ill-suited for a chase, and it rattled and jostled as it careened over one bump after another. On more than one occasion Guinevere found herself airborne for a moment, before slamming painfully back into her seat.

With another glance out the window, she saw that the carriage's flight was doing little good. Kay and his men were quickly overtaking the clunky-wheeled vehicle, and with a whip of red hair, Guinevere watched as Kay leapt from his horse and landed atop the carriage with a resounding crash overhead. Her breath caught in her throat as she heard Kay's cocky voice barking at the old driver.

"You've lived a long life, old man," Kay said. "Stop this carriage, and live a bit longer."

The carriage quickly came to a halt.

Guinevere did her best to steel her nerves and steady her breathing as she heard the other three rebels arriving moments later. Her senses were screaming at the danger, and her ears rang in terror, but her face remained still and impassive. She might be terrified, but she was utterly determined not to show it. In the past twelve months, she had done her best to rise in the estimation of

King Vortigern and his regime. She had been raised a lady and she had intended to stay that way, so with no shortage of quick thinking she had wormed her way into Vortigern's good graces. This had afforded her the luxurious life that she had been born into, but it also made her a target. Vortigern had many enemies, and now she shared them. Unfortunately, some of those enemies had now overtaken them.

In what felt like mere seconds, the rebels were pulling the ladies-in-waiting from the carriage. Guinevere would be the last to climb out, but before she did, she took a deep breath and then forced herself to take in a little more. The extra oxygen filled her belly, and she felt her nerves soften and her mind clear. It was an action that she had made many times in the months since she'd become a prisoner of Vortigern. She'd learned the importance of silencing her fear, and now was no exception.

Kay jabbed his crossbow at Guinevere as she gracefully stepped out of the carriage. Her foot wobbled as she touched the ground and her legs felt like jelly, but she had become adept at hiding any moments of weakness. Kay didn't seem to notice that anything was out of place, as he grinned and leered at the proper lady that stood before him.

"Well, well, well, I'm sorry to interrupt your pleasant afternoon, Lady Guinevere," he said, "but I think this gold would be better in the hands of the people."

Kay nodded to his three rebel friends, and they eagerly climbed into the carriage and began ransacking it in search of coins, jewelry, and other loot. Guinevere made a slight movement toward the carriage, but Kay stopped her with the careful aim of his weapon. The two of them circled one another as Kay moved between Guinevere and the carriage.

"Although I must say," continued Kay as he eyed up Guinevere, "I doubt we'll find anything more valuable in there than King Vortigern's favorite lady."

"Please," said Guinevere, her voice soft and measured, "leave the carriage. You'll find nothing but—"

BOOM!

The carriage exploded into a massive fireball. Flames licked the treetops, and splintering wood flew in all directions. The three rebels, now fully engulfed, would never emerge. Kay was knocked forward by the blast and fell hard to the ground. Guinevere heard him gasp, and she knew that his breath had left him as he took a painful gasp to refill his lungs. The fall was hard enough that it knocked the crossbow from his fingers and it fell at Guinevere's feet.

"As I was saying, you'll find nothing in there but Merlin's black powder."

And for the first time, Guinevere's voice wavered. But not with fear. With perverse pleasure. Her plan had worked. Dazed and at her feet, Kay crawled over the ground, desperately reaching for his crossbow. But Guinevere easily got there first. She raised it with the ease and confidence that had come with countless hours of practice. While under Vortigern's protection, Guinevere had continued her usual training as a lady, taking classes in languages, etiquette, and even cooking. Unbeknownst to the king, however, Guinevere had enacted a completely different kind of study for herself as well. In secret, at every spare moment she could find, Guinevere practiced tirelessly the skills of survival. She taught herself deception, guile and lies. With deft fingers she had learned how to escape knots, or palm a vial of poison. She had become more than proficient with a crossbow or the golden dagger that had been her father's final gift to her.

In reality, it was her father that had been driving her self-improvements. After that terrible night when Tintagel had fallen, she and Leodegrance had been pulled away from each other, and he had been taken deeper into the embrace of Vortigern's cruelty. The kindly old lord had vanished from all view, and no one seemed to know where he was being held. Every so often a letter in his handwriting would arrive, but there was never any real information. More often than not it was simply to reach out to foreign kings and lords, since Leodegrance still held sway with other powers. However, Guinevere knew that he was somewhere, probably in terrible danger, being forced to assist Vortigern's purposes. There was a strange irony in the fact that the reason Leodegrance was cooperating was almost certainly because Guinevere's wellbeing was threatened if he didn't. It was this that Guinevere always kept in mind as she herself did the king's bidding.

"I'm sorry, Sir Kay," said Guinevere, and she truly did sound sorry as she aimed the crossbow directly at the forehead that was now framed by a mane of wild, red hair, "but in these dark times, only the strong survive."

And with that, Guinevere pulled the trigger.

~   ~   ~

CHAPTER 6

The Wizard In Waiting

Merlin was bored. Matters of court had never interested him all that much. There were far more complex and fascinating subjects for him to pursue. The migration of geese, the alignment of the planets, the mastery of dragons, the dark arts that granted control over the minds of men, the as-yet-to-be-written works of Charles Dickens. He would've preferred nothing more than to quietly sequester himself away in his cottage, conjure a good book out of thin air, and indulge his curiosities.

Yet King Vortigern had demanded that Merlin stand at his side from time to time in order to remind the people of the new king's power. And the wizard's magic bound him to whoever controlled the throne, so there was nothing Merlin could do but stand there and wait patiently until Vortigern had been satisfied. Then Merlin would vanish in a whiff of smoke, or transform into an eagle, or, his recent transportation of choice, he'd summon a rain cloud and drift away with its precipitation. Finally, he'd be able to return home and curl up with a good book.

But at the moment, he would have to settle with being bored.

The throne room that once belonged to Uther Pendragon had been transformed under its new owner. King Vortigern now sat upon the throne surrounded by treasure chests, wooden boxes, and crates of all shapes and sizes. Trinkets, heirlooms, and trophies were scattered upon every spare inch of the cluttered throne room. King Vortigern himself, with his crown perched prominently atop his matted black hair, rifled greedily through his treasure as he took stock of the gifts sent to him from his frightened subjects.

Merlin stood silently as his eyes raked across the gold, silver and jewels, but his face remained impassive. There was a time when Merlin had enjoyed predicting what was in every single box, but it had annoyed Vortigern to no end, which Merlin had also secreted enjoyed.

Some people simply have a preoccupation with being surprised, thought Merlin sardonically. *If Vortigern really knew what awaited him, he'd want all the predictions I could give him.*

Nonetheless, the old wizard kept those observations for himself as he watched the king greedily hoarding his treasure. The huge wooden doors at the far end of the throne room creaked open, and a servant entered with eyes properly lowered to avoid the possibility of invoking Vortigern's rage. The servant quickly approached Vortigern and presented a long, thin box.

The dark king's lips curled into a smile of anticipation, but Merlin simply thought, *Just an old rusty sword. How boring...*

"Let me see, let me see... What have you brought me?!" Vortigern asked as he eagerly threw open the package. His face dropped as he pulled out, sure enough, an old rusty sword.

Noticing the king's souring frown at the poor gift, a thin smile broke across Merlin's lips, although it was mostly obscured by his long, white beard.

I could've spared him the disappointment, but no… thought Merlin. Then the wizard reflected, *Sometimes it's better not to know how things will happen. It does make things a bit more exciting.*

Vortigern grimaced as he tossed the old rusty sword aside, and his black eyes flashed with anger.

"Go back," Vortigern ordered the quaking servant, who clearly worried that this would all somehow come down on him. "See that they do better with their next gift. Or see that their home is burnt to the ground."

The servant hurried away, careful not to raise his eyes or even hint at dissent lest he evoke the mad king's rage upon himself.

As the servant reached the mighty oak doors that would provide his freedom, they suddenly swung open of their own accord, and the beautiful, slim figure of Lady Guinevere strode confidently into the throne room. She passed the servant with barely a glance, and the terrified man was only to happy to rush away and disappear into the hallway. Merlin watched as Guinevere navigated through the piles of treasure and headed straight toward Vortigern. The old magician's eyes narrowed as he surveyed her quick, confident steps and the determined look of a coldness on her naturally soft features. Without a doubt, Merlin liked Guinevere. Mostly it was because he always had a hard time figuring her out. It was easy to foresee events. The bigger they were the easier they were to predict. However, people were much more difficult and puzzling. They could even throw a wizard for a loop, because many people didn't always act in their best interests. They could be baffling, riddling, and enigmatic. And Guinevere had become one of the most enigmatic individuals that Merlin had come across.

It thrilled him.

Especially since it made Merlin suspect that one day he might have to destroy her.

For his part, Vortigern scurried over to his throne and threw himself into it with his legs draped across the arms, doing his best impression of a lazy, unquestioned monarch. As Guinevere drew closer, Vortigern bared his yellow teeth into a grin and clapped.

"Well done, my dear, well done!" Vortigern said, "The news of Sir Kay's demise reached my ears quite quickly. Yet another of my enemies has fallen at your hands. Come here, my dear! King Vortigern rewards his friends. And I have just the thing for you."

Vortigern's hands disappeared into a nearby box and withdrew a beautiful green gown.

"From a young woman to the north," he said. "She was saving it for her wedding. But I think you've earned it."

Guinevere bowed her head dutifully, and accepted the dress. With her face slightly inclined, Vortigern couldn't see the slightest grimace crossing her face. But Merlin could. Guinevere caught the wizard's eyes, and he could tell that he was unnerving her. She was doing her best to put up a strong front, and Merlin was able to put cracks into it.

Fun, fun, fun... thought Merlin.

"I live to serve, my king," said Guinevere, looking away from Merlin and refocusing all of her attention on Vortigern.

"With your help there may never be a need for my Red Dragon to reawaken from the great lake. Eh, Merlin?" said Vortigern, looking over to the wizard.

Merlin just smiled and shrugged.

"Your wizard's growing old, King Vortigern," said Guinevere. "Maybe he can't get his dragon to rise anymore."

Ah, there it was. That intriguing bold unpredictability of Guinevere. She had very little to gain by challenging Merlin, and yet she did so in order to upend the order and see what might come of it. In his musical lilt, Merlin finally decided to speak and his voice floated on the air, beautiful and deadly,

"A woman's wit,

Her sharpest lash,

But watch your tongue,

Or burn to ash."

And with a snap of his fingers, all of the torches in the great hall flared ominously.

Guinevere's eyes flashed with danger and alarm. Merlin's eyes twinkled. He loved to see the effect that he could have on people.

Klærent was one of the lesser known mystical swords, and that might have been partially due to its reputation as a "Sword of Peace." There simply wasn't the same demand for a peaceful sword as there was for a sword that promised to bestow the power to destroy one's enemies. In fact, the whole idea of a destructive weapon that was meant for peace was in itself confusing, and led many warriors and kings to disregard Klærent so as to seek flashier and more impressive-sounding weapons. But they were wrong to do so. For those who wielded Klærent found that while it did indeed seek for peace, it also seemed to imbue an innate understanding that sometimes peace can only be found on the other side of war. Klærent was an excellent instrument for battle, it was true, but even more impressively, it allowed its owner the ability to communicate with voices from the beyond that could aid in its quest for peace. It was a singularly powerful sword, and yet several decades earlier it had found itself plunged into a hunk of rock where it was doomed to gather moss until it would be claimed once more. Somewhere in history there was a genius swordmaker who must've been annoyed that a work of art like Klærent was so often overlooked.

That is, until Arthur set his sights upon obtaining it. From the moment that it had been mentioned Arthur sought to take control of the sword. His father's words rung in his ears: "It is meant only for the king. For me. And for you. Find it. And it will guide you." As is common for a son, Arthur looked up to his great father, and felt certain that there was a deep wisdom in Uther's last words to him.

"Now, now, you two," cut in Vortigern, with a perverse grin on his face, "there's enough bloodlust to go around. Here, Merlin, I have gifts for you as well."

Vortigern rifled once more and was quickly handing Guinevere a necklace to go with her gown. A moment later, Merlin received a book, Faeries Tales Culled from Egyptian Legend of the Pre-Christian Era, which seemed like an odd, overblown title which inspired little confidence that it would make good bedtime stories. Still, it seemed like Merlin had found his evening's reading material.

"Apologies, my king," said Guinevere, but she couldn't resist adding, "Merlin was instrumental in winning you the throne. But it is I who have helped you keep it."

She gave Merlin a menacing gaze. Merlin gave the merest lift of an eyebrow. Vortigern barely gave any notice at all to their interchange as he looked over Guinevere.

"I must say, Guinevere, I am most impressed by your initiative in killing those who vex me," said Vortigern. "Pray tell, how is it that I have been so lucky as to become the beneficiary of your considerable skills in treachery and guile?"

Merlin's eyes danced back and forth from Vortigern to Guinevere, and the old wizard would've given anything to be able to read her mind at that moment.

"You are my king. I would do anything for my true and brave king," was Guinevere's sly response. "Anything."

With the gown that Vortigern had just given her fluttering behind as she clutched it in her arms, Guinevere nodded to her king then swept out the door and was gone. Vortigern laughed gleefully as he watched her go.

But Merlin narrowed his eyes as she disappeared out of the mighty oak doors. Five minutes with Guinevere, and Merlin was no longer bored.

~ ~ ~

CHAPTER 7

Puppies and Crows

It only took a matter of moments for Guinevere to cross the castle and arrive at her lavish bed chambers. She was barely through the door when, in a burst of revulsion, she flung onto her large, canopied bed the gown and necklace that she had just been given. Almost reflexively, she wiped her hands off upon the thick bed curtains, and she drew in several sharp rasping breaths as she tried to expel her recent odious encounter with Vortigern. She steadied herself and brought her breathing back to a slow, controlled rhythm when she heard a slight whimpering.

A moment of panic tore through Guinevere as she spun around to take in her chambers. Had she really been so foolish to not thoroughly check the room before she allowed herself a brief moment of vulnerability? Had someone just witnessed her honesty? Could someone now guess that her loyalty might not be quite as strict as she had carefully cultivated?

She searched frantically for just a moment, before her eyes found the source of the tiny whimper. In an instant she had relaxed, although a heavy frown now lined her face as she looked at the source of the whimper.

An adorable black puppy.

It scampered out from beneath her bed, and playfully bounded over to Guinevere. The puppy's almost comically large paws charmingly petted at Guinevere's gown. Its soft, red lolling tongue dropped out of it gently smiling mouth just below its large twinkling eyes.

However, Guinevere didn't greet it with so much as a smile.

"It's done. Kay is dead," said Guinevere, addressing the puppy with forced formality. "Now, what have you got for me?

The puppy trotted back to the bed and disappeared once more beneath it. A second later, it returned with a small bag clutched in its jaws. Guinevere took the bag from the puppy's slightly drooling mouth, and opened it to find a small bounty of gold coins. With barely a glance, she tossed the bag aside.

"What news?" Guinevere asked with building insistence. "Any word of my father?"

The puppy only spun with its tongue bouncing and flopping around its mouth. But Guinevere refused to play with the little beast.

"Please. Anything. Where is he?"

And suddenly with a melting of fur, feathers, and reality, the puppy vanished and reformed itself into a large black crow. The ugly bird cawed at Guinevere, and she lurched backward to avoid its crooked beak. The crow leapt up onto the windowsill, and extended its leg.

Warily, Guinevere approached the bird, and untied a small roll of parchment from its leg. The moment the paper was free, the yellow-eyed crow spread its large wings and soared away. Forcing her hands to be still, Guinevere unrolled the parchment and her eyes absorbed the few words. Her brow furrowed in confusion as she allowed her latest order to take hold.

"Lancelot? But how can I kill a man who's already dead?"

~　~　~

CHAPTER 8
A Friend's Demise

The morning sun was cresting as Arthur swiftly darted across a wide open field toward a thick forest. He sprinted toward the heavy tree line, cutting through the thick grass, and staining his boots and pants with the morning dew. However, as he reached the trees, which were supposed to be his sanctuary, the young man came to an abrupt stop. His well-trained eyes and ears focused sharply, and his muscles tightened as he prepared for danger.

Sure enough, there was a rustle of leaves, and in a flash Arthur had Klærent the Stoneboure out of the sheath on his hip. He swung it with the expertise and confidence that he had cultivated over the past year on the run, and it clashed into the waiting sword of the man who had trained him.

Sir Gawain stepped out of the trees. Both he and Arthur relaxed and lowered their weapons as they took each other in. As always, Arthur couldn't help but be impressed with Gawain. Powerfully built and clad in war-beaten armor, as one would expect of a knight of his stature, he was also adorned with his preferred trinkets and decorations from his many journeys.

"Gawain, I might've killed you," said Arthur, as he resheathed his mythic sword. "I'm on a roll."

"You were supposed to be back yesterday," said Gawain. "I began to worry that something might've happened to you."

"You mustn't worry so much, old friend. Especially on your night off," Arthur said. "Which reminds me: I thought Kay was on duty. Has he neglected his post again? He's becoming more and more unpredictable. I suppose you and I need to have another talk with—"

"Kay's dead."

Gawain's blunt announcement cut through Arthur like a knife. All of his airiness drained away as Arthur locked eyes with Gawain, searching the knight's face for any sign of misunderstanding. But there was none, and the truth settled over Arthur that his friend, Kay, who had almost been like a brother during those long hard months, was gone. A crushing weight threatened to settle in Arthur's breast. He'd lost too many people over the past year, and here he was just barely a man. For a moment, his youthfulness threatened to overtake him, and Arthur almost allowed the tears that tickled the edges of his eyes to come. He yearned for a time when everything around him was no longer madness, and he might simply allow himself to study, to court, or simply to rest. However, that time still seemed far away and separated by still more blood and strife. There was no time to be weak, no time to be young, no time to mourn. Arthur forced away the sadness, and pushed forward.

"Who?" asked Arthur, doing his best to hide the soft tremble of his voice.

"We're not sure, though I have my suspicions," said Gawain, also refusing to bow to sentimentality. "I'm having them investigated. In the meantime, I ordered the camp to be moved again, in case this is a part of larger scheme by Vortigern and his men. But I doubt it. This feels like something else. I had worried that they might've gotten you too."

"You needn't worry about me," Arthur said, batting away Gawain's concern. Then, with a flush of vindictive pleasure, he added, "Sir Aggravaine, on the other hand—"

But Gawain was far from pleased by this boast as he cut across Arthur, "You killed Aggravaine?! His death won't go unnoticed! Arthur, I can't keep you hidden if you keep taking unnecessary risks."

"The time for hiding is past," said Arthur. "Vortigern demands his gifts. So I've sent him one."

The two men, the future king and his loyal knight, began to stride through the forest. Their feet beat against the undergrowth as they matched one another step for step, each of them trying to overtake their other, but neither ceding to the quickness of their fellow.

"You should've have discussed this with me," said Gawain. "You should've talked about this with the other knights. We're your men, Arthur. You have to trust our council."

"The sword and the stone gave me Aggravaine's name," said Arthur. "It meant for me to finally reveal myself. I'm sure of it."

Gawain gritted his jaw, and Arthur noticed a vein becoming more pronounced along Gawain's heavy bearded jawline, but the older knight kept his composure.

"And now you have a new name?" asked the grizzled knight.

Arthur nodded. And, absentmindedly, his hand fell to his waist and stroked the embroidered handkerchief that had been tucked in his belt for as long as he could remember.

"Not that it's your concern," said Arthur, "but I may be done with the names on the stone."

"I can't say I'm displeased," said Gawain.

Arthur couldn't help but bristle at Gawain's words as he shot back, "This sword has helped us, Gawain. Ever since I found it and was able to draw it from the stone, its guidance, while sometimes difficult, has been invaluable. It's undoubtedly helped us to increase our numbers. And to decrease Vortigern's."

"And yet you still refuse to share its..." Gawain carefully chose his next word: "...wisdom."

"My father instructed me to seek that sword. It and its messages are meant for me alone," said Arthur definitively.

"Arthur, I served your father for many years," said Gawain. "I traveled to far distant lands, and saw many remarkable things. I also saw many acts of cruelty, manipulation, and betrayal. Some of which were carefully crafted to appear as something else. I don't trust any power that refuses to show itself."

"You've made your concerns known, Gawain," said Arthur, "but there's still no evidence that there are any manipulations behind the sword and the stone."

"We've made many enemies," reminded Gawain. "The warlock of Loch Ness. The necromancer of Broceliade. The Queen of the Feys!"

"Who we don't even know exists," Arthur pointed out.

"Oh, she exists," said Gawain. "Although she may have concealed herself, I've seen her power, and I know that she had plans for your and your father."

"The only one that I am focused on is Vortigern," said Arthur simply.

"And I agree that our attentions should be on stopping Vortigern and reclaiming the throne," said Gawain with a forced reluctant nod.

Arthur shook his head as he pressed the point, "Then it makes sense we use every advantage available to us. Vortigern murdered my father. He terrorizes my people. And if killing the names that appear on that stone helps me to stop him then so be it."

"I thought you said you were done with those names?" Gawain reminded him.

Once again, Arthur touched the handkerchief at his hip.

"I'm not sure."

"The throne belongs to you," said Gawain, with the straightforward honesty and loyalty that Arthur had come to admire. "Just make sure you'll still be a good king once you've taken it."

SWOOSH!

Suddenly, an arrow flew out of nowhere and struck Gawain, embedding itself into a chink between his breastplate and shoulder guard. The grizzled warrior winced at the pain, and his knees briefly gave way. He fell to one hand and braced himself against the ground. In a flash, Arthur was at his side, but Gawain stubbornly waved him away.

"I'm fine. Fine!" he growled, and then added out of spite, "I've had worse."

Without a doubt, Arthur knew this to be true of his mentor. If there was any man in all of the kingdom who had faced down all manner of warrior and beast then it was Gawain. With that thought firmly in mind, Arthur had no hesitation in leaving Gawain behind and sprinting off in the direction of the arrow and its archer.

As Arthur raced away, however, he heard Gawain shouting after him, "Arthur, wait! It's too dangerous!"

But Arthur paid no heed as he delved deeper into the woods. From a young age he'd been trained in the hunt, and his tracking skills had always been excellent. Since the overthrow of his father, he'd pushed his abilities even further. There had been excursions where he'd followed a falcon for several days through thick brambles, putting off food and sleep in order to stretch himself to the limits. At this moment, all of that testing was about to pay off, when —

"KING!"

A gruff roar erupted from the trees to Arthur's left. He spun to face the voice, and his mind worked furiously to figure out how anyone could've gotten the jump on him. Arthur had only a vague instant to comprehend that he was dealing with an excellent tactician, a worthy foe, before he locked eyes on the man charging straight for him.

Lancelot.

Arthur drew his sword in a flash of reflexes, but it wasn't nearly enough against the mighty Lancelot. The errant knight already had his blade drawn, and easily batted Klærent the Stonebourne away. Then with the force of a furious bull, Lancelot slammed Arthur into a tree.

For the first time in over a year, Arthur looked upon the face of the once legendary knight, and Arthur knew that the months hadn't been kind. Lancelot's once full and handsome face was scarred and thin, his hair stringy and long. He looked thinner, gaunt and hungry. But his strength was undeniable. As Lancelot lifted his blade and pressed it into Arthur's neck, Arthur got another jolt of surprise as he took his first good look at the former knight's weapon.

Lancelot's sword was strapped to a stump of a forearm.

Where there should have been a hand, wrist, and fingers, there was now only long, cold steel. It was as if Lancelot had a sword for an arm, and he was now determined to run Arthur through with it.

"Nothing personal, King," said Lancelot, and despite his lean, rugged features, his voice retained much of the playful cockiness of the man Arthur once knew, "but if I kill you, I get my arm back."

With that, Lancelot cocked back his arm of steel and prepared to deal his death blow.

~ ~ ~

CHAPTER 9

The Greatest Warrior in the Kingdom

Lancelot took the briefest of moments to relish the situation. He was about to thrust forward his sword arm, and cut down the boy king before his prime. As soon as this task was accomplished, he'd be rewarded with a new arm and a feeling of completeness that he'd been lacking for the past year. After all the strife and pain that he'd been through, Lancelot's life was going to get back on track, and he could finally reclaim his rightful place as the greatest knight in all the lands. It was a sweet moment, and life afforded so few moments like this, so Lancelot wanted to savor it for just a fleeting instant.

It was an instant too long.

Another strong hand grabbed Lancelot by the shoulder, and blocked his ability to swiftly slice through Arthur.

Gawain had finally caught up.

Lancelot cursed his luck. He'd gotten so caught up in the moment he had ignored Gawain's lumbering arrival. Now, with his bear-like strength, Gawain spun Lancelot, and the two knights came face-to-face for the first time in many moons. Gawain's eyes took in Lancelot's thinner, more scarred appearance, and it gave Gawain a moment of pause. Which was all Lancelot needed as he quickly seized upon the hesitation and said,

"Gawain! It's been a lifetime!"

Then with a flick of his arm, Lancelot slashed at Gawain's throat. Just missed. Though slow to react, Lancelot had to admit that Gawain was still a capable knight and had deftly managed to lean back out of the way of the slicing sword arm.

"Lancelot...?" said Gawain, clearly not very quick on the uptake.

Just as slow on comprehension, Arthur rebounded from his tree, and scrambled to retrieve his dropped sword as he said, "We thought you were dead."

In all honesty, Lancelot was starting to like this situation. Both Arthur and Gawain seemed astonished at Lancelot's return. This gave the one-armed knight a distinct advantage. Both of his opponents would be confused and slow to respond. It was true that the presence of Gawain would make things more difficult, but Lancelot never minded a little challenge. In fact, he felt that it would make for an even more thrilling tale upon his inevitable victory. The mighty Lancelot had returned from the dead and immediately slain the disgraced king and dispatched his only rival for the title of greatest warrior in the kingdom.

Lancelot grinned. *It all had such a nice ring to it.*

With his intact hand, Lancelot drew a second sword from his hip and pointed it. His sword arm was now fixed upon Arthur, and the full sword was at the ready for Gawain. The three men circled each other warily. It was clear that Arthur was no longer just a boy: he had trained himself for any circumstance, and therefore couldn't be underestimated. Gawain, as well, wasn't the kind of man to be intimidated, and presented a formidable foe. But Lancelot was the stuff of legends, or at least he considered himself to be, and he had recently even managed to claw himself out of the clutches of certain death. He may have looked worse than before, but that only served to enhance his advantage of unpredictability.

Lancelot was really starting to feel bad for Arthur and Gawain.

"You think this is wise, Arthur?" taunted Lancelot. "Challenging the kingdom's greatest warrior?"

"You were never the kingdom's greatest warrior," Gawain spat back, and Lancelot felt that the older knight sounded more than a little pouty.

"I will be, once I've slain both of you!"

And Lancelot struck. With amazing speed and skill, Lancelot managed to fight both Arthur and Gawain at once. Ever since he was a small boy, Lancelot had an undeniable genius with a blade. He was quickly able to master any discipline, no maneuver was beyond his grasp, and shifting between styles was only too easy for him. He had battled any and all challengers, and always emerged victorious and more confident in his prodigious skills. With his preferred right hand, Lancelot was a furious, unbeatable menace.

Unfortunately, Lancelot no longer had that right hand.

He couldn't deny that it had been a blow that dark and stormy night in which he had lost half of his dominant arm. Lancelot had prided himself a swordsman without equal, and now his greatest asset was gone. Where weaker men would've fallen to despair, however, the loss of his hand had only driven Lancelot forward. As he lay dying, Lancelot urged himself to breathe, willed his heart to beat, and his mind worked furiously to design a means to reclaim his former greatness. The healing process was slow, but Lancelot wasn't idle in his downtime. His brain churned with plans to rise again, as strong and capable as ever. He plumbed into all of his considerable skills and knowledge to concoct new, heretofore unknown techniques of combat. Nonetheless, as he lay barely able to move or even stay conscious, everything that he dreamt was merely theoretical. When he finally emerged from off his deathbed, Lancelot quickly sought out a way to reunite himself with steel. Through long days and nights of trial and error, Lancelot had devised the sword that was now strapped to his wounded arm.

Then the real fun began.

There were no masters to learn this art from. There were no books from which Lancelot could study. This was a fighting style that he would have to create for himself. No problem at all. He was Lancelot, the ill-made knight, and it only seemed natural that he should be destined to create something new and unique for himself alone. Over weeks and months, Lancelot drew upon all his varied knowledge of combat, he revisited all of his many battles and contests, and he rebuilt himself to be a warrior the likes of which the world had never seen.

Now his sword arm had become an extension of himself as it slashed and jabbed with deadly precision and tireless strength at the young man before him. Lancelot could tell that Arthur knew how to duel, and he had learned from his own life experiences that young people tended to be brash and aggressive. It made it important to keep Arthur on the defensive, which Lancelot did with dazzling skill and ferocity. Lancelot could see Arthur desperately seeking for an opening, but the young man was destined to be disappointed. The legendary Sir Lancelot was back, and he had no intention of ever showing weakness again.

To Lancelot's other side, however, a different story was unfolding. Gawain was taking the fight to Lancelot, and Lancelot was forced to cede a bit of ground to the older, more experienced knight on his left. Although he would've been loath to admit it out loud, Lancelot's left arm was his weaker arm. At his prime, he knew that there wasn't a man alive who could've challenged him with his right arm, but with his left hand there were maybe a handful of men who could match Lancelot. And Gawain was certainly one of them. Nonetheless, Lancelot didn't allow a glimmer of doubt to enter his mind. He exhibited boundless vigor and flawless technique as he locked swords with the older, more seasoned knight.

If there had been anyone there to witness the match, it would've been undeniable that it was one for the ages.

As their steel clashed with resounding tones of adventure, Arthur surprised Lancelot with a tactic the fearsome knight hadn't expected. Arthur reached out a hand of friendship.

"I don't want to fight you, Lancelot," said Arthur, although Lancelot noticed that Arthur was indeed still fighting and refusing to die. "Join me. I could use a good man like you."

"What makes you so special?" asked Lancelot, as Arthur deflected a blow that would've cleaved a lesser man's arm from his torso.

"Show some respect," growled Gawain. "He's the rightful King."

"Why? Because his father was?" said Lancelot, ducking a swing from Gawain. "Why should Arthur be King?"

Arthur had no answer. And in that moment of hesitation, Lancelot viciously kicked Arthur in the chest. Arthur sprawled backward and gasped for air.

"Not impressed," said Lancelot.

"Traitor!" roared Gawain as he charged at Lancelot.

The two experienced knights squared up, and Lancelot couldn't help but think that any poet in history would have loved to witness the epic battle that was about to ensue. Lancelot, the mightiest warrior the world had ever seen, was about to finish off the over-the-hill, gone-to-seed, formerly great Sir Gawain.

Lancelot mused that perhaps he'd be the best person to write it.

However, Gawain was quick to get down to business, and shifted his fighting style to compensate for Lancelot's two attacking blades. For a short time, when they had both served under Uther Pendragon, Lancelot had trained with Gawain, and he knew that Gawain had always preferred to operate alone. Having Arthur out of the way gave them both a little breathing room. Now they could fight man-to-man, and Lancelot was sure that Gawain hoped to show him a thing or two.

Lancelot didn't seem particularly impressed as he tried to throw Gawain off-balance, saying, "I'm amazed to see you, Gawain. Say, where were you a year ago? When we needed you."

"I was crusading for Uther," shot back Gawain.

"Lucky you. In a distant land while the rest of us lost limb and life."

"I won't apologize to you."

"Aw, Gawain, you used to respect me."

"You used to have honor."

"I used to have two arms."

And, crossing his two swords, Lancelot bound up Gawain's blade. Then Lancelot thrust his head forward, colliding with Gawain's lined forehead and knocking the older knight to the ground. As Gawain fell, Lancelot grinned with an air of triumph.

"Though it seems you'd need three arms to best me," said Lancelot.

Suddenly, a fist cracked Lancelot across the chin, and sent him staggering backward in surprise. Arthur returned, and Lancelot spit blood out on ground at the young man's feet.

"We have four arms," said Arthur. "You can't win this. Drop your sword."

A crazed laugh escaped Lancelot's lips as he waved his stump of a sword arm. "Was that supposed to be a joke?!"

"How'd you like to lose your other arm?" said Gawain as he stood beside Arthur in a combined show of force. "And your legs besides?"

Both Arthur and Gawain advanced slowly. Lancelot cocked his head as he struggled with what was clearly a difficult decision. Finally, he winced and said, "I admit... I would not like to lose any more limbs. Well, you win some —"

Without finishing the thought, Lancelot turned and sprinted away. Just behind him, he could hear that Arthur had taken off after him with Gawain just a breath behind, shouting, "Arthur, stop! He's too unpredictable!"

Arthur's voice called back, "That's why we can't let him get away!"

Deeper and deeper into the forest Lancelot led his attackers. The one-armed knight maintained a small lead as he darted between trees and leap frogged over fallen stumps. Arthur and Gawain were well up to the task as they cleared small streams and knocked aside gnarled branches with ease while keeping up their pursuit.

Until, suddenly, the race stopped.

With an abruptness that must've confused his pursuers, Lancelot halted in the midst of a small clearing and spun to face Arthur and Gawain.

"You're not one to run away, Lancelot," said Gawain, panting slightly.

"It's not running away, Gawain," said Lancelot as he slashed at the rope that he had camouflaged amongst the tangled brush. "It's retreating to favorable ground!"

A massive log suspended by thick, worn ropes swung in seemingly out of nowhere. Gawain was once again slow to react, and the swinging battering ram hit him square in the chest. His armor took the brunt force, but he nonetheless stumbled backward with a heave of pain.

Lancelot locked eyes with Arthur, and there was a maniacal glint in the knight's gaze. "I've been planning this for a long time, King."

With another slash, Lancelot severed another deceptively hidden rope. From the crook of an old, dying tree, several crossbow arrows tore through the air. But Arthur didn't seem to be intimidated in the least. The young man who hoped to be king dove and expertly rolled out of the way of the flood of arrows, then with expert skill he returned to his feet just as a loud clunking sound erupted from a hollowed tree trunk. A double-headed ax flew at Arthur, flipping end over end, but Arthur gripped his sword tightly with both hands and batted the ax away. It flew off its path and embedded itself deeply into the soft ground.

Lancelot would have complimented Arthur if he believed in giving his opponents compliments. As it was, the great knight simply flung himself at Arthur and kept up his blistering attack.

In a flurry of hacks and slashes the two men battled, and Lancelot noticed that Arthur kept sneaking glimpses at their strange surroundings. There were ropes and traps everywhere! Even as they continued to duel, Lancelot sensed that Arthur's courage might be wavering under the overwhelming odds against him. On all sides were snares and foils. In even the slightest opening, Lancelot would cut another binding and Arthur would be forced to defend against another barrage of darts, hooks, blades, and spears. Not only that, but Arthur, who was barely a man, had to hold off the wild swings from two swords wielded by the full-grown, immensely powerful Lancelot himself. The knight couldn't help but be somewhat impressed that Arthur didn't simply give up, throw down his sword, and accept his fate.

Which was why Lancelot was completely thrown off guard when Arthur took the attack.

The young man who would be king gritted his teeth and pressed forward against Lancelot. In his prime, no one would dare take the attack on Lancelot, and he was shocked as Arthur increased his speed and forced Lancelot to match him. Their swords careened through the air so quickly that the glints of sunshine that broke through the trees barely had time to reflect off of the hot steel. Their blades were nearly invisible now as Arthur improbably put Lancelot on the defensive. Despite the attack, Lancelot grinned.

"Gawain's trained you well, King!"

"I'm raising an army to overthrow Vortigern. I never assumed it would be easy. And I could use a man like you," said Arthur even as he did his best to defeat the man he was offering friendship to.

"You've got a few dozen knights at your command, and many of them are miserable cowards," scoffed Lancelot as he sent another well-hidden volley of darts at Arthur. "You're constantly on the move. Hunted nearly to extinction. I'm sorry, Arthur, but I've already been on the losing side."

As he pivoted out of the way of the deadly tipped points, Arthur said, "You were loyal to my father once."

"And your father's dead. Loyalty to kings hasn't treated me well."

Then Lancelot lunged forward, causing Arthur to sidestep into a trip wire. It closed around Arthur's foot, and yanked Arthur upside down into the air. Lancelot had clearly won, and yet—

Arthur continued to fight!

The young aspiring king insisted on continuing to duel with Lancelot despite the world having been flipped on him! What was wrong with this boy?!

"Can't you see, King? You've lost!" shouted Lancelot.

"My people are hungry, poor, and dying. I will never stop fighting!" was Arthur's determined reply.

And Arthur stretched out to the nearest rope he could reach. The young man with golden hair desperately slashed at the taut rope, and a large boulder came swinging in. Whether it was because he hadn't fully recovered or because of utter astonishment at Arthur's unexpected boldness, Lancelot turned too late. The boulder smacked him in the head, and sent him stumbling onto what appeared to be a pile of leaves, but one he knew would quickly give way to a hidden pit below. Lancelot fell and was engulfed into the darkness.

Dazed and struggling to remain conscious, Lancelot lay on the soft earth at the bottom of his own trap. He felt the warm trickle of blood down his forehead where the boulder had clipped him. Some ten feet above him, he heard another slashing and a dull thud. Arthur must've cut himself free. Lancelot tried to push himself up, but his arms wouldn't obey. He fell back to the soft soil. He would rest for just a moment, just a single moment, then claw his way out of here and continue the fight.

His single moment of rest quickly became two.

And then three.

Then, as Lancelot lay there willing his head to stop spinning, he heard two sets of footsteps gingerly hobbling to the edge of the pit. Although he couldn't summon the strength to lift his eyes, Lancelot knew that the two men were looking down on him. The mentor and his expert pupil were gazing down to see Lancelot collapsed at the bottom, but neither of them was in much better shape. They were both clearly limping and gasping for air, and Lancelot knew that they were all but finished. They'd be easy pickings now. Almost too easy. He'd defeat them in mere moments. If he could only get his eyes to refocus...

"He was a good man once," said Gawain, and his voice sounded distant.

"Let us see if we can bring that good man back," said Arthur. "Bind him in the caves."

"It's too risky. The caves are too close to the new campsite."

"We have no choice," said Arthur. "If he's taking orders from someone, especially someone powerful enough to promise to return his arm, then we must learn who he's working for."

Lancelot laid his head down in the mud. They were going to take him as their prisoner. They were going to give him a chance to rest. They were going to willingly give him the opportunity to battle them to the death again. Sometimes life really could be wonderful.

"How did you know to cut that rope?" asked Gawain.

"I didn't," said Arthur. "But I had to try something! He was the greatest warrior in the kingdom!"

"I was the greatest warrior in the kingdom!"

Arthur laughed and patted the disgruntled Gawain on the shoulder. "Come on, old friend, let's get him out of there before he wakes up."

The two men rustled up above, and Lancelot allowed himself to slump completely. His eyes closed, his breathing slowed, and the greatest warrior in the kingdom allowed himself to be taken by darkness.

~ ~ ~

CHAPTER 10
Two Battered Knights

With each passing minute, Gawain wished more and more strongly that he had just left Lancelot at the bottom of that pit.

As the grizzled knight trudged deeper and deeper into a damp, dark system of caves, he shifted the uncomfortable weight of the still unconscious Lancelot on his aching shoulders. Gawain couldn't wait to toss Lancelot down like a sack of potatoes. The older knight was sore and tired from their recent duel. He was fairly sure that he had broken a rib when Lancelot's swinging log trap had struck him in the side.

Not to mention, Gawain's knees had been hurting him for a weeks now, and his back hadn't exactly been right for years.

Gawain wasn't an old man, but he had been a knight for nearly two decades now, and that sort of thing took its toll. If he could help it, Gawain preferred not to be lugging around two hundred pounds of crazed knight on his shoulders.

Fortunately, it was only a little bit farther to the makeshift prison. Gawain had stumbled upon these caves a few months earlier, and for a short time they had been used as a hiding place for Arthur, Gawain, and their small band of allies. They had erected some rudimentary torch brackets that now flickered with flames, and dimly illuminated the dripping rock walls. Ultimately, as their numbers swelled and they took on more and more refugees from Vortigern's oppression, Arthur had decided that they must abandon the caves as a permanent residence. They were only used now in rare instances. Chaining up a surly former knight who seemed hell-bent on killing them seemed like the perfect reason.

Gawain reached a large room in the cavern where several heavy sets of manacles had been pounded into the stone walls. With a little too much relish, Gawain dropped Lancelot to the stone floor, and then slapped a heavy, steel cuff onto Lancelot's left wrist. When he reached for Lancelot's right wrist, however, things became a bit more difficult. It was hard to bind a man who didn't have a hand. Gawain grumbled as he latched the cuff around Lancelot's large bicep. It would have to be good enough. Only now did Gawain allow himself to sigh and sag from his hard work. However, his moment of relief wasn't meant to last long, and Lancelot soon began to stir.

"Gawain...?" Lancelot murmured, as he took in his strange surroundings through half-opened eyes. "It's not possible you got the better of me..."

"You were hit by your own boulder," said Gawain, not bothering to disguise the hint of pleasure in his voice.

"You set traps, and sometimes you just set one too many," was Lancelot's reply.

"You also fell in your own hole."

"Sometimes you set two too many."

Gawain settled down on the stone floor beside Lancelot, which caused Lancelot to uncomfortably force himself into a sitting position. It was no easy task considering he was chained up.

And he only had one arm.

Gawain was only too happy to watch as Lancelot struggled. Suddenly, Gawain's ribs didn't hurt so bad. As he twisted his legs into a suitable sitting position, Lancelot eyed Gawain with a mix of confusion and bemusement.

"Are we going to be friends now?" asked Lancelot.

"You were always too cocky for my tastes," said Gawain.

"You were always too cowardly for my tastes," Lancelot fired back.

Gawain clenched his jaw and wouldn't have been surprised if he produced sparks between his grinding teeth. He really wanted to hit this guy. However, he simply held Lancelot's gaze with a supreme test of will. Then, finally, he seemed to buckle and he raised his hand, looking like he wished nothing more than to knock Lancelot's teeth out. Instead, he reached down and lifted a bottle of mead.

"I killed the Black Giant of Broceliade," said Gawain.

The older, more decorated knight then took a deep swig of mead. A bit of the drink dribbled down Gawain's chin into his wild beard, and wetted the wooden adornment that was woven in there. Gawain wiped his lips, and tossed the bottle to Lancelot.

Beat that.

Lancelot, of course, was up to the task. "I hunted with the Forest Men of Arden."

And Lancelot tipped his head back and took a long drink of his own. The bottle went back to Gawain, who snatched it up and motioned to a small vial of liquid dangling on his belt.

"I rescued the Lady of the Fountain."

Another drink, and the bottle was forced back upon Lancelot, who drank and said, "I defeated the Copper Knight by the Lake."

Drink. Pass.

Gawain took his longest drink yet, and declared with relish, "I freed the entire country of Brittany from venomous snakes. I wrestled tigers. And ripped beasts apart with my bare hands."

This time, Lancelot had to snatch away the bottle as he said, "Well, you're a lot older than me."

"I'm a better knight than you ever would have been," said Gawain. It was a statement and the knight stood by it.

But it was clear that Lancelot didn't agree.

After a long moment of reflection, the younger knight's face became hard and determined as he defiantly lifted the bottle high, poured all of the hot liquid down his throat, and drained the bottle dry. Then Lancelot locked eyes with Gawain and showed the terrible fire that burned in him when he sought to conquer someone fully, completely, and irrevocably.

"I fought an army single-handedly. Lost my arm. Then literally fought them single-handedly. I slew over fifty men before they brought me down. Lost nearly every drop of blood I had. And still I lived. And if you think a little drink is going to break me, then you're a bigger fool than I thought."

The now empty bottle exploded as Lancelot smashed it into the ground with a flick of his good, strong arm. Shards of glass scattered about the cave floor between Gawain and Lancelot. One particularly large piece settled near Lancelot's left hip, but Gawain didn't seem to mind as he twisted around and, with a shrug, picked up another bottle. That was the other good use for the cave. It not only served as a passable prison, but it was also a nice cool place to store bottles of mead. Once again, Gawain wrenched the cork out of the bottle with his teeth and spat it aside.

"Oh good! More mead," said Lancelot, instantly more affable.

"I'll find out what I want to know," said Gawain, as he took the first drink from the newly opened bottle, "from you, or someone you trust."

But as Lancelot took the bottle, he shook his head and smiled. "You can try. But there's not a man who knows I'm alive."

~ ~ ~

CHAPTER 11
The Spy's Reward

At the corner of the darkest, most secluded, most conspiratorial section of Tintagel's outer walls, Guinevere stood wrapped in a heavy, dark cloak. Waiting. Uneasily. She pulled her black hood tightly around her ears as she braced against a chilling breeze that could only partially explain the shivers that ran through her thin frame. She hated being here alone in this remote corner of the castle grounds. She felt utterly exposed standing there in the darkness with the towering castles wall to one side, and behind her the softly lapping waters of a massive black lake. The lake reached right up to the castle walls and then extended out into the formless dark of the night. Less than a year ago, this lake hadn't even existed. However, shortly after Vortigern's rise, Merlin had lifted his crooked staff and commanded the skies to turn black and the clouds to pour down upon this corner of the castle. Within hours a dark lake overtook the western wall of the castle and made it nearly unapproachable. More remarkable still was the rumor that at the bottom of this new lake slept the Red Dragon that Merlin alone could control, and that merely standing near the water's edge could incite the beast's hunger. At this moment, though, Guinevere wasn't worried about any of that. The dark corner at the edge of the lake was the perfect spot for a secret meeting precisely because it was so indefensible. If anything went wrong with her meeting, Guinevere would have nowhere to run. There was only one solution to this problem. She couldn't let things go wrong.

After waiting for many long agonizing, unpredictable moments, a twinkling light appeared in the distance. Guinevere steadied her breath as the light grew closer and formed into the flickering torchlight of a skeletally thin man with knotted, stringy, black hair and jagged, yellowing teeth. He held his torch aloft, giving Guinevere a clear view of his gnarled features curled into a repulsive grin as he slowly approached her.

Guinevere gave him a stiff nod as she called, "Hello, Claudas."

At Guinevere's use of his name, Claudas grinned wider and showed more of the gaps in his teeth as he hissed, "This is truly a strange place to meet, Lady Guinevere."

"Have you ever seen another soul here?" asked Guinevere.

Claudas licked his lips and made a subtle movement toward her with his free hand. In a flash, Guinevere flipped back her cloak and drew the long, golden dagger that she had received as a gift from her father. When it had first been given to her, Guinevere had been shocked even at its weight. Now she gripped it with the comfort of a favorite toy that she knew every crevice of. The expertise with which Guinevere flicked it from its sheath and pressed it to Claudas's throat showed that it had been a long time since she was intimidated by the weapon.

"I have learned to use this well," said Guinevere. "Do you wish to test me?"

Claudas pulled back, but his sly grin remained. It seemed clear that he understood the delicate power he held in this situation, and he was smart enough not to overplay his hand. Guinevere lowered her dagger, and after a moment's hesitation, she resheathed it. Claudas seemed to notice the hesitation. Turning away from him, Guinevere gazed out at the lake.

"Do you believe the stories, m'lady?" asked the thin man, his rasping breath wafting over her shoulder as he too examined the unnatural lake. "That the Red Dragon lies sleeping beneath the black waters?"

"Whether it does or not, the lake now defends half the castle. Making it virtually unassailable," said Guinevere with a shrug that was much more casual than she felt.

"Praise to the power of Merlin."

"What news do you have for me?" asked Guinevere as she turned to face Claudas once more.

"Lancelot is dead," said Claudas. "My men found the grave. And defiled it."

"I have reason to believe he survived the Battle of Tintagel."

"He was a great warrior," shrugged Claudas. "People will always whisper. Legends never truly die."

Guinevere nodded, then withdrew a small leather pouch from the folds of her cloak. Claudas greedily snatched at it, but with swift dexterity Guinevere pulled it away from his grasp.

"Nothing can be traced back to me?" asked Guinevere.

119

Claudas shook his head dismissively and grabbed for the bag again, but still Guinevere kept it from him.

"I need to hear it," she said. "Your men were thorough? No one can know that I've had any contact with you or them."

"Of course not, m'lady," said Claudas impatiently.

Satisfied, Guinevere handed over the small leather pouch. Claudas seized it and plunged his hand in. Almost as quickly, he gasped and yanked his hand back out again. His tight, leathery skin now bore two dripping black holes. Claudas's shocked, bloodshot eyes connected with Guinevere's just as a massive, hairy spider crawled out of the bag of coins and clambered over the spy's hand with its many legs.

Claudas tried to shriek but his voice was already becoming choked and muffled. "You — you — betrayed!"

"I said I would pay you to find Lancelot, but it seems you didn't find him," explained Guinevere. "I don't pay for failure."

His voice reduced to nothing more than a weak gurgling as Claudas collapsed to the ground. Guinevere casually brushed away the spider and picked up the bag of gold pieces. Then she stepped over the fallen man and followed the castle walls away from the lake and into the darkness as Claudas's mouth began to foam. Guinevere allowed a small grin to cross her face. Her plan had worked perfectly.

Nothing had gone wrong.

~ ~ ~

CHAPTER 12

The Baffled Knight

Back in the cave prison, both Gawain and Lancelot had also started to drool quite a bit. After several more bottles of mead, Lancelot was forced to admit that he was rather enjoying himself as the two normally serious knights had now boisterously broken into a chorus of the "The Baffled Knight."

"These words she had no sooner spoke
But strait he came tripping over:
A plank was saw'd it snapping broke
And sous'd the unhappy lover!"

When they finished singing, they both broke down into peals of laughter. They hunched forward, and Gawain jovially slapped Lancelot on the back. Despite his chains, Lancelot was surprised to realize that he felt completely at ease. It may have been the mead talking, but Lancelot thought that Gawain was a man among men, truly an excellent fellow. It was almost a shame that Lancelot felt such a burning desire to kill him.

Once they had calmed down a bit, Lancelot balanced himself and sought out what was left of their fifth bottle. On his third attempt, Lancelot finally managed to grab hold of the nearly empty bottle. As he tipped back the delicious warming drink, Lancelot felt compelled to press upon his friendly captor.

"Speak the truth, Sir Gawain," said Lancelot, doing his best to steady his words. "You've served many kings in this land and beyond. Is Arthur truly a king?"

"He can be," replied Gawain, also struggling with his uncooperative tongue.

"Not impressed," mumbled Lancelot, and he went to drink again, but Gawain quickly snatched the bottle away and took another long drink.

Wiping away a small dribble of mead, and refusing to look Lancelot in the eyes, Gawain said in a low tone, "If you tell anyone I said this, I'll kill you, but... I envy you."

Lancelot could only stare at Gawain with mouth half agape. How drunk was he?

Gawain continued, "You were here. You fought. You laid down your life. I would have done anything to be here."

"Looking back, I would have done anything to be somewhere else," said Lancelot.

"You're as bad as Merlin. Miserable traitor," grumbled Gawain as he tipped up the last of the bottle. "Why do you want Arthur dead? Who are you working for?"

"Someone even more steeped in darkness than I," said Lancelot, but the ominous tone was undercut by an unexpected hiccup. "If I do my deal, and kill Arthur before he's able to become a king, then I'll get my arm back. Can you offer more?"

"I can offer you your life," said Gawain.

Lancelot laughed a low, mirthless laugh. "I think you'll find it's near impossible to kill me. And not a force in this world will stop me from killing Arthur. Not even you."

Suddenly, Lancelot moved like lightning. He straightened his stump of an arm, and the cuff around his right biceps slipped free. He hooked Gawain into the crook of his elbow and pulled him in close. Then with his chained left hand, Lancelot snatched up the piece of broken glass from the shattered first bottle of mead and pressed it to Gawain's throat.

"Poor Arthur. First his adopted brother Kay is killed. Now his closest advisor. Not the makings of a strong royal court," said Lancelot.

"You—you killed Kay?" cried Gawain as he struggled against Lancelot's ferocious grip.

"No. Even better. It was Guinevere," said Lancelot, his voice dripping with pleasure. "Do Arthur's losses never cease?"

"ENOUGH!"

Arthur's voice echoed out of the shadows of the cave, and Lancelot's smile widened as he turned his head to see Arthur emerge from a dark corner of the cave.

"Arthur! Welcome! Come closer and watch me slash—"

But Lancelot was cut off as Arthur raised a crossbow, and without hesitation, fired an arrow at Lancelot. The point found its target and embedded into Lancelot's left arm. The already well-scarred knight shouted in pain as he dropped his shard of glass and released Gawain. Gawain pulled away from Lancelot and sucked in several deep gasps of air as he frowned at Arthur.

"I had it under control," grumbled Gawain.

But Arthur ignored Gawain's protestations as he slammed Lancelot into the cave wall and demanded to know, "IS IT TRUE? Did Guinevere kill Kay?"

With a little too much enjoyment, Lancelot replied, "I swear by my life. She's as cold-blooded as you and I."

Arthur drew a knife from his belt, and now it was his turn to press a killing weapon to someone's throat. Lancelot felt the cold, sharp steel against his throat, and he saw the fury in Arthur's eyes. The disgraced knight knew that Arthur could do it. He could even tell that Arthur wanted to do it. Knowing it might be one taunt too far, but saying it anyway, Lancelot added,

"Three killers. It's like we're made for each other."

Arthur stayed his hand, and dropped his knife as he turned and stormed out of the cave. Lancelot had to appreciate the amount of self-control Arthur must've had. In spite of his wish to believe otherwise, Lancelot admitted to himself that Arthur was shaping up to be a decent king after all.

~ ~ ~

Moments later, Arthur emerged from the cave into the forest now shrouded in the darkness of night. He blinked furiously as his eyes became hot with tears, and his hand drifted to his belt. He found and stroked the embroidered handkerchief that Guinevere had given him a lifetime ago. Or had it just been a few months?

Could she really have changed so much? The woman she'd become in the past year seemed to be someone that he had never met. But the thing that really plagued him was the worry that this was all his fault. He had left her behind that night. He had been unable to rescue her from Vortigern's fortress in all these many moons. He had left her to her own devices to survive. Of course, he had always intended save her one day, but was he too late? Was the Guinevere he had known and loved already gone forever?

As Arthur pondered what to do next, Gawain came out of the cave and joined him.

"Lancelot must've known you were listening. He's toying with you," said Gawain.

"Guinevere's name is next on the stone. He couldn't have known that," said Arthur.

"And now what? You're planning to kill her? Because a rock told you to?"

"It is not a rock. It's Klærent the Stonebourne!" said Arthur. Then seeing that this did nothing to persuade Gawain, Arthur added, "It's the sword of legend!"

"I don't believe in swords. I believe in the men behind them," said Gawain, as he held Arthur's shoulders and burned into the young king's eyes with an insistent gaze. "Who controls that sword?"

"I control it!" shouted Arthur. "Because I am destined to be king. And every name it has given me has brought me that much closer to the throne."

"So now you'll kill your friend?"

"No," said Arthur as he took from his belt the embroidered handkerchief that had been the last gift from his former love. "Now I'll kill a killer."

And he tossed the handkerchief to the ground at Gawain's feet. Then, with the terrible weight of his destiny threatening to overwhelm and break him, Arthur stormed forward into the night and prepared to face the darkness that lay before him.

~ ~ ~

CHAPTER 13

A Feast Upon the Floor

Guinevere took the steps two at a time as she quickly ascended the grand stone steps that led up to the feasting hall. She'd gotten used to always walking at a quick pace, finding that it helped to convey a sense of strength and purpose. Also, she found that it gave her a way to go almost anywhere unquestioned. It had been a pleasant little surprise when she had discovered that as long as she could project the image that she was headed somewhere that she was supposed to be, most people wouldn't stop her. It also made her legs feel good.

In her year of captivity, as she had carefully planned each move, Guinevere couldn't deny that keeping herself toned and ready had proven to be invaluable. She had always sought to better herself, and stay prepared for anything. Which was why her meeting with Claudas had been so frustrating. His network of spies was as good as any throughout the entire kingdom, and if he couldn't find any sign that Lancelot was still alive then what was she to do? Her mind had been churning ever since her talk with the master spy, and now she only saw one course of action. She had to see the king. And she hated seeing the king. Some days were worse than others.

She turned the corner and approached the hand-carved doors that depicted mythic tales of bravery and love. Guinevere barely recognized that sort of story anymore. She paused briefly at the doors, her dress and cloak billowing softly at her side, and Guinevere took a deep steadying breath.

You can do this. Be strong, she thought. And the mere fact that she even had to remind herself of that fact lit a fire inside. Her face became cold as she grabbed ahold of the door and wrenched it open.

The feasting hall was a marvel to behold. It was absolutely massive, with towering stained-glass windows overlooking the long table that could seat dozens of dignitaries and guests. The floor was finely finished and extravagant statues and fixtures lined the walls, many of which had been added since Vortigern had taken control and demanded his tributes from all over the kingdom.

But the most striking part of the feasting hall was how filthy it was.

Easily the largest room in the entire castle, and every last inch of it was wrecked. The table had been flipped onto its side. Dozen of chairs were knocked over or reduced to rubble. Piles of food were strewn about amidst puddles of wine.

And, on the ground, sitting in the center of the mess was Vortigern as he chewed on a mostly stripped turkey leg.

Disgusting, thought Guinevere. *It suits him.*

She was careful, however, to hide her disdain as his eyes lifted and gazed upon her. His breath was heavy and sullen with drink, food, and undeniable disappointment. Guinevere had to be very careful not to smile.

"Arthur is back," said Vortigern as food dripped out of his frowning mouth.

Guinevere was fighting very hard to restrain her smile now.

"So you took it out on the table?" she asked coldly.

Vortigern threw his turkey leg at her. It missed by a mile, and it wasn't like Guinevere was flinching anyway.

"He killed Aggravaine. And probably Balin. And Catigern. And WHO KNOWS HOW MANY OTHERS!" roared Vortigern like a spoiled child.

"So it hasn't merely been Gawain leading the rebels," said Guinevere. Her mind was moving quickly now. So many factors to consider. But she still hadn't found her father. She couldn't go back to Arthur yet. Not yet.

Vortigern sulked amongst his mess. "The finest meats, cheeses, and wine from all over the land, and I can't even enjoy it."

"You have nothing to worry about," Guinevere said as she boldly approached the king. "Arthur runs away. He hides. He never comes back."

"No. He's more dangerous than that," said Vortigern. "Just his name brings hope. Hope of rebellion. Hope of war. Hope to overturn the beautiful country I've worked so hard to build."

Vortigern's voice actually wavered, and Guinevere could've sworn she saw tears in his eyes. It made her want to kill him all the worse. Instead she sat down in the mess next to the sodden king.

"The people would never turn against you. Look at all gifts they've given you. They love you," she lied.

With an unceremonious flop of his slightly hunching body, Vortigern dropped himself upon Guinevere's lap and laid his head into the folds of the gown that she now swore to never wear again. Hiding her revulsion, Guinevere petted his greasy, filthy hair.

"What would I do without you?" sighed Vortigern.

Guinevere eyed a small dinner knife nearby. Hell, they were scattered all over the place. It'd be so easy. But—

"Where is my father?" she dared to ask.

Vortigern sat up in fury, and spat, "How can you ask me that now?! With everything that's happening?!"

"You promised me—"

"A father!" Vortigern shouted. "I promised you a father! And haven't I been that to you? I've given you so much. And it would be so easy to take it all away."

His voice turned silky as his threat hung in the air. Guinevere looked away from the knife. It wasn't the time yet. Not yet.

"Leave Arthur to me," she said, and her mind raced again, calculating several moves ahead.

Vortigern took Guinevere's palm and caressed it, rubbing the turkey fat that still stained his hands into Guinevere's soft skin. "I recently received the most perfect candelabra. It was made of pure silver. Shimmering. Beautiful. But as soon as it was out of its box, it became stained. Smudged. No matter what I did, I could not get it back to its former perfection."

His voice was almost a whisper. It had no trace of the roaring or the crying from just a few moments ago. It was now measured and cold.

And deadly.

Guinevere had to carefully control her breathing. Keep it still, calm, and smooth. But underneath it all, she was terrified.

"So what did you do?" she asked.

"What I had to," said Vortigern with a small shrug. "I put it into the fire until there was nothing left."

The king's black eyes looked deeply into Guinevere's soft brown eyes, and the look said everything he didn't need to. Don't fail me.

"You have two days," continued Vortigern, "and after that, I burn this kingdom. I stamp out any rebellion. I punish anyone who dares to oppose me. There won't be any people left for Arthur to lead."

"I'll find him," Guinevere assured him, and then she made her daring move. "But the usual spies won't be enough."

Vortigern grinned. "I know just the man."

~ ~ ~

CHAPTER 14

An Unwelcome Guest

Merlin just wanted to read. That's what he wanted to do most evenings. He always marvelled at the amount of ink that was constantly being put to paper. Being more clever than most men, Merlin was able to read at a dizzying pace, and yet he was absolutely swamped in books to read. Some of it was genius, some of it was average, most of it was drivel. But there was only one way to find out what was what, and that was by slogging through it all page by page. Most nights he could sit quietly hidden in the woods in his stone cottage and read to his heart's content.

But having the gift of foresight had its downfalls. And knowing whenever someone was about to knock on the door was one of them.

With a flick of his fingers, the rickety wooden door of his cottage opened of its own accord. Standing just outside was Guinevere, her hand raised and preparing to knock, and now struggling to contain her feelings of unease. She didn't say anything as she boldly stepped into the cottage and took in the strange sights. Merlin had always enjoyed observing people's reactions as they examined his home for the first time. Stray beams of moonlight wafted through holes in the ceiling and illuminated all manner of oddities. Archaic artifacts were strewn about. Models of flying machines hung from the ceiling. The old bent magician's cap that he hadn't worn in years sat in the corner gathering cobwebs.

Most of it was junk. But it was worth keeping just to see the looks on people's faces when they first caught a glimpse of them.

Merlin sat in his dark corner, with a book in his lap. He lounged in thin air, which was his favorite way to relax. Mostly because he had found it was the best thing for his old, weary back. Guinevere seemed surprised by Merlin's floating too. And the wizard loved it.

Guinevere crossed the room and glanced at a table that was loaded to the point of collapse with Merlin's books.

"'Human Regeneration.' 'The Art of Dragoneering.' 'Conversing with Owls,'" read Guinevere as she glimpsed the titles in pale moonlight. "It's so dark in here, Merlin. How do you read all of—"

Merlin spoke in his wispy, musical incantation.

"The moon, the stars,
the dark black night.
Must now give way
to sun-less light."

Instantly, the room began to glow. Light seeped in from the cracks as if the cottage was illuminating itself. Once again, Guinevere seemed to be doing her very best to project an image of calm and ease. Merlin knew better. And he was still loving it.

He closed his book, and as he did all of the books on the table snapped shut at the same time. Guinevere jumped at the sudden burst of bindings, and in that brief moment Merlin rose to his feet and approached her.

"It's impossible to find this house, my dear," Merlin said, with his piercing eyes probing at her, "except by those who've already found it."

"Your voice? I thought—" began Guinevere, but she was cut off before she could finish her question.

"That I only speak in rhyme? Could you imagine? It'd be dreadful."

In point of fact, Merlin mostly spoke in rhyme. Very few people ever heard him speaking in verse. It made moments like this, when he surprised people with a break in cadence, that much more delicious.

"So then, why do you—?" Guinevere started again, but was cut off again.

"It's only for spells, Guinevere," said Merlin dryly. And then he added, "And sometimes for dramatic effect. Now, how did you find me?"

Guinevere's hands disappeared in the folds of her cloak for a moment and she pulled out a scroll. Merlin snapped his fingers and the scroll vanished in a wisp of smoke.

"I don't need to read the decree."

Guinevere was getting heated now, and her frustration was coming through in her voice as she said, "King Vortigern's most powerful knights have been—"

"I am aware," cut in Merlin.

"I need your help. To find —"

"Arthur?" offered Merlin.

"Lancelot," corrected Guinevere.

And for the first time in this unexpected visit, Merlin was surprised. The lady must've been even more clever than he supposed. He was beginning to like this game.

"The King wants you to find a dead man?" the wizard asked with a hint of accusation.

"The King has given you orders to assist me however I see fit," said the lady with a hint of defiance.

Even though it was mostly buried beneath his thick beard, a smile grew across Merlin's face. *What did this woman know? Does she know things that I don't know? I must know.* His thoughts were dancing now as he reached out his hand toward Guinevere's forehead and began,

"Though deaf and dumb

And weak and blind.

Awake to me,

To read your — "

This time, Merlin was cut off. Literally cut off, as Guinevere drew a long golden dagger and with a flick that trimmed off the ends of Merlin's beard, she pointed it at Merlin's lower right abdomen.

"As a woman, I am used to men trying to violate my body," said Guinevere. "But try and violate my mind, and it will be the last thing you ever do."

Merlin pulled back his hand. Guinevere did not pull back her dagger. After a moment, Merlin gazed down and observed the unusual spot at which she had her blade pointed.

"I believe you're confused about the human anatomy, my dear," said Merlin, "Perhaps you meant to target—"

"Your heart? Your brain?" asked Guinevere with a wry smile. "There's more than one small spot that can destroy a man. And you're not an ordinary man, are you?"

She pressed the point into his lower right abdomen, and Merlin found himself conceding that this was an inconveniently sharp woman. And an inconveniently sharp dagger. Merlin winced as Guinevere dug her weapon just a little deeper, and for the first time he finally abandoned any hope of going back to his peaceful reading.

"So—Lancelot?" asked Merlin.

Guinevere nodded. "Lancelot."

~ ~ ~

CHAPTER 15

The Green Knight

The graveyard had been tricky to find. Gawain had gleaned enough information from Arthur to get an idea of its general location, but it had been surprisingly hard to track the young man in order to find the exact spot it was hidden.

The problem with teaching someone everything you know, thought Gawain in regards to his young pupil, *was that it made it extremely difficult to put one over on that person.*

Nonetheless, Gawain was thoroughly impressed by Arthur's skill and tenacity. He had managed to keep this graveyard a secret for at least several weeks after he had found it and retrieved the sword that he now swore was left to him by his father. Gawain wasn't so sure. While he had come to have complete confidence in Arthur's physical abilities, due in no small part to Gawain's own training, the seasoned knight worried that Arthur was being led astray by the mysterious messages that were appearing with the sword and stone. Gawain had become determined to see the stone for himself and thoroughly examine it. He'd seen all manner of magic and marvels in his many travels, and he felt that he'd be able to sniff out anything suspicious about this particular brand of enchantment.

And the moment he stepped into the graveyard, Gawain was pretty sure that something wasn't right there.

A heavy fog hung over the crumbling tombstones. That wasn't necessarily unusual; after all, this was Briton. But there also seemed to be an unnatural coldness that hung over the cemetery. The various grave markers were covered in moss, and many of them dated back hundreds of years, or were illegible altogether. It gave Gawain a headache. He was hoping to put dark magics behind him. He'd had enough of them for a lifetime, but as he approached the massive rock at the center of the graveyard, it seemed certain that his desire wasn't meant to come true.

The rock stood empty, and Gawain grumbled, knowing that Arthur must've drawn the sword and gone off for his next kill. At this very moment, Arthur might be tracking down his former intended, and given Gawain's recent experience with Arthur's tracking skills, Gawain didn't care for Guinevere's chances. Nonetheless, this gave Gawain a clear opportunity to examine the rock. There were no names written on it now, no messages, no clues, nothing. There didn't seem to be anything out of the ordinary with it, and that made Gawain grumble again.

He'd have to use more enchantments.

From his belt, Gawain drew out a small vial of water. It was another procurement from his many travels, and one that he had been quite fond of. He'd even been glad to brag about it to Lancelot earlier. Now he uncorked it and poured the small amount of liquid over the stone as he said,

"By the power of the Lady of the Fountain. Wash away these enchantments. Reveal your magics."

Immediately, one of the largest graves began to rumble and the earth broke. Gawain grimaced and he drew his sword. As the ground burst and emitted an unnatural roar, Gawain cracked his neck and shook his shoulders loose. The nice thing about most of these dark creatures was that they liked to make a big show out of their entrance, and it gave Gawain a chance to warm up. He kicked some of the stiffness out of his legs, and prepared for battle without the least bit of concern.

Until an enormous glowing Green Knight clawed his way out of the grave.

It took a lot to scare Gawain. But this did it.

"My god... You…" cried Gawain as his mouth fell open. "I-I killed you."

"And while you were killing me," boomed the Green Knight, his voice echoing unnaturally through the graveyard, "who was killing Uther?"

The Green Knight twisted his massive frame, and took a huge double-headed ax off of his back. He strode forward, and towered at least a foot over Gawain, who was no small man.

"You were not here for your king," denounced the Green Knight as he swung his ax at Gawain.

Gawain finally broke himself out of his stupor, and clumsily ducked the mighty arc of the Green Knight's killing weapon.

Gawain dropped his shoulder and rolled away from the massive glowing knight's reach.

"I would've died for him," said Gawain, as sweat began to pour from his brow. Was it from the fog? Or from the fear?

"And yet he is the one who lies rotting in the ground," the Green Knight boomed.

Gawain thrust his broad sword and stabbed the Green Knight, who didn't even try to deflect it. It turned out that there was no need, as the sword didn't even leave a mark. The Green Knight casually knocked it away.

"I still serve Uther..." said Gawain, but his resolve was weakening, "by serving his son."

The Green Knight swung his ax again. It struck Gawain straight to his armor, and Gawain was hurled backward. He slammed into a tombstone and broke it in half.

"You will fail Arthur, just as you failed his father," said the Green Knight as he closed in on Gawain and raised his ax for what would surely be a third and final time.

"Who controls you?!" shouted Gawain desperately. "Who leaves the messages on the stone?!"

"Uther," said the Green Knight with savage resolve. "He sends me from the grave to punish your failures."

"Well, at least now I have an answer," said Gawain with a shrug, and he was able to stop pretending to be afraid. That was the other nice thing about these dark creatures: they weren't too bright.

Now that the Green Knight had seemed to name his master, Gawain could get down to business.

"Now, if you won't stay in the grave," said Gawain as he picked up the broken headstone that he was laying against, "I'll bring the grave to you."

The Green Knight looked confused, but he swung his mighty ax once more. Gawain easily dodged it, and then using all of his strength he bashed the Green Knight in the face with the headstone. The stone crumbled in Gawain's hands, and the force of it was enough to cause the Green Knight to lose his grip on his ax. Gawain seized it, and lifted it high over his head.

"Stay in the grave this time," shouted Gawain as he brought the huge, double-headed ax down with a thud.

The Green Knight collapsed as his head and body were separated. Gawain sagged and heaved from the effort, but he couldn't deny: "He was a lot easier to kill this time."

Despite his exhaustion, Gawain examined the body of the Green Knight. Between his shoulder blades, where there used to be a head, there was a painted symbol of a dragon surrounded in flames. It was Uther's symbol. In a moment it was gone as the Green Knight's head and body dissolved into a green mist and was lost among the heavy fog.

Gawain tossed the ax aside as he weighed all this new information. The Uther Pendragon he knew wouldn't operate like this through murder and deception. But the Uther Pendragon he knew was dead, and if he had chosen to communicate from the other side then who was to say how he might choose to do it? Perhaps this was the only way he could reach out to Arthur and help his son reclaim the throne. Yet whoever was behind these enchantments decided to taunt Gawain with his greatest regret. The great knight hadn't been there for his king in the moment of his most desperate need. Was Uther determined to punish him?

Regardless of the enormous toll this excursion had taken on him, Gawain only had more questions. And he needed more answers. He needed to see the wizard.

He grumbled some more. He realized he'd been doing that a lot.

~ ~ ~

CHAPTER 16
Guinevere's Visit

For the first time in her life, Guinevere had made her way to one of the outer villages, and she was shocked by what she was seeing. As a lady of privilege, she'd been educated about the mutually equitable state of these small villages filled with peasants. They worked hard in the soil and happily paid taxes to the local kings in fair exchange for protection. That was the theory, anyway. The reality seemed to be very different.

As she rode her horse down a dirt path, stray animals darted out of her way. She was quickly swarmed by people dressed in rags who all looked thin and sickly and distinctly unhappy.

"Please, M'Lady. Mercy," cried a woman as she reached out a free hand and clutched a baby in another.

"Anything. My family. Help us," called a filthy child with both hands out.

"Haven't eaten in days. Please," gasped an old man who was hunched over with hunger.

Guinevere couldn't have hoped to maintain her steely demeanor amongst all of this despair. She'd always been safely sheltered away in the castle, unable to see any of this. On some level she had known things were bad under Vortigern's rule, but now seeing it and experiencing the pain in front of her eyes, she was infuriated. She knew she had to do something, but wasn't yet sure what. For the moment, she dug her hand into her cloak and pulled out every last coin she could place a finger on and tossed them to the people. It would have to do for now.

As she watched, the beggars scrambled and fought over the handful of meager coins, and Guinevere silently vowed to herself that she would soon help them much more. With any luck, that would involve freeing them once and for all from Vortigern's cruelty.

And things will be better once Arthur has been returned to the throne, she thought with a flush of excitement.

Having crossed the small village, Guinevere reached a tiny hut which was her destination. She'd rarely seen anything so humble in her life. The small home couldn't have been more than one room with crumbling walls, and a single tiny chimney puffing smoke into the air. Altogether, it looked like a strong wind could've knocked the place over.

Guinevere dismounted and tied her horse up alongside the hut. Then she circled around to the front door and raised a hand to knock, when something caught her eye. Out in the distance, she spotted a powerful gray horse. The rider was silhouetted by the sun at his back, but Guinevere couldn't shake the feeling that he was watching her. A moment of fear seized her and she wondered if it was possible that Vortigern had had her followed. She suddenly felt very exposed, but she also knew that she had come this far and couldn't turn back now. It had been very difficult to get this woman's name and the location of her small hut, and Guinevere had to see it through. Guinevere raised her hand and knocked forcefully on the old wooden door.

No answer.

She knocked again. Still nothing.

"Woman! I need to speak to you," demanded Guinevere in her most regal and authoritative tone.

There was the clumsy scuffling of feet, and the door finally opened.

"What is it you want?!" shrieked the old woman as she appeared in the doorway. Guinevere had to look away in revulsion at her first glimpse of the woman. She was hunched over, gnarled and toothless. The years had not been kind.

As she squinted at Guinevere through milky, nearly white eyes, however, it was the old woman's turn to gasp. "Begging your pardon, m'lady. I didn't know. Please. Mercy, m'lady."

Guinevere ignored her sputtering and said, "May I enter?"

The old woman paused in shock, but after a small hesitation she moved aside and allowed Guinevere in. For the second time in a few short days, Guinevere found herself taking stock of her very strange surroundings. The floor was dirt. The meager furniture was cobbled together with uneven wood. The walls looked like they could go at any moment. In a corner, a small fire crackled with a cauldron bubbling over top it. Out of the heavy black pot there seemed to emanate an unnatural orange glow. Almost immediately, Guinevere felt herself overcome by a stifling heat that slightly muddled her brain.

"You are a healer, are you not?" asked Guinevere, shaking off the heat, and turning to face the old woman who seemed to be doing her best to prostrate herself.

"I have limited skill, m'lady," said the old woman who couldn't seem to bend very far and was on the verge of toppling over. "I haven't much to work with. Perhaps I could offer m'lady a simple beauty potion but—"

"No, I don't want that," dismissed Guinevere as she rushed over to the old woman's side and helped her into a nearby chair. "I assure you, I'm not here for anything so mundane."

"I am at your command, m'lady," the old woman huffed, as she gasped for breath. The simple action of going to the door and back seemed to have taken a lot out of her.

"You once lived in the castle, did you not?" asked Guinevere. "You saved a wounded man at the Battle of Tintagel."

"I saved many, m'lady," said the old woman, "but I lost many, many more. Forgive me, m'lady, I'm but a meager healer."

"I am only interested in one man," said Guinevere, and leaned closer to the old woman to make sure that she didn't miss a word. "He was a knight. Said to be the greatest knight in all the kingdom."

A smile flickered upon the old woman's lips.

"I should've thought m'lady could have any man for her pleasure. But she chooses well."

Guinevere flushed as she cried, "No! That's not why I—I seek him for other purposes."

"Beggin' your pardon, m'lady," said the old woman with a bow of her head. "You wouldn't be the first to yearn for him. Yet I warn you, no woman yet has been able to tame him."

Guinevere couldn't help but be taken in by the old woman's strangely seductive words. Maybe it was the heat from the fire, or the effort of the journey, but Guinevere was starting to feel light-headed. Her head was swimming slightly, but instead of feeling sick, Guinevere was feeling lighter than she had in over a year. A warmth was spreading through her, and she felt for the first time in months that she was on the verge of success. Guinevere felt a surge of hope.

"So you did save him?"

"I kept him alive, m'lady," said the old woman. "I'm not sure anyone could save him."

"You mean he's weak?" asked Guinevere.

"No. He's strong. Unnaturally strong," came the strange reply. "I found him piled amongst the dead. But breath he still had. It took all my meager skill, and many times I was sure he had passed on. But he clung to life like a sickness clings to its rotting host."

"What happened to this man?"

"Over many moons he rebuilt himself. But was never satisfied. Never finished. Never able to rest."

"He must have a weakness," pried Guinevere.

The faint flicker of a smile flashed again on the old woman's face, and she said, "I am an old woman, m'lady. A woman like you may still be able to put his soul to rest."

"You said no woman could tame him."

"No woman... yet," said the old woman, and then she added almost as an afterthought, "M'lady."

A shadow passed by the window, and Guinevere snapped out of her trance. She nodded to the old woman and hurried to the door.

"Thank you for your help," said Guinevere with a quick bow of her head. She was about to rush out the door when she stopped and dug her hand back into her cloak. For a few moments, Guinevere rummaged deeply, and her hand finally emerged with a spare coin that had missed her notice earlier. Guinevere left it on the old woman's table.

Before she could get out the door, however, the old woman called out to Guinevere once more and asked, "M'lady? If you find him... Will you bring him back? He was my greatest. I'd like to see him."

Guinevere paused, and without looking at the old woman, she said, "No. You will never see him again."

With a quick swish of her cloak, Guinevere was out of the hut and had the door closed behind her. The air around her was cool and refreshing, and Guinevere already felt the haze lifting from her mind. Her thoughts were less cluttered as she took a small pleasure in the fact that she had gotten what she'd come for.

She knew how to kill Lancelot. He was a great warrior, and no enemy could bring him down. Only a lover could do that. She, herself, was the best weapon against him.

Guinevere circled around the small hut to find her horse still securely tied, but now there was another horse bound up nearby. The powerful gray horse that she had seen upon the hill was grazing on a close patch of yellowing grass. Guinevere approached the animal and was in the process of examining the bridle when a shadow fell over her. Her survival instincts overtook her and she ducked to avoid a blade slashing through the air. With her expert reflexes, she drew her long, golden dagger in the space of a breath and spun to face her attacker.

It was Arthur.

The boy she had loved had finally come for her. But not to save her.

He'd come to kill her.

~ ~ ~

CHAPTER 17

The Girl He Loved

Arthur had tried to do it quickly. He didn't have the heart to do it any other way. From the first moment that he had glimpsed Guinevere in the distance, his heart had been pounding in his chest. He couldn't deny that she looked different. A bit taller. A trifle thinner. Her beautiful strong hair bound neatly into a crown of braids. She was still the girl that he had once loved, and yet she was also a woman that he could not recognize.

He had been tracking her for two days now, and in that short time he'd come across a trail of bodies that all led to her. Most of them were spies and thieves and probably deserved their fate. Arthur admitted that he would've also struck down many of those villains if he were given the opportunity. Some of her victims, however, were like Kay, and seemed to meet their demise at the hands of a woman who simply wanted to advance her own cause. It was undeniable that Guinevere had risen in Vortigern's favor with astonishing quickness.

That was what Arthur tried to keep in his mind when he swung Klærent the Stonebourne at the neck of the girl he had once loved.

Kill her quickly. Be done with it. She's not the girl you once knew.

But she had foiled him with her unexpected speed and reflexes. Arthur couldn't help but muse that she'd always been full of surprises. Then with a spin and flash of gold, Guinevere turned to face him. The brown eyes that he had known so well were now locked into his green. And both of the young people were breathing much more heavily than the brief amount of action would've called for.

"Arthur...?" said Guinevere, and her voice was soft and tender and it caused Arthur's own voice to vanish.

Arthur didn't want to give her a chance to speak again. He gripped the ancient sword with its smooth stone-encrusted hilt. The sword that hadn't failed him yet. The sword that had helped him strike blows against Vortigern's strongest lieutenants. The sword that had brought him allies. The sword that now instructed him to kill the girl that he was once promised to marry.

In his moment of hesitation, however, Guinevere didn't strike with her dagger. She didn't breathe fire or claw at his eyes or slash out his entrails. She flung herself at him and wrapped her soft arms around his neck, and the smell of lilacs flooded Arthur's nostrils.

She had gone for his heart.

"You came," she cried as she hugged him tightly.

Arthur was shaken more by this than anything else she could have done. Her hands caressed his golden hair and touched his face and she blurted out, "I knew it. I knew you'd come! I knew! You'll take me with you."

But Arthur stilled his heart, and he pulled her arms away from him as he mustered all of his strength to say, "Guinevere. Stop. I'm not here to take you with me."

Those beautiful eyes of hers stared at him blankly. Her jaw quivered. She seemed to be blinking more than was necessary. And Arthur's eyes were hot as he clenched his jaw.

"Do you really think I could take you back?" he asked her. "After what you did to Kay? After what you've become?"

"Kay?" she cried in confusion. "But I thought that you would be happy that he was gone."

"How could you think I would be happy that you murdered my friend?!"

"Kay was going to betray you, Arthur!" cried Guinevere so genuinely that Arthur had to force himself to remember that it was all just an act. "I would never have hurt him if I thought it would hurt you. I was trying to protect you."

Lies. They were all lies. Lies wrapped up in a beautiful package. Arthur shook his head, and tried to ignore her gentle words, and the lovely lips that they came from.

"No," said Arthur, "Kay was my friend. He was like a brother to me."

"Arthur, he was plotting against you," Guinevere tried to protest.

But Arthur cut her off. "No! He's not the only one you've killed. Word of your deeds has reached me even in my darkest hiding places. I shudder to think about what you've become."

THE LEGENDS OF KING ARTHUR BOOK 1

Guinevere was clearly blinking back tears now. She was trying her best to put on a strong face. To hold it together. But her voice came out in an incredulous rage.

"You think I want to be like this?!" she cried. "Do you have any idea what I've had to do to survive since you left me that night? Since you left me, and never came back. Daggers and crossbows and fires and lies have become my life."

"And this is more lies," said Arthur as he gripped his sword again.

"No! Put me in chains," pleaded Guinevere, "but give me a chance. You can still save me."

Arthur could see the desperation in her eyes, and he knew that she would say anything to save herself now. She had killed his friends and who knew how many more. She had aligned herself with the monster king that had killed his father.

"Vortigern's planning something," she said as she circled him. "I can help. I know his weaknesses."

Arthur did his best to block out her words as he raised his sword.

"I know how to raise the White Dragon!" shouted Guinevere.

Whatever Arthur had expected her to say, it wasn't this.

He lowered his sword a bit.

"The White Dragon hasn't been seen in a hundred years," he said as they continued to circle each other. "It's just a legend."

"It's not a legend! You'll need it to defeat Vortigern's Red Dragon," said Guinevere. "And we can bring it back. Together."

She reached out a hand for him, but Arthur pulled away from her touch. He didn't know what to think anymore. He didn't know what was right and what was wrong. Now that he was seeing her again, he felt utterly lost. So he had to remind himself,

"I don't know you anymore."

With all of his determination, he tightened his grip on his sword. He raised it.

"Arthur, please!" came Guinevere's last desperate cry. "What you don't understand is that through all of those murders. All those killings..."

And suddenly she grabbed the reins of his gray horse. In all of the confusion, Arthur had barely noticed where they were, he hadn't noticed that she had manipulated him into position just beside his own horse. With a deft movement, she tossed the reins of the gray horse over Arthur's head. The reins tightened around his neck as Guinevere ducked under Arthur's arms and slapped his horse on the rump. With a mighty gallop, the horse charged off, and dragged Arthur behind it.

"...I got really good at it..." was Guinevere's last sad simple statement that Arthur barely managed to hear as he was pulled away.

Stupid. He had been so stupid, Arthur thought as his free left hand scratched at the reins digging into his throat, while his right hand clutched his sword along behind. He had her and he let his own weakness get in the way.

Even as Arthur was being dragged by his own horse into the barren fields nearby, he couldn't help but chide himself. And yet he still struggled with it all. He had looked into her eyes. There had been real tears there. Real pain. Or was it all a lie? A clever deception? After all, she had now tried to kill him too. He was now fighting to not be trampled behind his own rampaging horse.

Five minutes with Guinevere and his whole world was upside down.

He tossed his sword aside and it stabbed into the earth. With both hands free, Arthur was finally able to get control of himself. He loosened the reins around his neck with one hand, and with his other he grabbed ahold of the pommel on the saddle of the horse. He kicked hard off of the ground and, using the saddle for leverage, he twisted himself in the air to land coolly upon the horse as he wrenched the leather reins away from his neck.

As kids, they had always ridden together. Both he and Guinevere had always been gifted on horseback. The memories of those happy times flashed through Arthur's mind as he turned his horse and began to gallop back in the direction of the village. Up ahead of him, he saw that Guinevere had remounted her own horse and was now tearing off in the opposite direction through the barren earth of the fields. She knew that her plan had failed, and now she was trying to escape him. But Arthur wouldn't let her get away again.

As he passed where he had tossed his sword aside, Arthur leaned in his saddle and snatched it back out of the dirt. This time he wouldn't hesitate.

Guinevere was bearing down on her horse. Trying to put as much distance as possible between them. It was no use, though, as Arthur urged his horse forward and quickly gained upon her. He was now close enough to her to watch as she looked over her shoulder at him and shouted,

"Is this the kind of king you want to be? Gaining power by murder?"

She wouldn't fool him again, though, and he shouted back, "No worse than you and your master, Vortigern."

"So now you're aspiring to be like Vortigern?" she demanded.

Arthur rode up alongside her, and sprung out of his saddle. He tackled Guinevere, knocking her off of her horse, and the two former lovers fell into a loveless heap upon the ground. Tangled up in each other's arms in a deadly embrace that neither could've predicted just one short year ago.

In a flash, Arthur sprang back to his feet, and looked down on Guinevere as she coldly said, "I don't know you anymore either."

The young man who was destined to become king raised his sword and ignored the tears that were now pouring down Guinevere's face. He barely noticed the tears that were streaking down his own cheeks, snaking through the dirt caked on his skin. It was only a small stream that wasn't nearly enough to wash away all that had come between them.

But then her soft words cut through him.

"Through fire or storm…" she whispered. "I will always come for you…"

Her brown eyes closed, and her beautiful face clenched into a grimace as she braced herself for the inevitable blow that she could no longer avoid.

And Arthur brought the sword down with a terrible finality.

Moments later, or was it an eternity, Guinevere opened her eyes to see the sword thrust into the dry, cracked earth. Arthur stood beside it and shuddered with sobs.

Despite all his strength, despite all his determination, he could no longer fight back the tears as he cried, "I won't do it. I don't care what it means. I don't care if I never get to be king. A true king should be better. You deserve better."

Arthur stretched out his hand to Guinevere. Her tiny fingers reached out to his, they twisted around each other, their palms touched. And Arthur lifted her up out of the dirt and despair.

It didn't last long.

A burst of flame exploded out of the earth not ten feet away from them. Arthur watched it rise high into the sky then arc downward and strike the ground a mere arm's length away. In the years that followed, Arthur always took pleasure in the fact that he didn't suspect Guinevere for an instant. Of course, there wasn't a lot of time for thought, as he watched in amazement and horror as the flame rose up and shaped itself into a massive serpent. Twenty feet high, crackling and spitting, as it bared terrible fangs of molten fire.

The serpent made of flames dived at them, and Arthur grabbed Guinevere around the waist and pulled her out of the way just in time to escape the serpent's lunge. She turned to Arthur and cried breathlessly,

"I didn't do it! Did you know that was going to happen?"

Arthur shook his head, then rethought it as he added, "Things do tend to go wrong when I ignore the sword. But this is new."

The serpent of flames rose again, poising itself to strike.

"Who wanted you to kill me?" asked Guinevere as the towering serpent was reflected in her astounded eyes.

"The sword. The stone," said Arthur, and in that instant, he dove for the blade that was still half-buried in the ground. He snatched it up just as the flame serpent struck for the second time. Arthur swung the sword and the serpent burst apart, scattering into several smaller piles of fire.

"That's quite a sword," marvelled Guinevere.

"Klærent the Stonebourne," shrugged Arthur. "Standard sword of legend."

But the two of them noticed that the small piles of fire were now moving of their own accord and merging together like drops of water forming into a larger puddle. Arthur's eyes raked across their surroundings, looking for shelter, and quickly found an old, crumbling stone farmhouse out in the distance. He pointed with the sword.

"You want to run away?" cried Guinevere in surprise.

"It's not running away," said Arthur, recalling Lancelot's words from their recent battle. "It's retreating to favorable ground."

He grabbed Guinevere by the arm and they began sprinting in the direction of the farmhouse as the flames reshaped themselves into the monstrous serpent. It snaked along at incredible speeds and quickly cut them off. Without breaking a stride, Arthur swung the sword again, and scattered it into several smaller pieces. In the moments it took to reform, Arthur and Guinevere reached the farmhouse. The place was in terrible shape, and Arthur worried that it wouldn't provide much shelter, but they didn't have many options. He grabbed Guinevere's foot and boosted her up to a large hole in the stone wall. She scrambled up and disappeared inside. Arthur turned to see the flame serpent charging once again. He looked up, and Guinevere was still gone. The hole was just out of his reach, and now he was pinned against the side of the farmhouse. The serpent was coming closer. Closer. Arthur gripped the sword again. It had worked to keep the serpent at bay but it had done little to hurt it. The serpent was upon him, it reared back to strike, but —

It was hit by a splash of water.

The beast fell back, scrambling and spitting, and Arthur looked up to see Guinevere standing at the hole in the wall clutching an old wooden bucket. She hadn't abandoned him. She thrust a hand down to him, and Arthur took it. In a moment, he was into the farmhouse with her. They could hear the serpent hissing as it prepared for another attack, and Guinevere rushed to the far side of the raised platform that they stood on. The other end of the farmhouse was also falling apart, and revealed a spinning water wheel. Guinevere dipped her bucket in the churning water just as the entire farmhouse rattled.

The flame serpent had bashed itself into the dilapidated side of the building. It was now encircling the frail stone structure and was setting fire to the creeping vines and moss upon it. Whenever, he could get a clear shot, Arthur took swings at the serpent and scattered its flames. Guinevere would then hit the smaller parts with buckets of water. Little by little it was taking its toll, but the farmhouse might not hold up long enough for them to finish the monster off.

As they worked together, Guinevere panted, "So the legend was true? Only you were able to pull the sword from the stone?"

"I found it in my darkest hour," Arthur said as he deflected an attack from the snake. "It has guided me."

"And now you want to kill me because a rock told you too?" asked Guinevere incredulously.

"It's not a rock! It's Klærent the Stonebourne!" shouted Arthur, and he was really getting sick of people saying that. "It's the sword of legend!"

The entire farmhouse was aflame now. The ceiling was collapsing over their heads, and suddenly the serpent poured in from a hole in the roof. It balanced on its tail as it faced them on the raised platform. Arthur and Guinevere backed up to the water wheel. He looked over his shoulder and saw that the water wheel was fed by a fast-moving river some twenty feet below.

"Are you still going to listen to that sword?" asked Guinevere breathlessly.

Arthur shook his head. And he sheathed it. Then he grabbed Guinevere's hand and the two of them leapt out of the farmhouse just as the serpent of flame dove at them one more time.

The three of them fell toward the river, but while Arthur and Guinevere plunged into the raging waters, the serpent struck the surface and sizzled as it died.

The currents mercilessly dragged them along, but fortunately both Arthur and Guinevere were strong swimmers. Once again Arthur had flashes of days long past when he and the young girl with the long, braided hair had snuck away from the castle to play in the nearby waters of the sea or to splash in the moats that surrounded Tintagel.

Finally, the river widened and slowed and they were able to reach the banks where the current wasn't so strong. Arthur pulled himself upon a sandy embankment and fell beside Guinevere, whose sodden dress clung to her legs. They sat beside each other and for a moment, Arthur felt that nothing had changed. They were just kids again, and the world still made sense, and it was possible to be happy. Arthur felt Guinevere place her hand upon his.

And he didn't pull it away.

"For a long time, I've felt lost," Arthur said, "trying to stay one step ahead of Vortigern. Trying to keep people safe. Trying to find allies. But unable to make a stand. And never truly knowing what to do next."

He looked at the sword on his hip and sighed, "Maybe I've been following the wrong thing."

Now he looked at Guinevere. Her hand upon his. The girl he had once loved. The girl who was once going to be his queen. If they could only survive that long.

"I don't know if I can trust you," Arthur admitted.

In answer, Guinevere held her wrists up to him. "I'll do whatever it takes, Arthur. Tie me up. Cuff me. Where do you want me?"

~ ~ ~

CHAPTER 18

Prisoners in a Cave

Being imprisoned in a cave was boring.

It was true, Lancelot probably had more freedom to move around than the average manacled person. After all, he only had one hand to chain to the wall. Nonetheless, time dragged on insufferably when you had no idea how much time was actually dragging by. He couldn't see the sun rise and fall. He couldn't hear the noises from outside to discern the calls of the nocturnal animals. At least when Sir Gawain was around he had someone to plot against. And possibly get drunk with. Being alone, however, was nearly intolerable.

Which was why Lancelot was so surprised when Arthur brought him a woman.

It had seemed like Lancelot had been in there for weeks, although he'd never been a patient man, and he allowed it could've only been hours. Yet he still was determined to kill Arthur, so there was no point in attempting to escape. His best option was to wait here until Arthur inevitably returned, and then Lancelot could look for an opportunity to strike. Sure enough, now Arthur was returning, but he wasn't alone. The young man was leading a thin, beautiful woman with long hair that appeared to still be wet. Lancelot dared to hope that he might find a way to cut down

Arthur and then woo the maiden. This might not be a bad day after all.

"King, and here I thought you didn't like me," said Lancelot as he smiled at the woman.

"Touch her and you lose your other arm," came Arthur's terse reply.

Oooh, he likes this one, thought Lancelot.

Arthur set about chaining the woman to the wall with another set of manacles. Lancelot noticed that Arthur seemed to be taking trouble to make sure that the woman wasn't too close to him. Lancelot also noticed that the woman seemed to be stealing several glances at his mighty visage.

And she seemed to be trying to keep from smiling.

Lancelot was more than happy to smile broadly at her. He couldn't blame her for being intrigued by him. He was, after all, an incredible specimen of stunning manhood.

"I'm sorry to leave you like this," Arthur told his female captive. "I'll be back as quickly as I can."

Arthur straightened up and turned to leave, but as he rose, he quickly traced one finger along the woman's cheek. Arthur was trying to be subtle and discreet, but Lancelot had noticed. It seemed that Arthur didn't just like this woman. He loved her.

A moment later and Arthur had gone. Lancelot smiled at the woman again, and because he was no dummy, he said, "I take you to be the notorious Lady Guinevere. I've heard lots about you, my dear. I would even dare to call myself an admirer. Allow me to introduce myself. I'm Lance—"

"Oh, I know who you are," cut in Guinevere.

And, once again, it seemed like she was trying to keep from smiling.

~ ~ ~

CHAPTER 19

Missing Advisors

Arthur strode into camp doing his best to project the confidence that he felt all of his followers needed him to project. They looked to him to be a paragon of hope shining through the darkness of the wretched conditions that surrounded them. Yet it took more effort than Arthur liked to admit. His heart fell slightly every time he walked through the camp and saw the poor state of his followers. Thin, dirty children. Tired, ragged mothers. Old men dressed in torn clothes. He knew that the few hundred refugees that relied on him and his knights for support from Vortigern's oppression had come to count on his strong presence. Despite their terrible lot in life, there were always grateful people who wanted to shower him with praise and treat him like their savior. It still made him uncomfortable to be doted upon like this, especially since they were all still destitute and struggling, but he'd come to understand that this was more for the people's benefit than for his own. These people needed to be led, they needed a paragon of hope to look to. Almost immediately upon their return to the forest, Gawain had explained this to him, and now Arthur sought Gawain's guidance again.

However, his most trusted advisor was nowhere to be found.

The camp had grown out of necessity as their numbers swelled, and this made it grander but also much more difficult to coordinate. There was a constant expanding need for more shelters and beds, but there was also the need to always be prepared to move. Then there was a need for more surveillance and more defense. It was a tricky balance to strike. However, Arthur's supporters had risen to the occasion by looking to the trees. They had designed a system of tree forts that could be easily attached and detached from the high branches of suitably strong trees. A system of pulleys and levers was created so that a small group of men could lift the forts up high and then anchor them to the trunks of the forest. All of the tents upon the ground had been carefully planned so that they could be dropped at a moment's notice and packed up to go on the move.

The camp had become a marvel of ingenuity, and the unlikely architect of all this was hurrying Arthur's way now.

"A-Arthur!" called Percival. "Arthur! Hello! Good to – good to have you back."

"Hello, Percival," returned Arthur.

If he was being honest, Arthur had never been particularly impressed with Percival when they used to periodically cross paths with one another at Tintagel Castle. Percival seemed a little weak, a little soft-spoken, a little cowardly. Arthur still thought most of these things about Percival, but he couldn't deny how invaluable Percival had been in the planning of the camp. The man had a gift for engineering that he didn't have when it came to fighting or bravery. However, Arthur had come to rely on Percival as much as any man in his small army.

That didn't mean Percival didn't bug him sometimes, though.

"I don't have much time, Percival," said Arthur, hoping that Percival wouldn't press the matter. "What can I do for you?"

"Th-the camp is nearly set!" stated Percival proudly. "A new best. Less than ten hours."

"That's wonderful," said Arthur. And it really was; not that long ago it had taken several days to set up the camp. But Arthur's mind wasn't on the camp at the moment. "Percival, I'm looking for Gawain. I need his council."

"Gawain?" repeated Percival with confusion, which annoyed Arthur because he was in something of a hurry. Percival's next statement, however, threw Arthur. "I-I thought he was with you."

Arthur turned to face Percival. "You mean Gawain isn't here?"

"He left yesterday morning. Around the same time you did."

~ ~ ~

CHAPTER 20
Gawain's Dark Path

Gawain was trudging through a much different part of the forest than he was used to, and it had none of the comforts of home. The trees here created a canopy overhead that blocked out nearly every ray of light. Otherworldly noises emanated from impossible to discern places. Gawain recognized several bird calls, but also the unnerving howls of a wolf. He also thought he heard laughing of a monkey, but he could've been imagining things. Gawain pushed it from his mind as he finally laid eyes on his destination.

A tiny stone cottage sat in strange relief to these bizarre surroundings.

The old knight took a step toward the cottage, but as he did he looked down and noticed another unusual trait of this particular stretch of forest. A vine was acting of its own accord and wrapping itself around his leg. Gawain grumbled and drew his sword. With a quick slash he cut the vine, and then pressed forward as a dozen more began to creep toward him. He hacked his way through the strangling forest as he pressed on toward the stone cottage that held his old friend.

As Gawain ripped through several more writhing plants, he had a funny feeling that Merlin was already expecting him.

~ ~ ~

CHAPTER 21

Bound Together

In the flickering torchlight of their cave prison, Lancelot was really starting to like this Guinevere woman. Mostly he was really enjoying the chance to talk about himself, and he was happy to find that Guinevere seemed to be a very rapt audience. She had started out trying to ignore him, and for a while he had suspected that she was just another boring noblewoman. Slowly but surely, though, he had been able to wear her down. Now he had her right where he wanted her as she listened to his grand stories of adventure with downright glee.

"You didn't?!" laughed Guinevere.

"I did!" boasted Lancelot proudly. "Won the tournament. With a wooden sword. Beat ten grown men!"

"But you were only fourteen!" she said as she gaped in amazement.

"Thirteen!" stated Lancelot, although Guinevere had been right: he had said that he was fourteen at first, but now he felt that it was more impressive to revise his age downward. "They'd have been fools not to take me on as a knight's apprentice. Youngest in a century."

"All that without a scratch," marvelled Guinevere.

"Well... Not without a scratch," said Lancelot, and he pointed to a scar on his collar and then another on his brow.

He knew that he really had her now. When she tried to examine the scar on his forehead, Lancelot was able to lock eyes with her for just a moment. She looked away quickly, of course, but that just confirmed that she was entranced by him now. It was time to press his advantage.

"I've always thought it wasn't a good fight unless you've got some scars to remember it by," Lancelot said.

And with a mighty tug, Lancelot ripped his shirt wide open and exposed his massive, muscular chest. His shoulders and stomach were a sight to behold, there was no doubt. And his thick chest hair was a point of particular pride. But it was the scars that he knew would really draw her in. There was barely an inch of Lancelot's torso that didn't bear the marks of some battle or another.

"I've had many good fights," Lancelot said with relish.

Guinevere gasped and was clearly amazed by Lancelot's tapestry of war wounds. From everything he knew about Guinevere, Lancelot had guessed that this was a woman who wouldn't be impressed by proper manners and boring dignity. She was a woman who liked men. She was drawn to sweat and hair and scars. As she crept slightly toward him, transfixed by his masterpiece of bloody triumphs, he knew that he'd guessed right.

"I'd say you could touch them, if we weren't chained up," he said.

Guinevere froze in place, and she seemed to be considering something as she looked down at her cuffs. After a moment, the

171

heavy manacles fell open, and the clever woman sheepishly tossed them aside.

"I picked them almost as soon as I arrived. They were hurting my wrists," Guinevere said, and it was tough to say by the flickering torchlight, but Lancelot could've sworn she was blushing. As far as he was concerned, it made her even more desirable.

"Impressed," he said. "Well, I am a man of my word."

With another fierce tug, he ripped his shirt cleanly off. He gazed at her silently and waited. Daring her to touch him. It took a long moment, but Lancelot wasn't going anywhere. And it paid off when Guinevere finally, slowly reached out to touch his chest. Her fingertips were inches away. But she stopped. And pulled back.

"I shouldn't," she said, and she shuffled a few feet away from Lancelot. "I'm trying to get Arthur to trust me."

Lancelot laughed, "I don't know what a woman like you sees in a man like him."

"I am a lady."

"Maybe you were once," Lancelot said, shaking his head, dismissing her own suggestion of herself, "but now you're like me. A wild beast yearning to run free."

"I'm already free," Guinevere reminded him.

"I didn't mean from the chains of this cave."

Once again, Guinevere began to slowly creep toward Lancelot. She seemed so tentative, so afraid. It was intoxicating, because Lancelot knew that she was not a weak woman. She had killed people. She had survived under the worst of conditions. She had overcome dangers that would destroy most men.

And yet Lancelot made her nervous. It was wonderful.

Cautiously, gently she touched one of Lancelot's scars. He exhaled softly yet audibly to reward her boldness. She touched another scar, giving it a soft caress. This time he moaned faintly. Another touch. Another moan.

But then she reached out to touch his stump of a right arm. Lancelot pulled away reflexively, and turned his face away from her. Even he was surprised by his reaction. He wasn't the kind of man to be ashamed of anything, but as he moved his arm away from her he realized that it was the one scar he wasn't proud of. All of the other scars were from battles that he had won. They were reminders of his victories. But this was his greatest and most memorable marring, yet it only served to commemorate his greatest defeat. And Guinevere had gone right for it. Now Lancelot could barely bear to look at her.

After a moment, however, Guinevere reached for Lancelot's chain.

"I learned to pick locks a few months ago. Before that it was a crossbow. And before that I killed my first man," she said, and her voice dripped with the same bitterness that Lancelot felt burning deep inside himself. "It's all come so easy. And I hate it."

Her deft fingers began to work at the cuff around Lancelot's one good arm.

"You could escape from all of this," he said.

"I could never leave my father," Guinevere replied, shaking her head. "But... I'm afraid, Lancelot..."

The knight's cuff fell away.

This time she looked deep into his eyes, and he saw that her brown eyes were full of tears as she asked, "In freeing my father, am I losing myself?"

Guinevere looked away suddenly, blinking back tears, as she continued quickly, "I'm being silly, of course. You wouldn't understand. You've never been weak. Never been scared."

Finally, Lancelot understood that she had never been afraid of him, but that she had been afraid because she saw herself in him. Somehow this cut to him even deeper, and while before he had desired her, now Lancelot ached for her. He reached out with his newly freed hand to brush away her tears. But she pushed it away, and now she was the one who refused to look at him.

"I thought I was going to die," he told her, and this time there wasn't even a hint of boasting. "Any moment. Any breath could've been my last."

He stretched out his hand for her again. And again she pushed it away.

"I forced myself to live," he continued. "I forced my lungs to breathe. Forced my heart to beat."

He reached out again, but this time with his missing hand. Using the rounded end of his half-missing right arm, Lancelot touched Guinevere's chin, and raised her eyes to look into his own.

"For weeks, for months really, I was sure that if I let myself sleep, even for a moment, I'd never wake again. So you may think that I've never been scared, but I was too scared to let myself die. And that's the only reason I'm still alive." And then he added with a slight wink, "Plus I really want to slay that Red Dragon."

A quick laugh escaped Guinevere's lips, and the torchlight danced on her tear-stained cheeks.

God, she was beautiful, Lancelot thought as he brought his face close to hers.

"You must be so tired," she whispered to him.

Their lips were inches apart now. Centimeters. Millimeters.

"Be with me. You can finally —"

Lancelot closed his eyes and his lips traced against hers, and he felt her say the last word.

" — rest."

But as their lips touched something exploded inside of Lancelot. He wrenched backward, pulling away from her as something darker than anger boiled up inside of him.

Fire raged within his belly and he shouted, "REST?! NO! No rest! No sleep. Rest is sleep. Sleep is death. I cannot sleep! I will not die!"

In his sudden madness, he seized Guinevere's face with his left hand, and pulled her close to him as he spat, "YOU WILL NOT KILL ME!"

With vicious savagery, he shoved Guinevere away. And as she tumbled backward, Lancelot watched a small white ball pop out of her mouth. With a wild look on his still crazed face, Lancelot picked up the ball, and crushed it between his fingers. A black liquid oozed out and dripped onto the cave floor.

Guinevere tensed, and then her shoulders dropped, and Lancelot realized with a jolt that she was finally speaking honestly with him for the first time as she said, "I almost had you."

"What is it?" he asked, and his confusion was actually overtaking his momentary rage.

"A wax capsule. Filled with poison," she explained.

"You've been holding this in your mouth for what? Hours?"

"It took a lot of doing to get into this cave with you," said Guinevere. "I couldn't count on bringing my dagger."

"That was all a lie?" said Lancelot, and now it was his turn to marvel.

"Sometimes the truth is a more dangerous weapon than a lie," Guinevere said.

"You're very good."

Guinevere smiled as she picked up a rock from the ground. It was a well-chosen rock, small enough that she could wield it effectively, but large enough to do the job. Once again, Lancelot had to admit to himself how good she was.

"You know I would've kissed you at almost anytime," admitted Lancelot. "Why go through all of the dramatics to make me truly want you?"

"Just any kiss wouldn't have worked," said Guinevere. "It had to be passionate enough that you would allow death down your throat. And, anyway, you're the mighty Lancelot. You deserved to be sent off in style."

She gripped the rock tightly but kept a safe distance. Lancelot knew enough about killing to know that she was still debating the perfect way to strike. She was skilled enough to know that she wouldn't get more than one chance at this. Lancelot welcomed the attack. If he was going to die today, then dying at the hands of this woman was a good way to go.

"I wanted to send you off pleasurably," she said as she positioned herself to strike, "but I guess we'll do this the hard way."

Lancelot just broke into a broad smile as he laughed, "We really should be working together."

Guinevere lowered her rock just a bit. Intrigued. And, once again, Lancelot was sure that he had her right where he wanted her.

~ ~ ~

CHAPTER 22

Another Unwelcome Guest

As the door to his cottage burst open, Merlin thought to himself, *Will I ever get a chance to read in peace?*

The surly, grizzled knight that now stood in his doorway seemed to suggest that Merlin wasn't going to get his wish anytime soon. The wizard sighed as he closed his book with a snap. Gawain slammed the door shut behind him with a bit more force than seemed strictly necessary, and several strangling vines that had been creeping over his shoulders were cut cleanly off.

Does he even care that they have feelings too? wondered Merlin.

It didn't appear to be the case as Gawain growled, "I think you were expecting me."

Without warning, Gawain heaved his sword like a spear straight at Merlin. Generally it was tough to ruffle Merlin's feathers, but even he realized that at this moment, time was of the essence. With a rapid-fire precision, Merlin enchanted,

"You strike at me,
I will not yield.
My will is strong,
My pow'r my shield."

Gawain's sword froze in mid-air. Inches away from Merlin's lower right abdomen.

"Does everyone know about the appendix?" huffed Merlin indignantly. "It hasn't even been discovered yet!"

"You're not as clever of a man as you think you are," said Gawain.

"I would've expected you to aim for my heart, old friend," Merlin said.

"Why would I do that? You haven't used it in quite some time."

Merlin flicked his hand, and Gawain's sword flew away, burying itself deep into the wall.

"Even years ago, I should never have invited you here," sighed Merlin.

"We used to be friends," said Gawain.

"And now my friend's come to kill me?"

"No," admitted Gawain with a shrug. "I just wanted to see how tough you still were. I've actually come to ask for your help."

The old wizard laughed as he snapped his fingers. New vines flew in from beneath the door and windows. They wrapped themselves around Gawain's arms and torso, and bound him tight. A final vine whipped over the ceiling beam and twisted itself around Gawain's neck in a taut noose. But the knight's feet remained firmly planted on the ground. Sure, he wasn't going to get to read his books anytime soon, but Merlin figured he still might learn something interesting tonight.

"All right," said Merlin, "I'm listening."

~ ~ ~

CHAPTER 23

Percival Speaks Out

The counterweight rose swiftly into the air as Arthur deftly swung down from one of the tree forts. He gracefully plummeted to the ground and broke into a stride moments after he had landed. He still had Klærent on his hip since he hadn't completed his most recent order. Considering that the sword had already sent a serpent of flames after him, he didn't particularly want to know what it might do if he tried to return it to the stone.

Arthur strode toward the outskirts of camp, thoroughly determined to go out and find Gawain. From the many times that he'd been chided by his mentor for disappearing for days on end, Arthur felt certain that Gawain's disappearance wasn't something to take lightly. Something was stirring, and Arthur intended to get to the bottom of it.

He hadn't gotten far, though, when he felt a familiar dogging presence at his heels and he heard the faintly hesitant call, "Ar-Arthur!"

Percival jogged up alongside of him as Arthur tried to simply explain, "I'm going to find Gawain."

"I'll—I'll go with you," Percival stated certainly with an uncertain nod.

But Arthur impatiently waved his knight away. "No. Stay here. Some of the towers aren't fully secured. Make sure—"

"Arthur! Stop!" demanded Percival, and it was hard to tell who was more surprised by the forcefulness of the demand. Flushing but persistent, Percival continued, "We can do more than this. The men want to get out there. They want to take the fight to Vortigern."

Arthur shook his head. "That's how Kay got himself killed."

"Kay got himself killed because he was tired of being left behind while you went on your secret missions," argued Percival.

"Then he should've brought it up with me," said Arthur. "If any of you have concerns with my leadership, then I'm happy to discuss it."

"No, you're not," disagreed Percival. "You're always hurrying off to who knows where. You won't talk to us. That's why Kay was going to—"

Percival suddenly stopped short, but Arthur couldn't unhear what he'd just heard. He spun on his lieutenant and asked, "What was Kay going to do? Was he planning to betray me?"

"Yes," said Percival after a long moment of hesitation. "He wasn't happy about being left out. He'd been planning a coup for some time."

Arthur could barely believe what he was hearing. Kay was like a brother to him. He was Arthur's closest friend. Sure, Arthur hadn't chosen to confide in Kay about the commands he was receiving from the sword and the stone, but they were meant for Arthur alone.

"Was he planning…" Arthur started to speak, but paused as he found the words. "Was Kay planning to hurt me?"

"No!" said Percival forcibly. But then he winced as he added, "I don't really think so. Sometimes he would say things. But you know how Kay was. Always brash, sometimes he would get carried away. He—he would never actually follow through on some of the things he said. Probably."

"But I thought…" stammered Arthur, "Kay trusted me."

"He did," said Percival, "at first. But we don't know what to think anymore. You—you don't talk to us. You used to treat us all as equals. You used to value our opinions. But ever since you've decided that you're our leader and that you're above us, you've pushed us away."

"That's not what I'm doing," Arthur said.

"Then what are you doing?" pleaded Percival. "Arthur, we're your men. We'll follow where you lead. But you have to lead us. And you have to trust us."

Falling silent, Arthur saw the truth in what Percival was saying. Without meaning to, he had moved away from his own men. So he took the first small step back toward them when—

BOOM!

An explosion rented the air about one hundred yards away. Instantly alert, Arthur spun and looked to the source of the blast.

"The explosives wagon," he said as his mind raced forward, trying to determine if his worst fears were being realized.

"If someone blew all the explosives," said Percival, "it should've been much bigger."

BOOM! BOOM! BOOM!

Several more explosions rang out through the camp. In mere moments, the once peaceful stretch of forest was dissolving into chaos. Terrified women were calling for their children. Small boys and girls were crying for their mothers. The hundreds of refugees were all seized with terror, convinced that Vortigern had caught up with them at last. However, Arthur knew that this wasn't the work of the mad king. There was a far simpler explanation for this.

And it was all his fault.

"Clear out the women and the children!" barked Arthur to several of his knights who were scrambling into action. "Get them to safety."

Arthur spun to Percival. "You wanted to come with me? Come on! We have to secure the armory."

With Percival at his heels, Arthur sprinted across the camp, and several thoughts tore through his mind. How could he have been so foolish? How could he have not seen this coming? How could he have thought he could trust either of them?

Arthur arrived at his destination. The armory was a larger tent that had been reinforced with large wooden beams due to its importance. It was also the only tent that had guards constantly stationed outside. Two guards, to be specific. Two guards who were currently sprawled out unconscious on the ground. Arthur warily approached the tent that held all of their weaponry, and just as he did, a bare-chested Lancelot emerged, strapping a sword onto his handless arm. Beside the warrior who had sworn to kill the future king was Guinevere, with a crossbow clutched in each of her hands.

As Arthur stared at his former love and his current enemy, one question repeated over and over in his mind: how could he have left those two together?

~ ~ ~

CHAPTER 24

A Tangle in the Trees

"I do love the feeling of cold steel on my hot flesh," said Lancelot with a wicked grin spread across his handsome face.

The former knight tightened the leather straps that bound his blade against the skin of his forearm. It had taken him quite a bit of trial and error to get the sword just right and attach it so that it felt like a natural extension of his arm. As he had rebuilt his strength and come back from the point of death, he trained for hours on end to get to a place where swinging this death weapon had felt like second nature. All in all, Lancelot felt that it was extremely considerate of Arthur to keep it for him.

"Oh God…" whispered a tentative, familiar voice, and Lancelot's eyes fell on the slight frame of a man that had lifted Lancelot out of his darkest hours with grand dreams of revenge.

"Percival… you cannot imagine how I've longed to see you again," said Lancelot with relish dripping from his voice. "I can't wait to bathe in your blood."

The thin man who had left Lancelot for dead so long ago swallowed hard and looked like he might pass out from fright. Lancelot loved it. He felt the leather straps biting into his right arm, and he gripped a full sword in his left hand. Lancelot couldn't help but think that this day was just getting better and better. He'd been looking forward to a rematch with Arthur, but now he'd also get the chance to finally introduce Percival to his sword arm.

Sometimes it really was possible to get everything that you asked for.

"Percival, get everyone out of camp," came Arthur's order with his knack for getting in the way.

For a second, however, Percival didn't move, and Lancelot wondered whether this nervous man had finally found some courage between his legs. But it didn't last long.

"Percival, go!" insisted Arthur. "I'll handle this."

It seemed that Percival's determination only went so far, and he nodded before he turned tail and ran. Lancelot watched Percival sprinting away, and he promised himself that there'd be time to take care of the cowardly knight later.

"It's very noble of you, King," said Lancelot, "but you're only buying a few more days of air and sunshine for your cowardly follower. I'll find him soon enough."

Arthur drew his sword and pointed it at Lancelot, saying, "This is between you and me."

"Did you forget about me?" asked a soft voice, feigning offense, and Lancelot turned to see Guinevere step up from behind him.

~ ~ ~

These men certainly do get carried away, don't they? thought Guinevere as she positioned herself at equal distance between Arthur and Lancelot, completing a three-pointed deathmatch.

She hefted a loaded crossbow in each hand, but didn't point them at either of her targets yet. Not yet. She had trained herself to lift and aim the clunky, heavy weapons with relative ease. Nonetheless, she was smart enough to know not to waste her strength until the moment was perfect. He didn't know it, but that's why she hadn't gone for the kill with Lancelot in the cave. It was too risky. But now with two precision death instruments at the ready, it was only a matter of waiting for the proper moment, and that moment hadn't come quite yet. Not yet.

Arthur turned to her. "Do I have you to thank for blowing up my camp? And terrorizing the people under my protection?"

"I've gotten good with explosives," she admitted. He couldn't blame her for playing to her strengths.

The man who had once been the boy that she knew so well seemed uncertain as his sword point delicately bounced back and forth between Guinevere and Lancelot. Lancelot, the brash warrior who had been fairly easy to manipulate so far, had no such issue as he directed his sword arm toward Arthur, and kept Guinevere on point with the blade in his left hand. Guinevere took stock of the situation calmly, and the three of them began to circle one another.

"You knew I was following you in the village, didn't you?" Arthur asked her. "I didn't bring you here, did I? You let me bring you here."

"To bury me with a dead man?" said Guinevere, completing Arthur's thought. "Yes."

"But the lady and I have come to an understanding," boomed Lancelot pompously. "She's going to help me cut you down, Arthur. And then I'll help her find her father. I'm sorry to say, King, but your reign ends today."

With Lancelot's full attention on taunting Arthur, Guinevere decided that her moment had come, as she said, "Of course, there's always my original plan. Thanks for the crossbow, Lancelot."

In less than a second, she lowered her arm, took dead aim on Lancelot's head, and pulled the trigger.

~   ~   ~

The time has come, thought Arthur. *Not all of us are going to leave here alive.*

He had been doing his best to stall Lancelot and Guinevere so that Percival and the other knights had plenty of time to clear the camp. There was no telling what kind of damage Lancelot and Guinevere could cause, and Arthur wanted to do his best to protect anyone else from getting caught in the crossfire. As the arrow leapt out of Guinevere's crossbow, streaking toward Lancelot's head, Arthur realized that there was a chance this could be over far more quickly than he had expected.

But whereas Guinevere seemed fairly single-minded in her pursuit, Lancelot was a bit more unpredictable. He was also undeniably formidable. Arthur could barely believe his eyes as he witnessed the speed at which Lancelot was able to wrench himself backward and clear his head from the path of Guinevere's arrow. Guinevere didn't give Lancelot a moment to retaliate, however, as she quickly pointed her second crossbow at his leg and fired. The second arrow found its mark and buried itself deep in Lancelot's thigh. The fierce warrior roared in pain as he stumbled backward and fell.

In less time than it took to draw a breath, Guinevere dropped her fired crossbows, dug her hand into her bodice, and drew out the long, golden dagger that she had used on Arthur once before. Arthur only had a moment to consider how unwise it had been to keep both Guinevere and Lancelot's weapons of choice on hand, when he found the dagger being used on him once again.

As the woman with the crown of braids slashed at Arthur, he leapt back narrowly and escaped her dagger's deadly touch, then perhaps not at his most clever, he said, "So I take it you're not working with him?"

"I've been promised my father back," said Guinevere as she slashed again and again, forcing Arthur to retreat rapidly, "but only if Lancelot stops breathing."

The fact that he could only hope to avoid her insistent attacks for so long forced Arthur to ask, "So why are you coming after me?"

"I'll happily drop my weapon," answered Guinevere as she showed no sign of dropping it, "but you have to drop yours first. Then, I swear, I will help you reclaim the throne."

Continuing to dodge Guinevere's attacks, Arthur said, "You've destroyed my camp. Put my people in danger. I'm sorry to say, but—"

And, sensing a small opening in her arc of attack, Arthur darted forward and shoved her with his free hand. Guinevere slammed backward into a tree trunk.

"You don't inspire much trust," finished Arthur.

Then, gritting his jaw and pulling together all of his determination, Arthur raised his sword to do what he had known would eventually have to be done. Once again, the Guinevere he had known had proven herself to be long gone.

This new woman had to die.

Before he could deal his killing blow, however, her golden dagger flashed again and Arthur found it pointed at his stomach. Apparently she had decided that he could no longer live as she said with cold determination, "I'm sorry, Arthur, but in these dark times, only the strong survive."

She was about to force the point deep into his intestines when they both heard a bellow.

"KING!"

Guinevere lurched backward as Lancelot came charging back into the fray. The crazed knight dove and tackled Arthur, sending the two men tumbling end over end. As they flipped and rolled, Arthur tried to get his bearings both on gravity and on the current alliances of the fighters. Both he and Lancelot quickly regained their stances, and the bare-chested warrior threw himself at Arthur with a flurry of blades. Yet again Arthur found himself astounded at the skill with which Lancelot was able to balance two very different styles of attack. More precisely, Arthur would've been astounded if he wasn't so busy fighting for his life.

"King, I'm having a thought…" said Lancelot as he continued to force Arthur backward. "We men must stand together. It may be our only chance to conquer the fairer sex."

Arthur's head was spinning now. Lancelot had proven himself once again to be quite unpredictable as Arthur asked, "How does that get your arm back?"

"It's not much good having an arm if I lose my head," explained Lancelot, and Arthur thought it was not an unreasonable explanation.

Something else occurred to Arthur as he asked, "Does it bother you that she hasn't rejoined the fight?"

Lancelot frowned, and for the slightest instant both men turned their attention away from each other. It only took them a moment to realize that their lives were still very much in danger, and not from each other. Guinevere stood some twenty yards away and aimed two newly reloaded crossbows. One for each of them.

Twang! The arrows flew. And Arthur and Lancelot disengaged from their battle with each other, and dove in opposite directions to narrowly avoid Guinevere's expert aim.

As he rolled into a new attack position a few yards away, Arthur heard Lancelot mutter, "I offer them a chance to live, but no. I tried to take the high ground. But I guess I'll have to take the high ground."

Trying to decipher this strange muddle of words, Arthur watched as Lancelot dropped the sword in his left hand, and leapt into the air. As he soared, the knight slashed with his right sword arm, and neatly cut one of the ropes that suspended a tree fort some thirty feet above the ground. Lancelot was pulled high up into the trees as the tree fort, which was now ablaze from Guinevere's explosions, came crashing down.

Once again Arthur found himself diving out of the way to escape oncoming danger as the cascading fireball of wood missed him by mere feet. Regaining his footing, Arthur found himself next to Guinevere, who had also just dived to avoid the falling fort, and was now once again pulling an arrow into position for her next attack.

"I guess it's every man for himself," Arthur said to her.

"And woman," corrected Guinevere with a hint of annoyance. "Come now, Arthur, we will be half of your kingdom. That is if I let you live once I've finished with him."

She darted away, and with surprising dexterity Arthur watched her run up the crooked remains of a fallen tree trunk. From her higher position, she took aim at Lancelot once again, who was now positioned several feet above them in another suspended tree fort. Guinevere's crossbow fired again, but Lancelot batted the arrow away easily with his sword arm.

"I was really starting to like you!" roared Lancelot.

"I tried to send you off pleasurably," was Guinevere's quick reply.

Arthur barely had time to try and make sense of their unusual exchange as he watched Lancelot charge forward and fling himself out of the safety of his fort and into the air toward Guinevere. With a war cry, he knocked Guinevere off of her perch, taking it for himself, and sent the lady plummeting toward the ground. It was a well-planned move, because Guinevere was sent spiralling not toward a soft bit of grass but for the still burning wreckage of the fallen fort below.

In the instant that Guinevere fell, Arthur made a decision. He didn't want her to die. It didn't matter what she had done or what she had planned to do; Arthur wanted to save her. And even though Lancelot was determined to kill him, Arthur didn't particularly want Lancelot to die either. With his new course of action firmly in mind, Arthur sprang to work.

Determined to be the protector that the kingdom needed, Arthur leapt to save Guinevere. Mimicking Lancelot's earlier move, Arthur slashed a suspension rope, and grasped the newly cut end. As the tree fort that had been attached to the rope fell, Arthur was pulled sharply upward, and in the arc of the swing he caught Guinevere.

It had all taken the space of a few seconds, but Arthur now knew that he wasn't going to let her go again.

Of course, it would still be necessary to explain that to her. The two former lovestruck children landed on the fort that Lancelot had just recently vacated.

As she regained her footing, Guinevere drew her dagger again and held it defensively as she asked with apparent confusion, "I think you just saved me... But I thought you were trying to kill me? Who's on whose side again?"

"I've been rethinking that," started Arthur, but he didn't get very far before a battle cry interrupted him.

Lancelot bellowed once more as he came leaping in, and joined them on the already unstable suspended platform. The entire tree wobbled, and Arthur heard a distinct cracking sound as the trunk buckled under the stress of the three warriors. However, there wasn't time to worry about that yet, as Lancelot slashed his sword arm at Arthur's head.

Arthur deflected Lancelot's blow, and he said, "Thank you for joining us, Lancelot. I had something I wanted to discuss with you, as well."

The three of them were all engaged in combat now, as Lancelot hacked and slashed, while Guinevere's dagger danced through the air, and Arthur did his best to avoid the attacks while he laid out his grand vision for the three of them.

"Lancelot," said Arthur, deciding it was best to try and first persuade the more unstable of the two, "you were the greatest knight in the kingdom once."

"Still am!" declared the bare-chested windbag as he tried to add kingslayer to his list of accomplishments.

"And, Guinevere," added Arthur, as she made a stab for Lancelot, "you have the ability to get close to Vortigern."

"I'd worry more about how close I can get to Lancelot," she said as Lancelot caught her wrist just in the nick of time to stop her from plunging her dagger into his heart.

"This may be surprising to hear, given our current state of engagement," said Arthur as he pulled Guinevere off of Lancelot and slammed her into the tree trunk, causing them all to stumble off-balance, "but I need your help. Both of you. I am going to become king. I am going to bring peace and stability back to this nation. But I need us all to work together to overthrow Vortigern."

Lancelot tossed his head back in laughter, then took another swing at Arthur. She didn't make an outright attempt on his life, but Guinevere didn't look real close to accepting Arthur's offer either. If he was being honest, Arthur hadn't expected it to be easy to convince them, but that didn't mean he was going to give up.

"Guinevere, once I'm king I can free your father," Arthur said, determined to end the fight as he slammed his full weight against the trunk of the tree. "And, Lancelot, I'll use all of my power to find a way to restore you."

The entire tree buckled as Arthur hit it, and the three of them tipped off-balance as Arthur shouted, "The three of us are strongest if we're together. Join me!"

And as the tree fell, Arthur slashed at the leather bindings that held Lancelot's sword arm in place. The blade flew up into the air just as they were all pitched off of the falling fort. Arthur deftly leapt into the void and neatly snatched Lancelot's blade out of mid-air. Then the future king flipped through the air as he fell.

Guinevere and Lancelot hit the ground hard, but Arthur stuck the landing and forcefully thrust both his own sword and Lancelot's blade forward, and held them just beneath the chins of his assailants.

"Or I can kill you both now," finished Arthur, slightly digging his points home. "What do you say? Can we talk?"

With swords to their throats and their lives potentially on the line, both Guinevere and Lancelot nodded agreeably. They weren't unreasonable after all.

Thank goodness, thought Arthur as he maintained a look of deadly determination. *I don't know how much longer I could've kept this up.*

~ ~ ~

CHAPTER 25

The First Round Table

This feels right, thought Guinevere, doing her best to keep her face impassive so as not to betray the optimism she was feeling for the first time in many, many moons.

While she was feeling good at the moment, Guinevere still knew that this wasn't the time to do anything rash like showing unabashed enthusiasm. Instead, she was following dutifully behind Arthur and secretly relishing in glimpses of the greatness in him while doing her best to maintain a straight, even expression. Bitter experience had taught her that optimism about a promising future shouldn't be taken as prophecy. For the time being she'd go along quietly, listen attentively, and hope against hope that her life wouldn't collapse again into a pile of rubble and flame.

The three exhausted warriors stumbled through the remains of the camp, and passed a few smoldering fires that were quietly burning themselves out. Glancing around, Guinevere felt slight pangs of remorse for the destruction that she had brought down on this little refuge. She reminded herself, however, that Arthur was threatening to kill her, and Lancelot wasn't exactly trustworthy, so she had done what she needed to do to survive. As she followed a few steps behind Arthur, she secretly hoped that her days of constantly worrying about her own survival were nearing an end.

Arthur led them into the longest tent in the camp, and as soon as they had ducked their heads beneath the canvas flaps of the door, Guinevere's eyes swept through the new surroundings and searched for any signs of ambush or betrayal. It was empty save for several long wooden tables and benches, and a handful of overturned smaller tables and chairs. There was still food on the tables, some of it steaming slightly. Apparently it had been meal time. Guinevere's pang of remorse returned.

She couldn't wait for the day when she wouldn't have to check every room she entered for traps, or worry that she'd ruined someone's dinner.

Arthur strode over to the longest wooden table, and he motioned for Guinevere and Lancelot to sit while he indicated that he intended to the take the head of the table for himself.

"Sit," said Arthur with all the air and dignity of the great king that was now shining through.

Nevertheless, even a king can only do so much, and Lancelot and Guinevere weren't about to sit.

"Are you out of your mind?!" shouted Lancelot. "I'm not letting you sit in my blind spot."

"No," said Guinevere, shaking her head as she carefully examined the situation and quickly dismissed it. "You could kill either of us at any moment. We'd never see it coming."

"Fine. You choose," sighed Arthur, and he swept his arm in a do-as-you-please gesture.

Guinevere pointed to a small square table.

"There," suggested Guinevere.

But Lancelot exploded just as forcefully at this suggestion as he had at the last. "So she can use the corners to stab me under the table?!"

"She's not going to do that!" said Arthur, and it was clear that his kingly dignity was straining now.

"Actually," admitted Guinevere, "that was my plan..."

For someone so stupid, thought Guinvere, *Lancelot can be inconveniently paranoid sometimes.*

Rummaging through the fallen wreckage of multiple tables and chairs, Arthur extracted a small round table amongst the mess. He flipped it over, dusted it off, and offered it to the other two.

"The Round Table," said Arthur. "No head. No sides. No advantages. No weaknesses. We all sit as equals."

After a long moment in which they were both clearly trying to find a fault in this line of reasoning and in which they both came up short, Guinevere and Lancelot nodded.

"You two make Vortigern look trusting," said Arthur under his breath, and Guinevere had to admit to herself that Arthur had a point.

~ ~ ~

CHAPTER 26

Vortigern's Gifts

Deep beneath the bowels of Tintagel Castle, flickering torchlight illuminated a dank, nightmare-ish dungeon. During the reign of Uther Pendragon, even the basest of criminals was treated with some respect and locked in cells that had at least a modicum of fresh air and sunshine. King Vortigern thought that was absolute rubbish. He believed in making his enemies pay for their sins with torture and pain. In fact, Vortigern took pleasure in it.

In the first months after he took the throne, Vortigern quickly decided the merciful prisons of his predecessor would be one of the first things to go. He sought deeper, darker corners of the castle and quickly found the cool, dark catacombs that had once been used to store certain kinds of salted meats and liquors that benefitted from lower, constant temperatures. Vortigern quickly found better uses for the space that once held bloody animal carcasses, and those dark corners of the castle were now used to tenderize the flesh of those who dared oppose him.

The resourceful king was now using the hidden recesses of the castle for still darker purposes. Today he had ventured down into the depths, despite sullying still more fine clothes, to find the dungeons filled with his most vicious, brutal disciples. Dozens of Saxon warriors had volunteered to chain themselves to the walls, volunteered to starve themselves, volunteered to subject themselves to excruciating pain for the chance to serve their king.

As Vortigern pulled a red hot poker from the sizzling flesh of a particularly massive and ugly Saxon, he looked the beastly man in the eyes.

"Make me a gift of your anger," said Vortigern, his words dripping with perverse pleasure. "Make me a gift of your cruelty. And I will reward you with all the miserable, cowering, pathetic prey you could hope for. Do you love your king?"

The Saxon warrior gritted his teeth as he sought to silence his agony, and then he nodded. Vortigern smiled as he turned to the throngs of barbarians who all seemed only too eager to take his pledge of pain in return for the chance to dispense their cruelty. The mad king's lips curled upward as he spoke again.

"Who's next?"

~ ~ ~

CHAPTER 27

Raring for a Fight

Lancelot was raring for a fight. Again. Sure, he had arguably just lost one, although he'd be damned if he was ever going to outright admit that. His feet bounced anxiously, and his good left hand snapped against his taut thigh that yearned to leap back into battle. Lancelot already felt fresh again, and his blood pumped through his veins as he sought to get back out into the fray.

Instead, they were talking. A lot.

With all the determination he could muster, Lancelot focused his attention on Arthur and Guinevere's words, because despite his willingness to throw himself into action, Lancelot knew that strategy was important. On top of that, he knew that a good strategy always led to another good thing. A good fight.

"Vortigern's been conditioning his army to be more vicious and merciless than ever," said Guinevere as she leaned across the table to address Arthur and Lancelot. "Aggravaine was to lead them."

"I can happily say that he's no longer a threat," Arthur said.

"And thank you for that," said Guinevere, and her entire face seemed to glow as she looked at Arthur. "Although I wouldn't have minded if you had waited a while so that I could join you in that particular good deed."

Great... this again... thought Lancelot, rolling his eyes. *What does she see in him anyway?*

"But nonetheless," Guinevere continued, "tomorrow Vortigern plans to send out every single one of his warriors to ravage the country. He'll wipe out a quarter of the people by supper."

"My God..." said Lancelot as his cry of disbelief slipped past his lips unbidden. If there was one thing that Lancelot liked more than a fight, it was a noble battle. Based on the cruelty that Vortigern was showing, this was shaping up to be a crusade that the poets would write songs about. And Lancelot just didn't feel like there were enough songs written about him.

"He hopes to crush any last hope of rebellion before it can start," said Guinevere.

"He really thinks he'll succeed?" asked Arthur, clearly sharing in Lancelot's disbelief.

"You've been to the villages. Who's going to mount a defense?" said Guinevere. "The starving throngs of beggars? Or your old blind woman?"

She turned to look at Lancelot now, and the knight shook his head as he bowed it slightly.

"We will," came Arthur's simple promise.

"Your small group of men can't be everywhere all at once," said Guinevere.

"So we take the fight to him," said Arthur, and his voice grew strong, his words filling Lancelot. "I will attack the castle. I will protect the people at all costs. I will stop Vortigern."

The youthful face of the hopeful monarch set itself with a look of deadly seriousness, and Lancelot found himself grinning slightly. He was starting to recognize something in this young man that he had once mistaken for a spoiled, reckless upstart.

Arthur, too, was raring for a fight.

And Lancelot was finally starting to understand what Guinevere saw in him.

~ ~ ~

CHAPTER 28

Two Old Friends

"Arthur has the ability to inspire," croaked Gawain through the vine that was still wrapped tightly around his neck.

His throat was dry. His lips were parched. But Gawain stood strong in the center of Merlin's cottage. The wizard may have had the knight at his mercy, but Gawain was determined to fight to the last. With enchanted plants binding his legs and arms, Gawain only had his words to battle with. He would've preferred to have a sword, but he would work with what was available to him.

"His army is a few dozen men. Hardly an inspiration," said Merlin with a lazy flick of his hand, and the rope around Gawain's neck tightened.

"Do better," said the wizard.

"His numbers are growing," Gawain said. "More and more people put their faith in him."

"Yet Kay died waiting for Arthur to lead. And you're not far behind, old friend. Do. Better."

Once again the old wizard waved his hand, and the rope tightened still further around the knight's neck. Gawain was pulled up to the tops of his toes, struggling to breathe.

"I've trained him," said Gawain, his voice shuddering with the effort. "He's accepted his destiny. He understands what it means to be king."

"A short time ago, a sword telling him to kill people broke him from his apathy," shot back Merlin. "Would he even be attempting to fight if it weren't for a sword in a stone telling him to?"

Merlin tensed one more time, bringing Gawain to the tip of his toes. His boots scraped against the ground as he struggled to get a purchase. Grimacing and choking, Gawain sucked in what little air he could manage and he continued to argue.

"I believe Arthur's being misled by the sword," said Gawain, "but you and I could set him back on the path."

"What's in it for me?" asked the wizard.

"Once Arthur is king…" gasped Gawain, his legs on the verge of giving way under his precarious position, "I'll give you an honorable death."

And Gawain turned his slightly bulging, oxygen-deprived eyes at the wizard and glared with all the fury he could muster. He might die any moment now, but he refused to be broken.

Merlin had to chuckle. And with another sharp wave of his hand, the vine loosened around Gawain's neck. Gawain's feet slipped back down to the floor and he drew deep, ragged breaths, doing his best to keep them measured and in control, while he kept his stern gaze upon the all-powerful magician.

"A rope around his neck and he offers me my life," said Merlin, still smiling through his overgrown beard. "All right, Gawain, let's start again. Why should I believe in Arthur?"

~ ~ ~

CHAPTER 29

The Mysterious Messages

Arthur was beginning to think that if he could convince
Guinevere and Lancelot to join him, then the rest of the country
would be easy in comparison. He gently rubbed his temples as
Guinevere pressed him.

"Can we really trust you, Arthur?!" demanded Guinevere. "Or
will you turn on us again as soon as your legendary sword and
stone tells you to?"

"Is that where he's been getting his orders?" asked Lancelot.
"From a rock?"

"It is not a rock! It is Klærent the Stonebourne!" cried Arthur,
once again getting sick of everyone's doubt. Then he continued,
"It's a legendary sword. It's a sword of peace!"

His speech didn't seem to come across as impressively as he
had hoped, however, and all he received were blank, unconvinced
stares, so he turned things on Guinevere. "Fine, please enlighten
me. Who was giving you instructions then?"

"A large black crow," she said, trying to muster a tone of
conviction, but her voice came out much smaller than usual.

Lancelot shot a look of disbelief at Guinevere, and Arthur felt a
little less silly.

"Sometimes it's a puppy!" she said, her voice rising now, but her eyes still weren't exactly making contact. She spun on Lancelot, asking, "Who told you that you would get your arm back if you killed Arthur?"

"Someone very powerful," said Lancelot, and leaving it at that.

However, Guinevere wasn't about to let that lie as she asked skeptically, "More powerful than his sword of legend? Or my shape-shifting crow?"

"A voice from beyond the grave," said Lancelot.

"Tell us who," demanded Arthur as he leaned in toward Lancelot. "We need to know everything."

Lancelot gazed at Arthur now, and his look was difficult to read. Arthur had the sense that Lancelot was wrestling with a decision. He clearly had something to say, but wasn't sure how to say it. In the end, it seemed that Lancelot, who was a man of action, chose to be simple and direct.

"It was your father," said the knight.

Arthur lurched back at the absurdity of this statement. His father? Why would his father have given Lancelot orders to kill him? His father had sent him the sword which was his birthright and which was now helping him to regain the throne. Arthur's head was swimming trying to make sense of it all, as Lancelot continued.

"I barely escaped death. He seems to be doing the same," explained Lancelot.

"How did he contact you?" asked Guinevere.

"Magic," said Lancelot, then added for good measure, "Powerful magic."

"Why would my father want me killed?" Arthur finally managed to ask.

"He was a great king. Maybe he sees that you won't be," offered Lancelot.

"No," said Arthur, shaking his head. He refused to believe that his father would be plotting against him. There had to be another explanation; he just wasn't sure what it was.

"That sword of yours? Klærent the Stonebourne. The sword of legend," said Lancelot. "Who else could leave messages on it but another legend?"

Arthur sat silently for a long moment, weighing the strange omens in his mind. Finally, he shook his head definitively.

"The messages have always been cryptic. If it is him, I can't believe he wants me dead," said Arthur.

"Just me?" asked Guinevere, cocking her eyebrow.

"Just us," corrected Lancelot.

"No. I think he wanted to bring us together," said Arthur, the answer coming to him unbidden, but as soon as he said it, he knew it was right.

"Why should we believe that?" began Lancelot, but Arthur pounded on the table, finally letting his frustration get the best of him.

The young king stood as he gazed upon the two whose aid he now sought with furious intensity.

"Because I believe it! Someone or something has brought us together. Whether for good or for ill, we three now sit at this table as one. The greatest knight in the kingdom. A woman for whom, as far as I'm concerned, there is no equal. And myself. The three of us together are a force that can not be matched. And I say we use our strength to take back this land!"

Arthur finished his speech and fell silent. His eyes darted back and forth between Lancelot and Guinevere as he allowed them to take his words to heart. He didn't dare to say anything else to them, because he knew that they needed to come to this decision on their own. They had to choose to join him with free hearts. And his most desperate hope was that they would.

"I'm in," said Lancelot after a long moment of silence.

Arthur's heart leapt.

Then Arthur turned to Guinevere, and she caught his eye. A lifetime of memories and future dreams passed between them. And then she too nodded. Arthur was starting to feel as though he might become king after all.

"We need to strike at Vortigern in a way that will truly hurt him. And that means Merlin," said Arthur as he started to lay out a plan.

Guinevere and Lancelot turned to Arthur with looks of surprise. Arthur held their gaze. He knew it was bold, but he also knew it was the right move.

"It will take the most powerful man in the kingdom off the board," Arthur explained.

"And neutralize the Red Dragon," added Guinevere with a slight nod of her head, "taking away Vortigern's greatest weapon."

"I've been wanting to slay that dragon ever since I first laid eyes upon it," said Lancelot, "but it might be just as satisfying to slay the wizard."

The mighty knight nodded, and they were agreed.

"If we're going to strike at Merlin, first we have to find his home," said Arthur.

"Impossible," said Lancelot. "It's shrouded by impenetrable enchantments. You can't find it unless you've already been there."

"I've already been there," Guinevere cut in.

Lancelot's mouth fell open, then curled into a smile as he said, "You're very good."

Guinevere popped her eyebrows at Lancelot and then she said, "Why, Sir Lancelot, you sound as if there was ever any doubt."

A warm look passed between the knight and the lady, and Arthur began to have hope that their new alliance would hold. Nonetheless, he felt compelled to add, "If we're going to pull this off, we have to all be together. Can we put aside our differences? Can we trust each other?"

The three of them sat as equals at the small round table, and considered the question. They had each faced trials and tribulations that had pushed them to their absolute limits. They had tried to kill one another, and they had fought to protect their lives from one another. Arthur knew that asking them all to trust each other was like asking for a miracle. The young man who sought to be king silently asked for that miracle to come true.

~ ~ ~

CHAPTER 30

A Gathering of Villains

Vortigern lounged in his throne room with one leg draped across the arm of the massive golden chair that had he claimed through murder. Once again he had dressed himself in the finest garments that he could get his hands on, and once again he had managed to spill, stain, and sully them before he even made it out to present himself.

This was a particularly important occasion, however, as his throne room was filled with nearly a dozen men whose reputations could all rival his own. It had taken months of machinations and devil's deals, but a notorious collection of tyrants, warlords, and dictators from all across the country had finally consented to appear before King Vortigern.

They didn't seem too impressed with Vortigern's slovenly demeanor.

"How dare you summon us here, Vortigern!" said Yder, on the verge of drawing the two scimitars that were his trademark. "Only to smugly sit upon your throne above us. I should cut you down by the knees and make you gaze up to me for the rest of your days."

Vortigern merely nodded lazily. Looking bored.

"You claimed to have an offer worthy of my consideration," said King Lot, an old man draped in a long bear-skin cloak. "You certainly begged and grovelled enough to convince me to appear. Was it all just some ruse to try and make us look silly in your presence? Because I will not be made to look the buffoon."

"King Lot, Lord Yder, all my distinguished friends," said Vortigern, finally placing his feet on the ground and leaning forward to address them, "I asked you here today to offer you a unique opportunity."

Each of the men in the room had killed for much less than having a bit of their time wasted, and they presumed that Vortigern was no fool, so they bit their tongues just long enough to hear him out. Vortigern had them all right where he wanted them as he licked his lips and made his grand request.

"Join me. Pledge your allegiance to me as the king of all kings to rule over you all. Or die."

Rage flashed across the faces of every last man in the room. Vortigern's eyes raked across all of their scowls and he relished the power he had over them, knowing that in one moment they'd have no choice.

"Will no one willingly offer me their devotion?" asked Vortigern with a look of mock indignation. "Or shall I force you?"

Yder was the first to move as his hands flew to his sides and he drew both of his arcing scimitars. He advanced toward Vortigern, as several of the other men also extracted various weapons. Before any of them had a chance to ascend the few steps that separated them from the throne, however, Vortigern clapped his hands together once only. The twenty-foot-tall doors to the grand throne room flew open, and his army of blood-thirsty Saxons flooded into the room. Each of them towered over the villains who had concentrated themselves in the center of the hall. The Saxon warriors were covered in fresh scars and war paint. Their yellowing teeth were bared to show that they had been ground into fangs. At least a hundred hulking behemoths encircled the small group of men who just a few moments ago thought that they were in charge.

"Now," said Vortigern, once again getting his fellow tyrants' attentions, "I think it's becoming clearer to you all. I have trained my army to seek out any and all who oppose me. Tomorrow they will ride out through the country and ask every man, woman, and child who they serve. Who they love. And if they are given even a moment's hesitation, they'll strike at any who oppose me."

Vortigern's hungry eyes now roamed over the men he had at his mercy.

"I can't seem to remember if there was any man in this very room who dared to oppose me? Or do you all wish to pledge your allegiance to me?"

One by one, each of the warlords and kings bowed before Vortigern's throne. He broke into a wide grin, and his drool dripped down to leave a new stain on his once beautiful shirt.

~ ~ ~

CHAPTER 31

Preparing for Battle

As she dressed for combat, Guinevere was fairly impressed by the range of options that were afforded to her by Arthur's arsenal. When she and Lancelot had come here earlier, she had simply grabbed for the dagger that she had become so comfortable with, and a couple of crossbows for good measure. However, now that she took the time to look around, she saw that despite the improbability of necessity, the armory was equipped for the needs of a lady. From the time that they were children, Guinevere had known that Arthur was uncommonly progressive, but in this instance he was proving to be chivalrous by his refusal to adhere to normal notions of chivalry. It was really quite sweet.

Guinevere looked through the weapons and found several lightweight throwing knives and even unconventional crossbows that she had overlooked before. They all seemed to be have been tinkered with precisely so that they fit a smaller, more feminine hand. She had also found a leather jerkin that seemed to be designed for a slim man, but with some minor adjustments it suited Guinevere quite well so that she had some protection, but also still had ease of movement. Of course, considering that they were about to battle a wizard, it was anyone's guess as to what would be the proper attire.

For good measure, she cut a long slit into one side of her gown to give her the ability to run, jump, and flee as the need determined. Since she also now had easier access to her own leg, she fashioned a holster and strapped her golden dagger to her bare thigh. It felt good to her to have it so near at hand.

Apparently Lancelot thought so too, as Guinevere caught him staring at the exposed flesh of her leg as she fastened the weapon to it.

"If you don't wish this to be buried in your heart," she said as she lowered her skirt back down and covered her thigh, "then I'd suggest you look away from now on."

Lancelot wasn't known for his bashfulness, but he did her the honor of looking away, although Guinevere caught a glimpse of a self-indulgent smirk as he turned. Guinevere fumed. They were about to go into war and Lancelot seemed caught up in the idea of a very different conquest. She shook her head dismissively and did her best to push away the girlish smile that seemed determined to creep onto her flushed cheeks.

Strange, she thought. *It must be because he's famous.*

Refusing to give it anymore thought, Guinevere approached Arthur, who had insisted on dressing in a different section of the tent to give her more privacy. He had also put on a layer of leather undergarments, but his was to help support the weight of the light chain mail he was now carefully putting into place. It was a light suit of armor, simply adorned with a breastplate and some shoulder guards, but Guinevere agreed with his decision to guard his heart. It was a most vulnerable target.

She brushed his golden hair across his forehead as she stepped up next to him and helped him to tighten the straps that attached the front and back sections of the armor. Guinevere smoothed over Arthur's protections, and brushed her hand over an exposed area along his left hip. He rippled at her touch, and gave a boyish giggle as he pulled away quickly. The lady smiled to match her lord, and their eyes met as a moment of silent longing passed between them.

"All right, let's go," said Lancelot, walking in and wrenching them back to the real matter at hand. "I'm ready to add wizard-killer to my list of accolades."

Guinevere felt that she had taken a somewhat minimalist approach to her preparations, but Lancelot had raised it to a whole new level. He was stripped bare to the waist, with only his sword arm strapped on to give his upper body any amount of cover. His legs, however, he had taken the time to cover with heavy metal armor.

"You don't think you might want just a bit more armor?" asked Arthur.

"You don't need armor if you don't intend on getting hit," said Lancelot wisely. "This, on the other hand," and here he knocked upon his metal codpiece, "is just good sense."

Arthur shrugged as he pulled on a helmet and covered his golden hair. "Well, then, let's go tempt our fates, shall we?"

And he strode out of the tent. For her part, Guinevere hefted up her crossbow, and followed her king.

~ ~ ~

CHAPTER 32

Even More Unwelcome Guests

Once again Merlin had brought Gawain to the tips of his toes.
The wizard was growing tired of this game. It had been nearly a
half-dozen times now that Merlin had brought his prey to the point
of death and then granted him a reprieve. It wasn't much longer,
though, before Merlin would have to actually follow through. Like
the father of a petulant child, Merlin knew that he'd soon have to
teach Gawain that bad behavior carried severe consequences.

"Your devotion to Arthur is touching, Gawain," said Merlin,
"but, you know, my magic binds me to the king."

"You've changed allegiances before," said Gawain.

"Vortigern's rise was inevitable," said Merlin, lifting his hand
just a fraction of an inch and urging Gawain ever higher. The
grizzled knight was tough, but Merlin knew that he could only go
so far.

"As is Arthur's," said Gawain almost silently through gritted
teeth as the vine cut into his neck.

"I'll be honest, Sir Gawain," said Merlin. "This has been great
fun. It truly has. I so rarely get to catch up with old friends. But
you've done nothing to convince me that Arthur is the savior you
believe him to be. I don't even understand why a knight such as

yourself, who has seen more kings in more lands than perhaps any other man alive, would choose to follow him."

Gawain's shoulders lowered and the noose choked him even further, but this time due to the knight's own effort. Or lack thereof.

Dear me, thought the wizard, his eyes going wide beneath his bushy eyebrows. *Have I actually broken the poor man?*

But Gawain raised himself back up again as he faced Merlin for what they both knew was the last time.

"I've lived too long, Merlin," said Gawain. "An old knight in service of a dead king. But Arthur has made me believe again. He will be the greatest king this land has ever known."

"Well, I finally agree with something you've said, Sir Gawain," said Merlin.

And with a fierce finality, the magician clenched his fist, and the rope jerked Gawain several feet into the air.

"You've lived too long."

The storied knight, whose very real exploits had already reached a nearly mythological status, twitched slightly as the last of his air slowly left his body.

It wasn't Gawain's time yet, though.

With a thunderous crash, the front door flew open and, in almost the same instant, a knife slashed through the air, cutting through the vine that suspended Gawain by the neck. The old knight crashed to the ground, and he breathed once more.

Although he was a clever man and had strong suspicions even without looking, Merlin spun to see who was now intruding upon his humble abode. His suspicions were confirmed and Merlin watched as the three people he knew to be the future king, queen, and traitor burst into his cottage.

"Well, well, well, Gawain's young king came for him after all," said Merlin.

With a gentle wave of his hand, Merlin sent Gawain's crumpled body flying across the room, where the pardoned knight crashed painfully against the wall near to where his trusty sword was still buried into the wood.

"Your voice? But I thought that—" said Arthur with a furrowed brow.

"I don't just speak in rhyme!" said Merlin, not really in the mood to clear up the confusion at the moment.

"We mustn't let him speak at all," said Guinevere, which Merlin found to be very rude considering they were in his home, and to make matters worse, she was talking about him as if he wasn't even there.

Twang! Guinevere fired her crossbow. Merlin accepted that he was getting on in years, but he could still catch an arrow in mid-air. Which he did to the amazed disappointment of his attackers.

Lancelot charged forward, and raised his sword arm high overhead in a gesture that clearly meant to cut Merlin down to size. In the few moments it took the surly knight to cross the room, however, the wizard wondered if Lancelot forgot that he was still holding the arrow. Merlin flung it at the charging brute, and Lancelot easily batted it away.

I guess he did remember the arrow, thought Merlin. *It's most fortunate that I still happen to have magics.*

And with another lazy flick of his hand, Merlin sent Lancelot careening across the room. In the instant that took, Arthur struck at Merlin. Klærent the Stonebourne, the legendary sword of peace, was on course to cut Merlin in twain. With unnaturally fast reflexes, however, Merlin raised his hand and the blade froze in mid-air.

"Well, you mustn't give yourself too hard of time," said Merlin. "You three did give it your best shot. Although, I must say, Arthur, why are you trying to kill me? I don't see my name on this sword. And I should know. I was the one leaving messages on the stone."

The wizard saw the young man's eyes go wide as understanding quickly took hold. Then Merlin sent Arthur sailing backward into a nearby wall. Guinevere, Merlin noted, had finally finished reloading her crossbow, and now she needed to be dealt with too.

"And, Guinevere, does anything look familiar?" the wizard continued.

A black crow soared in through the roof. It bit at her, then for good measure, it split into a dozen more crows. They flocked around her, pecking and cawing furiously, and her waving arms did little to deter them.

"Lancelot, you were the easiest of all," said Merlin. "I only had to write you a note with Uther's name signed upon it."

Arthur and Guinevere looked at Lancelot, who had stopped short just as he was about to launch another attack.

224

"A note?!" repeated Arthur in disbelief as he struggled to regain his footing from his heap against the wall.

"You said it was powerful magic!" shouted Guinevere through her circle of birds.

"I was supposed to be dead!" Lancelot cried defensively. "He would've needed powerful magic to know I was alive!"

"Oh, and I have powerful magic," said Merlin. "I admire your bold attacks against me, although you must've known you had little hope of success. Now allow me a chance to counter-escalate."

The wizard raised both of his arms into the air, and almost immediately a low rumble was emitted from the ground. The power of the wind was unleashed and filled the small stone cottage, causing Merlin's long beard to whip and tumble in the churning air. The already dim lights further tipped toward darkness.

As he began his incantation, Merlin took a moment to scan the faces of the three young people who had hoped to slay him. He was pleased to see that they all seemed to understand that this was going to be very, very bad.

"The darkest hex,

And blackest spell.

Now come to me.

To –

Merlin paused for a brief instant to savor this most delicious moment. The entire cottage was groaning under the force of his magic now. Books blew open. The fire roared. Statuettes of beasts and monsters came to life on their shelves. Then he spoke the final words to set them on their destination:

" – *unleash Hell.*"

And the world went black around them.

~ ~ ~

CHAPTER 33

Darkest Desires

The throne room felt so familiar. So warm. So safe. Arthur's eyes feasted on his surroundings as he took in the room that he had spent so much time in during his youth. It was clean, bright, and regal, and Arthur felt that it was all his at last.

Just a few short steps away stood the throne. There it was, his for the taking. A beautiful golden chair sitting empty, waiting for its new owner. Tentative at first, Arthur moved toward his birthright, and he was pleased to find that the floor didn't collapse beneath him, and the high vaulted ceiling didn't come crashing down on his head. His pace quickened as he reached the three steps that could rise him to the level of the throne. In the blink of an eye, he ascended those few small steps without any hesitation.

Stopping just an arm's length away from the throne, Arthur took a deep breath and realized that he felt freer than he had in a long time. His handsome face broke into a wide smile, and as he reached out to touch the throne, he heard a familiar voice.

"You did it, my son," said King Uther Pendragon.

Arthur spun around to see his father, fully adorned in his shimmering armor flecked in gold and bearing the crest of the dragon surrounded in flames. His father beamed at him, his eyes shining with tears.

Behind Uther the throne room was suddenly filled with people. Throngs of people huddled in the throne room with adoration on their faces. All of them were here for Arthur. All of them wanted to catch a glimpse of their new king.

Arthur looked down and was shocked to find that he was now dressed in armor to match his father, and yet Arthur's was even more spectacular. The gold-laid etchings shimmered in the rays of sunshine that poured in from every window.

His father approached him and lifted the majestic golden crown off of his own head. Arthur bowed slightly and felt the weight of the crown as it slipped perfectly atop his golden hair with surprising comfort. Uther's bright eyes locked on his son.

"You are truly a king," said Uther, and no father could've sounded prouder.

Every person in attendance burst into glorious applause.

~ ~ ~

Guinevere's heart was racing as fast as her feet while she sprinted down an empty corridor of the dark castle. Her aging father's arm was slung over her shoulder, and his prickly white beard tickled her neck as she did her best to support his feeble frame. Her chest burned with exhaustion but she knew she had to keep pushing them onward. For some reason she was terrified, and the fear infected her, causing her to irrationally strive on and on down a corridor that didn't seem to want to end.

"Father, we're almost there," Guinevere said, gasping for air and trying to ignore a painful stitch in her side. "We're almost—"

They had come to an old door with a large metal ring upon it. Guinevere grabbed the handle and wrenched the door open and gasped as she found —

Aggravaine.

The ugly, bald-headed, duplicitous knight was just as massive, hulking and abominable as he had been in Guinevere's many nightmares. With a vicious growl, the brute lunged for her. But Guinevere was no longer the type to cower. Not anymore. She gritted her jaw, and all of the finely trained muscles in her body tensed into fighting mode. Guinevere ducked under Aggravaine's outspread arms and with the speed and reflexes of a hundred sleepless nights spent training, she drew the long, golden dagger that her father had given her. It flashed through the air, and Guinevere buried it into the heart of Aggravaine.

The behemoth fell with a resounding thud and was dead.

Guinevere spun to her father as waves of relief washed over her and unbidden tears flooded into her eyes.

She struggled to form the words that she never thought she'd say. "We're free."

~　~　~

The field seemed to stretch on for miles. Green grass rippled in a soft breeze beneath a clear blue sky. But the most beautiful thing of all was Lancelot.

He stood in the middle of the field, stripped down to nearly nothing, and he was perfect. His body was without a single scar, without a single blemish, without a single fault. He turned and found a sword stuck into the ground and twinkling in the light of bright, full sun.

Lancelot reached out to draw the sword from the ground —

With his right hand.

The greatest knight in a thousand centuries flourished the sword expertly as he marvelled at the strength that surged through his fully restored arm. With an impressive show of skill and exhibition, Lancelot twisted and found to his surprise that he was suddenly surrounded. It was an impossibly large army. Hundreds. Thousands. Uncountable numbers. Against one. There was only Lancelot to oppose them.

Lancelot simply grinned. Bring them all.

All at once, the entire massive army charged upon Lancelot, and the greatest knight the world had ever and would ever see fought them flawlessly. Spinning. Blocking. Swinging. Every blow landed. Every strike was a kill.

"Is this all you've got?!" he roared as he cut down three men with a single swing.

The mighty Lancelot was finally back.

~ ~ ~

The throngs of adorning subjects continued to cheer for their new king, and Arthur had no desire to stop them. His heart swelled as he settled himself into the throne that was above them all, and placed him just out of the reach of their common hands. Still beaming, his father approached his son.

"My son, there's just one thing left to do," said Uther Pendragon, and then his face contorted into rage as he bellowed, "BRING THEM IN!"

A door along one wall of the mighty throne room was thrown open, and several guards led in a small group of filthy, shackled prisoners. Arthur's crowd of subjects hissed and booed and jeered at the men who were being led forward to stand in front of the king. They assembled before him, and Arthur quickly recognized the small band of knights who had stayed loyal to him during his darkest days. Percival was there. And so was Kay, shaking back his wild mane of red hair.

"He's not a king," spat Kay. "I knew him as a boy. He's no greater than I."

Uther leaned near his son and whispered in his ear, saying, "They've been disloyal to the crown. You must kill them, Arthur. Kill them all. And prove that you are king."

The former king handed the new king a sword, and Arthur looked at it to see that it was Klærent the Stonebourne, the legendary sword of peace, which had caused so much pain already. Arthur felt the smoothness of stone that was laid into the handle as he approached the prisoners. His guards forced Kay and the others to their knees, but their heads didn't droop as they continued to scowl at the great King Arthur.

Arthur's hands wavered, but he raised his sword high into the air and prepared to deliver his righteous blow.

~   ~   ~

Guinevere and Leodegrance were sprinting down a new hallway now. But both she and her father ran with a renewed vigor. Her legs felt fresh and light while her decrepit old father was now positively bouncing alongside her.

"We're free!" she cried. "Just a little further and we'll have sunshine forever. We're almost there."

They reached a large door, which Guinevere threw open only to find another long hallway. Her enthusiasm undiminished, she ran down the new hallway and found a new door. She threw it open too and found another hallway with another door at the end. Guinevere ran down that one, and another, and another, and another, and opened door after door after door. It seemed neverending, yet Guinevere forced herself to clutch at the last grains of hope even as they slowly slipped through her fingers like a handful of pure, white, ungraspable sand.

"We're almost there... We're almost there... We're almost..."

~ ~ ~

Lancelot was invincible. One man against an entire army, and Lancelot knew that he couldn't be beaten. Every man who came within his reach fell instantly. The great knight was bathed in sweat, mud, and blood from a thousand fallen rivals. And, finally, with as much ease as when he killed the first, Lancelot slew the last man that dared to attack him.

All was silent.

Alone in a battlefield covered in the corpses of an uncountable number of dead men, Lancelot heaved slightly then drew in a deep breath that filled his lungs, belly, and every last blood vessel down to the tips of his ten fingers. It burst out of him again as he laughed in triumph.

But Lancelot quickly realized that he wasn't the only one laughing.

"Is — is this all you've got?"

Lancelot turned to see the slight, unimpressive form of Sir Percival slowly approaching with sword in hand. A broad smile filled Lancelot's face as he spun and swung his mighty sword to cut down the man who had betrayed him.

And Percival blocked it.

Easily.

He even shrugged as he said, "Not impressed."

~ ~ ~

The legendary sword was raised high, but Arthur couldn't bring it down. Even as Kay and the other knights spat and taunted him, Arthur couldn't kill them. Not like this.

"I won't do it," said Arthur, lowering his sword and turning to face his father. "They were once my friends and they deserve a chance to redeem themselves. I'm no better than they."

Arthur expected another smile and a kind word from Uther Pendragon, who had always valued the virtue of mercy. However, there was no kindness to be found on the old king's face. Instead Uther scowled at his son as he advanced. Arthur stepped back and was surprised to find that the sword he had been clutching in his hand was now gone.

With a look of deepest disdain drawn across his regal features, Uther held Klærent himself and wielded it menacingly as he said to his son, "You are not worthy of the throne."

Uther struck his son, and the sword of legend hit the gold-flecked armor like a crack of thunder. Arthur fell backward and stumbled down the few steps that had elevated him to the level of the throne.

As he struggled to regain his footing, Arthur was suddenly grabbed from behind. One hand. Then another. And another. And another. A clawing, ripping, tearing throng of people fell upon him as they screamed at him,

"No King! Not my King! Never a King!"

~ ~ ~

Gasping with exhaustion, Guinevere and Leodegrance urged themselves to take one last step and they reached one last door. Struggling just to lift her hand, Guinevere wrenched open the door.

"It has to be…" she said as she used every last ounce of strength she had to throw this last desperate hope of a door open.

And she was finally rewarded.

It was undeniably freedom. A huge, bright sun shone down over a clear blue lake of shimmering water. The entire world was open before them. Guinevere's face lifted into a smile that was as bright as the sun overhead.

"We made it, Father," she said with tears sparkling in her eyes. "We're fr—"

But Guinevere never had a chance to say that last word as an arrow flew out of complete nowhere and struck her father in the heart.

The old man crumbled to the ground as his knees gave way.

"NO!" Guinevere screamed as she cradled the body of her slowly expiring father.

"Why...why..." And he forced himself to form the words as he whispered, "Why didn't you save me...?"

Guinevere melted into sobs as she draped herself over the lifeless shell of the father she had failed completely.

~   ~   ~

Lancelot couldn't win. He was locked in man-to-man combat with a smaller, slower, weaker foe. But he couldn't finish it. No matter how hard he swung, or how fast he attacked, Percival always blocked it. *Hell, Percival even looked bored.*

"We didn't leave you that day because we were scared," said Percival as he easily deflected another pathetic attack from Lancelot.

"We left you that day because you weren't good enough."

Enraged, Lancelot reared back and swung with every bit of his considerable might. Percival easily stopped it. Then with speed, skill and ferocity that Lancelot could scarcely believe, Percival spun, twisted and slashed.

And, once again, Lancelot's right arm was cut away.

As his arm was lost once more, Lancelot, who wasn't a great knight, who had never been a great knight, who was the weakest knight in a thousand centuries, fell to his knees, and a pitiful scream of defeat erupted from the deepest parts of him.

Looking on as Lancelot cradled his stump of an arm, Percival said, "You will never be good enough."

~ ~ ~

The throngs of blood-thirsty subjects had Arthur pinned into place. He couldn't break free. He couldn't fight. He could barely even struggle as his father strode toward him with the legendary sword in his legendary hands and declared,

"YOU ARE NO KING!"

And Uther plunged the sword into Arthur's chest.

~ ~ ~

CHAPTER 34

Merlin's Bargain

As his scream of agony died away, it took Arthur a moment to realize where he was. He was back in Merlin's small stone cottage again.

It had all been a dream.

But the grip of fear, despair and helplessness still felt very real. As he tried to catch his breath and still his nerves, Arthur looked around the tiny room and saw Lancelot cowering on the ground as he clawed at the ghost of his right arm, and Guinevere sobbed as she cradled a body that wasn't there.

"I offer you all a choice," said the wizard, and the words shook Arthur and his fellows out of their stupors. "Give in to your fears. Give in to your weaknesses. And turn on each other. And to whoever lives, I will grant you your greatest desire."

For a brief instant, Arthur remembered his vision of sitting on the throne, of wearing the crown, of being adored. He didn't know what had been promised to Guinevere or Lancelot, but he could tell by the hungry, crazed looks in their eyes that they were just as tempted as he.

"Or," continued Merlin, "you can nobly yet foolishly stand together. And I offer you no promises."

Arthur's eyes darted to Guinevere and Lancelot, who were doing their best to compose themselves, and Arthur saw madness in their eyes. He couldn't blame them, he felt it deep within himself too, and he wondered if it was all worth it. They couldn't defeat Merlin. And they didn't need to. Arthur could be king without all that trouble, and all he had to do was strike down the lady and knight who stood before him. Hadn't he already defeated both Lancelot and Guinevere in combat? He could do it again. Then, with the help of the wizard who had just thoroughly shown them the extent of his power, Arthur could finally ascend to the throne. Surely it would be easier that way. All he had to do was finish off the two people whom he was sure were plotting his demise.

Arthur lifted the sword of legend as he noticed Guinevere unsheathing her dagger and Lancelot strapping back on his sword arm. Then, with their weapons clutched tightly, they all turned as one.

And faced the wizard.

The glint in Merlin's eye vanished as Arthur took a step toward him with Guinevere and Lancelot at his side. The young king, his future bride, and the mighty knight all gripped their weapons and prepared to stay true to each other and fight on.

"It won't work, Merlin," said Arthur. "We know, we must stand united and togeth—"

But Arthur's speech was cut short as blinding pain ripped through him. He looked down to his left flank, and watched as Guinevere drove her dagger deeper into his side.

CHAPTER 35

Cut to the Core

The golden dagger dug into Arthur's back, and it hurt so much more than he could've expected. He looked over his shoulder and found the face of the woman that he had wanted so badly to trust again. She had chosen the bare spot along his left hip, the very same spot that she had tickled when she had helped him dress in the armory only hours ago. Or was it a different lifetime? Arthur had hoped then that her slight caress across that one vulnerable spot might mean that they could go back to being the kids they once were. But they could never go back. Everything had changed.

"It was only a matter of time, Arthur," she said, her voice barely above a heartbroken whisper, "until you turned on me."

"No. I would've stayed true to you," Arthur said, and his voice shook with pain.

Guinevere was unmoved, however, as she set her face and twisted the dagger, forcing it deeper into Arthur's back. A fresh wave of pain swept through him and Arthur's knees buckled. Guinevere drew back her dagger as Arthur crumbled to the ground.

Upon his knees and at her mercy, Arthur twisted himself to look at Guinevere as she raised her dagger high and prepared to bring it down with deadly finality.

She wouldn't have the chance, though.

Arthur watched as she was grabbed from behind and spun around. The dagger was slapped out of her hand. And Lancelot grabbed the front of her clothing with his powerful left arm and raised her up off of the ground with madness in his eyes. The tip of his sword arm lifted and pressed into the soft flesh beneath her chin. He held her there for a long moment, but the knight didn't finish the act.

"No!" shouted Lancelot, and suddenly the words were spilling out of him. "I can't. I'm a good man. Not anymore. Get out of my head. Stop. I won't be controlled!"

In a rage, Lancelot tossed Guinevere and she crashed to the floor. Then the crazed knight dashed over to the table that was straining under the weight of Merlin's books. Lancelot scanned the table, found the book he was looking for, snatched it, and sprinted out the door.

Arthur watched everything, but his mind was muddled by the pain of the wound in his back, and his head dropped to the floor from the effort of trying to make sense of it all. He was able to glimpse Guinevere's feet as she rushed over to Merlin and clutched the wizard's robes.

"Merlin, please," she begged, "Arthur has fallen. He won't last much longer. Lancelot is broken. Gone. I've done what you've asked. I've earned your reward. Please, tell me! Where is my father?"

But the wizard's eyes were cold as he said, "Poor, poor Guinevere. I fear that King Vortigern will be none too pleased when I tell him of your treachery."

Guinevere's jaw clenched in frustration and tears streaked down her cheek as she scowled at the old man before her. Finally, Merlin sighed.

"Well, all right. I am not an unfeeling man, after all, and you have earned something," continued Merlin. "I'll give you a short head start, my dear. Perhaps you can reach King Vortigern before I. Perhaps you can explain all this unpleasantness. I would love to see you try."

The lady's face fell with disappointment, and she allowed herself to sag for a single moment in her desperation. But then Arthur watched as she lifted herself up again, and pulled together the determination that had kept her alive for so long against all odds. Guinevere spat at Merlin, then turned and dashed out of the cottage.

Merlin didn't even bother to wipe the small amount of spittle out of his beard as he approached Arthur, who was still lying in a heap on the floor. The young man lifted himself slightly onto his forearms and felt a new stab of pain. Arthur winced, but he wasn't looking back now. He'd come this far, and even though he was now alone, he vowed to fight on. He struggled to lift himself as he faced the wizard.

Merlin seemed to have his own plans, however, as he surveyed Arthur's efforts to lift himself and continue the fight. The wizard swept his hand through the air, and a glimmer caught Arthur's eye. He turned his head and saw his sword lifting up off of the ground and floating toward him.

Pointed right at his heart.

"Hmmm. Klærent the Stonebourne. The sword from the stone," said Merlin. "Only the true king was supposed to be able to draw this from the stone. It was supposed to be the birthright of the man who was meant to bring peace to the land. It was supposed to guide him. To aid him. To help him with his quest to save this poor, wretched country..."

Then Merlin shrugged.

"I guess it made a mistake."

He pushed his hand through the air, and urged the floating sword forward. It flew straight at Arthur, who braced himself for the piercing blow. But—

"NO!"

The sword buried itself into the stomach of Gawain, who had finally freed himself of his bindings, and now threw himself in the path of the deadly blade. Klærent the Stonebourne now sunk deep into the man's flesh, and became still.

With a burst of adrenaline, Arthur forgot all about the pain in his back, and worried only about the pain of his companion. His mentor. His old friend. The only person he felt he could really trust.

In the frenzy of the battle and the madness of the enchantment, Arthur had barely taken notice of Gawain, but the war-weary knight must've cut himself free on his own sword, which Arthur now glimpsed still buried in the wall. As Arthur had fought against Merlin with singular focus, Gawain had thought only of Arthur.

With shaking hands, Arthur pulled the sword out of Gawain and tossed it aside.

"Gawain... Hold on..." Arthur said as pushed his hands desperately at the wound, hoping to staunch the lifeforce that was flowing all too freely.

Gasping from his wound, the knight looked into the eyes of the king that he would never get to see ascend to the throne. Without words, both of the men understood it wouldn't be long now.

"I finally get to die..." said Gawain with a slight smile on the face that was rapidly losing its color, "for my King."

The grizzled knight's hand fumbled as it dug into his belt. He drew out a crumpled handkerchief with crushed yet still beautiful embroidery. Gawain forced the piece of cloth into Arthur's hands and then said with his last breath,

"Be a good king."

And the life disappeared from Gawain's eyes.

A few moments passed before Arthur noticed the soft footsteps shuffling toward him. He turned and saw Merlin shaking his head at the sad sight before him.

"I'm sorry, Arthur, but it doesn't seem as if you're destined for greatness after all. Guinevere betrays you. Lancelot abandons you. And now the only one who believed in you lies dead. Is it really worth all this to you?" asked Merlin. "Just to sit upon a throne?"

Snatching up his sword, Arthur forced himself to his feet and faced the wizard.

"Even alone. I will fight you with everything I have," Arthur said with determination flashing over his tear-streaked face. With that, he raised his sword and prepared to fight to the bitter end.

"No," said Merlin, holding up a hand, and although there was no magic behind it, Arthur paused. Then the wizard continued, "I see your end coming. More terrible than you could imagine. I'm sorry, Arthur, but to kill you would too kind."

With that, Merlin picked up his wooden staff and his musical voice wafted on the air.

"Upon the wind,

The rain's own shroud.

Fly through the air,

On darkest cloud."

The robes, the beard, and the long white hair all dissolved before Arthur's eyes and transformed into a dark mist. The storm cloud that was once an old man floated up to the roof, wafted through a hole in the ceiling, and was gone.

And Arthur was left alone.

~   ~   ~

CHAPTER 36

The Wrong Kiss

Guinevere emerged out of the strange choking forest and onto a rocky beach. The waves of the sea crashed into the boulders that dotted the shoreline, and churning waters slowly ground them down into fine smooth sand over the course of a thousand years. Guinevere didn't know which way to go. She had stabbed Arthur in the back. She had betrayed Vortigern. She had failed in finding the location of her father.

Desperate to move and needing to make some decision, any decision, Guinevere turned and raced along the beach with the sea raging beside her.

"Guinevere! Wait!" came a voice.

Lancelot emerged onto the beach and chased after her. She stretched her legs and forced her muscles to outrun him, but it was no use. In no time at all he caught up to her, and grabbed her arm. The knight's strength was enormous and he spun her to look at him. Despite being unbalanced and confused, Guinevere's hands flew to her dagger. She drew it and raised it for a fight.

"Can we stop trying to kill each other for one moment?!" Lancelot demanded, and he stripped his sword arm away and tossed it to the sand.

"Tell me why I shouldn't kill you," challenged Guinevere. "Tell me how my life is any better with you still alive. Tell me what I should do now!"

"Leave here with me," said Lancelot, with his weapons stripped away and his soul laid bare.

It wasn't often that Guinevere was caught off-guard, but this did it. Her mind raced as she tried to get to the bottom of his most unexpected request. Was this just another one of his pompous overtures? Did he think that she needed him that badly? That she couldn't take care of herself? Or was there something deeper behind all of this?

"You and I aren't meant for this world," he continued. "After this, we can be done with Arthur. And maybe... we can finally rest."

He took a step toward her, and for the first time Guinevere truly looked into his eyes. Dark blue, and as turbulent as the ocean behind them. Ever since the moment when Guinevere had been told that Lancelot could be vulnerable to a ladies' charm, she had put her guard up around him, assuming he was just another philandering conqueror of women. But now as he got closer to her and she felt his hot breath tickling her neck, she understood the power he truly had over women. Whereas Arthur was a singularly strong and beautiful man, Lancelot was a different kind of beast altogether.

"What about your lost arm?" asked Guinevere, trying to sort through her suddenly muddled thoughts.

Lancelot hooked her with his incomplete arm, and cradled her in the crook of his elbow. Suddenly he was kissing her. It wasn't the tender, soft, loving kiss that she had been taught to expect as a lady. It was a rough, burning, all-consuming kiss.

After a moment that lasted an eternity, they broke apart.

"There are other ways for a man to feel whole," the incomparable knight said.

Guinevere dropped her gaze as she placed a hand on his chest and gently pushed Lancelot away. She was tired of fighting, and wanted to collapse into his arms and be warm and safe and simply to sleep forever. Yet she knew that she still had work to do, and she couldn't stop yet.

Not yet.

"You may be able to forget your arm. But I can't forget my father," she said as she took a step away from him.

"And so you'll just run away? Back to Vortigern?" asked Lancelot.

"It's not running away. It's retreating to favorable territory," Guinevere said.

For some reason the words seemed to overcome him with a fervor. He took a step toward her, and she didn't step away. Her breath came out as a thin fog in the cold night air, and it mingled with his.

"If you get into trouble, I'm not sure I can save you," said the knight.

"I'm not some silly little girl anymore," said Guinevere. "I don't wait for a brave knight to ride in on a gallant steed and rescue me."

She kissed him once more, but softly this time, the way that a proper lady was supposed to kiss a dashing knight. And it felt all wrong.

"You feel whole to me," she said to him as she placed a soft hand upon his wounded, mangled right forearm.

With that, Guinevere turned and dashed away along the wild sea that, given enough time, could wash away any and everything in its path. Lancelot didn't chase after her.

~ ~ ~

CHAPTER 37

Farewell to a Friend

Arthur held his torch high in the clearing of the forest that he had found back near the camp. He was exposed. He was unprotected. He was vulnerable. He didn't care. As he gazed upon the lifeless body of Sir Gawain lying atop a large pile of carefully stacked wood, all of Arthur's concerns vanished. At this moment, he wasn't plotting his rise to the throne. He wasn't concerned with the battles that he still had before him. He wasn't looking ahead to some grand and difficult future. He was just missing his friend.

"I should have listened to you from the beginning," said Arthur. "I should have questioned the sword. Maybe I wouldn't have had to trust Guinevere and Lancelot. Maybe then you'd still be with me."

He touched his torch to the funeral pyre and the flames began to consume the small twigs that lay beneath Gawain's body. Slowly they spread out to the tangled kindling. Then the longer branches. Then the strange pagan trinkets. The wooden beads, the metal trophies, the misshapen adornments. The wild beard and the war-beaten armor. It was all consumed as the flames danced upward and tickled the sky.

"I swear, I will be the King you believed me to be."

Arthur watched as his friend disappeared into a burst of radiant red, yellow, and orange heat and floated up into space and beyond him.

~ ~ ~

CHAPTER 38

Vortigern Victorious

Vortigern was surrounded in gold and jewels and rubies and diamonds. At his fingertips were candies and sweets and crystallized fruits. There were clothes and books and paintings and toys and statues and even a funny little spring thing that he wasn't exactly sure what to do with. Everywhere he looked there were prizes, tributes, and gifts.

But Vortigern was unhappy.

The wizard stood beside him, and the old man's words burned in his mind.

"I am so sorry, Great King, but I have the most distressing of news for your regal ears," Merlin had told him. "Guinevere is a betrayer."

Then Merlin had gone on to describe a confrontation he had just had with Guinevere, and all the events leading up to it. Each word cut deeper and deeper into the king.

The doors of the throne room swung open, and after a short glance at the wizard who stood at his shoulder, suddenly Guinevere was there and she was boldly striding toward him. Despite the copious stains upon his own garments, Vortigern couldn't help but look upon her tattered and dirty clothing with disdain. He couldn't help but note, however, that her hair was as shiny and well-maintained as ever. Delicate, complicated braids wove and danced around her head, and there was nary a hair out of place. It seemed to be mocking him.

"Guinevere," he said, pointedly avoiding her eyes, and casting his gaze downward like a sullen child, "I expected you back hours ago."

The lady strode confidently up to his throne, bended a knee, and bowed her head to him.

"My king, I come to report a brewing conspiracy," Guinevere said. "Arthur is planning an attack."

"With your help," Vortigern muttered under his breath, but still loud enough that she and everyone else in the room could hear him.

"No," stated Guinevere plainly. "I misled him. I—"

"WITH YOUR HELP!" the king cried, and suddenly he was yelling and his furious tirade was tumbling out. "I could scarcely believe it. You knew how important this was. I'm about to rise as the king of all the kings. And you nearly ruined it. And I gave you so much! Dresses! And flowers! And pearls! And love! You were like my own daughter!"

Guinevere's mouth fell open as she tried to find the words to respond to him. However, Vortigern wasn't interested in her excuses. She had hurt him deeply. He had trusted her and she had betrayed that trust. That wasn't the kind of thing he could just forgive. He was the king, after all. With a sloppy wave of his hand, he motioned for two of his guards to grabbed Guinevere.

"Please! I've stayed loyal. I turned on Arthur," she cried as the guards seized her roughly by each arm. "Merlin, tell them!"

But Merlin stood as a silent sentry alongside Vortigern.

"Toss her in the dungeon," said the king. "When the sun burns brightest, so will she."

Guinevere struggled against the guards, but she was just a woman. Just another woman. She could never have overcome them. With small consolation, Vortigern watched as she was dragged hopelessly toward the doors. She was nearly gone, down into the dungeon, sent to her doom, and out of his life.

At the last second, she shouted, "My father! Please! Where is he?"

With a wave of his hand, Vortigern signalled his guards to halt. The dutiful, loyal guards obeyed his command as they always had, as a good servant always should. And they held the traitorous woman tightly as she called to Vortigern from across the grand throne room.

"If you are truly done with me, my king," said Guinevere, "then you have no more use for holding my father. Please, let him go. Don't continue to punish him just to control me."

Vortigern took a moment to consider her request. He was a good king and he was fair, or so he told himself. He owed it to the lady to at least think on her words. And he saw that there was sense in them.

"Very well, Guinevere. I shall release your father," said Vortigern, his moping voice now transforming back to his usual serpentine hiss. "So he can burn with you."

"No!" sobbed Guinevere, and the tears of indignation that flowed out of her eyes gave Vortigern no pleasure. No pleasure at all. Not even a little bit.

Vortigern waved a hand, and the guards dragged Guinevere away. As she disappeared out of the throne room, Vortigern pulled himself together. He sat up straight. He wiped the tears away from his eyes. After all, no one ever said it was easy being the king.

~ ~ ~

CHAPTER 39

Lancelot's Departure

The hut looked so tiny, and yet Lancelot felt so small within its feeble clay walls. As he stepped through the creaking wooden door, his eyes took in all of the familiar sights. The uneven, cobbled chairs. The rain-warped roof. The large black cauldron softly simmering over the quietly crackling fire. And the old woman slowly stirring the smooth surface of the oddly glowing stew inside.

She turned at the sound of Lancelot's footsteps, and gazed at him through her white eyes as she croaked softly, "I knew I'd see you again."

Her unstable feet and crooked back stumbled slowly toward him, and she tenderly reached out a surprisingly soft wrinkled hand. She caressed his rough cheek, and a ripple of something Lancelot could not describe tickled his senses. He had come to warn her to get out before Vortigern's army stormed through the village, but he hadn't expected that once he got here he would feel so warm, so tired, and yet so peaceful.

"You have to go," said Lancelot. "By tomorrow it won't be safe here for you anymore."

"Look at me. Does it look like these old legs will get far?" she asked, shaking her head. "But you could stay. You could protect me."

He was afraid that she would say that. After watching Guinevere disappear the night before, Lancelot had raced off into the darkness, and finally decided for certain that he would leave the kingdom. He was going to run for miles, hours, as far as his legs could take him. Once his back ached and his lungs could no longer hold any breath, Lancelot intended to ignore it and keep going anyway. He was going to strive on and on and not look back.

Then thoughts of the old woman crept into his mind. At first he tried to drive them away, but they came back stronger and more insistent. He owed her so much, and he knew that he couldn't leave without at least warning her. Now that he had heard her words, her pleas for him to stay, he wasn't sure that he could abandon her.

Lancelot took out the book that he had tucked into his belt. It was the book he had stolen from Merlin, and it was filled with strange archaic writings and ancient incantations. He held it up to the old woman, hoping to make her understand.

"This book could hold the answers I've been looking for," said Lancelot. "This could finally make me what I was. But it'll take me far away from here. To places that no man should journey to. It will be terribly dangerous, do you understand? And I might not survive."

The old woman's face fell, but she nodded silently.

"Do what you must," she said.

In a way her simple acceptance was harder to ignore than anything else she could have done. Lancelot wished that she had cursed his name. Or that she had argued desperately with him, and tried to manipulate and trick him. Or even that she had wept in despair. Those things he could battle against and stand strong, but as he watched her turn away quietly and begin to hobble across her tiny hut, he broke.

"Curse it all!" he bellowed. "Come with me! I'll take care of you. I owe that to you. Just as you took care of me once."

She turned back to him, and shook her head. Once again, it was a small restrained gesture, and Lancelot could barely understand how she kept so calm.

"You still haven't found what you're looking for," she said as she crossed back to him. The simple effort of crossing back and forth across the room was taking a toll on her, and she breathed heavily as she touched his wounded right arm. "I started you along the path. I bear the responsibility for it. And I must accept that. You can't stay for me, and it was silly of me to ask. You have to go and find what you've lost. And until you do, I can't go where you lead."

"If you stay here, you will die," said the knight who owed so much to the tiny decrepit woman who stood hunched over before him.

She just smiled sadly, and once again gently shook her head.

"My time is coming," she said. "As sure as the winds and the rains will always come, so too my destiny is on its way. And I must wait here to meet it."

Lancelot placed his left hand on her shoulder. Then he lifted up her chin, so that he could look into the cloudy, nearly white eyes. He smiled at her, and she could see enough to smile back.

"Thank you for everything," said Lancelot, pausing before uttering her name: "Morgana."

Then he turned and was quickly out the door. The old woman's smile curled the edges of her mouth, and if Lancelot had stayed a moment longer, he would have noticed that a small bit of emerald green coloring had broken through the cloudiness of her eyes, simply at the mention of her name.

~ ~ ~

CHAPTER 40
Arthur, King of None

Arthur was exhausted. He was only eighteen, barely a man, and he felt like he had seen too much. Only a year ago life had still made sense. Things were clearly laid out for him, and it seemed like he was destined for greatness without even trying. Now he wasn't even sure if he wanted to be king anymore.

The two people he had convinced himself to trust had betrayed him, and were now gone, possibly forever. His closest advisor was dead. And before him was the promise of a massive slaughter of his people. Vortigern's army was poised to strike down anyone who even hinted at opposing him. Worse yet, after crushing any defiance in this kingdom, Vortigern was on the verge of uniting all of the other rogue kings and villainous lords throughout the entire country, and maybe even further. It would be an unmatched empire and if he wasn't stopped here, it was possible that he could never be stopped.

And Arthur wasn't sure if he could do it.

As he slowly limped back into his camp, the impossible odds weighed on Arthur's mind, and he wasn't sure if he had the strength to stand up to the king who had plotted his father's downfall and turned Merlin against him. He looked at the state of the camp, and saw that there were still smoldering tents and shelters. The rubble of fallen tree forts was still strewn upon the ground. Arthur had barely been able to protect this place against Guinevere and Lancelot. How could he possibly hope to protect the entire kingdom against a madman's army?

But the few strong, capable men that Arthur had at his command, his knights, were doing their best to pick up the pieces. A brief smile crossed Arthur's face at the sight of this small band of good men. His smile quickly faded, however, as he thought about the larger, more vicious army at Vortigern's command. Arthur's chivalrous knights were thoroughly outnumbered by the blood-thirsty Saxons who threatened to overrun the kingdom that the knights had sworn to protect.

Catching sight of Arthur staggering into camp, Percival dropped what he was doing and rushed to his leader's side. Arthur warmed at the sight of his loyal followers, and wished that he was better able to reward them for their goodness, but that wasn't destined to be.

"Arthur! Are you all right?" said Percival, breathing heavily and nervously. "You look… You look… uh…"

"I'm fine, Percival," said Arthur, then added with a small laugh, "and I'm aware of how I must look. It's very kind of you to spare me the details."

"All of the explosives are gone," reported Percival. "I can't believe Guinevere used them all. It seems like the entire place would be decimated if she had. We thought there was enough here to take down a mountain."

Arthur smiled at the swiftness with which Guinevere must've been able to act. For a moment, Arthur thought with fondness of the sweet, beautiful girl he had grown up with, and the strong, capable woman she had become. He wondered if he would ever see her again.

"Percival, I need you to gather the men. I need to talk to them all. I need to rally them all for battle," said Arthur with no tone of anger or annoyance in his voice. It was a simple command that he issued, and yet it was costing every bit of strength he had to give it.

The thin knight's already pale face lost even more color, but Percival swallowed and said, "Arthur... It seems hopeless. Our camp is in tatters. Our armory is depleted. If Lancelot and a woman could nearly undo all of this, how can we stand against Vortigern's army?"

Arthur nodded in understanding. These were all the same concerns that had been running through his head for some time now; but he said again, "Gather the men."

Percival nodded dutifully and began shouting to the various men to gather round. He hustled about and commanded the others to come and hear Arthur's words. For his part, Arthur barely heard what Percival was saying as he found a collapsed tree fort that had fallen in just such a way as to provide a makeshift stage that stood a few feet off of the ground. Arthur climbed up onto it and then turned to face the small group of men and women that had heeded his calls and had come to hear him speak.

"For a long time, I thought that because of who my father was, I knew who I was," began Arthur. "I thought that I was destined to be king just because my father was king. I thought that because his royal blood flowed through my veins, I was meant to rise above all others and rule these lands and all the people in them. But, I realize now, our lives aren't determined by our blood: they are determined by our hearts."

Klærent the Stonebourne weighed heavily on Arthur, and he drew out the grand, beautiful sword and held it out for all to see.

"The sword of destiny. The sword of peace," continued Arthur as he examined the fine weapon. "I was sure that this sword was meant for me. That I was meant to wield it and finally ascend to the throne with a blaze of glory and riches. But I was wrong. This sword wasn't meant for me."

In the corners of his eyes, Arthur saw his men shifting uncomfortably. One or two of them whispered to each other, and questioned what was happening. Arthur ignored it as he fell silent for a moment, then took a deep breath and urged himself on, his words now ringing with all the strength and conviction that he could muster.

"This sword is meant for you. This sword is meant to protect those who cannot protect themselves. This sword is meant to strike down tyranny. This sword is meant to free this kingdom!"

Arthur raised the Stonebourne high in the air, and it caught the sun's rays and showered light upon all who were there to see it. His courage was rising now, and Arthur could feel that his knights were now starting to share in his spirit. New life and energy was coursing through them all.

"I am no better than any of you. I was simply born lucky. But that does not make me suited to rule you. It makes me suited to serve you. Tomorrow, I will ride out with you. Not as your king. But as your equal. As your friend. And together we will free this kingdom! My brothers, my sword is yours!"

Once again Arthur thrust the sword high into the air, and the cheer that received it was deafening. The strong men who were his knights lifted their swords in solidarity. The tired, hungry women wept. The old and weary men straightened their backs a little taller as they were filled with hope. The children laughed and yelled, and all of them would dream that evening of becoming knights themselves, so that one day they could also serve this great king.

Arthur leapt off of the platform and strode forward into the crowd. All of those people who had heard his words reached out their hands to touch him for just an instant. His knights fell into step behind and around him.

At this moment, Arthur stood on even ground with those that had sworn their loyalty to him. He was nowhere near to a throne. There was no crown upon his head. He didn't wear armor flecked in gold.

But from that instant onward, throughout all history, he would always be remembered as King Arthur.

The king and his knights entered in the long mess tent, and Arthur led them over to the round table that he had shared with Guinevere and Lancelot.

"We will all sit at the round table," said Arthur. "I want to hear all of your voices, and see all of your faces."

But as they got closer to the table, they all realized uncomfortably —

It looked pretty small.

Arthur stopped for a moment and had to admit to himself that while this table was suitable for three people, there were dozens of them now. One of these days, he decided, he'd have to get a much larger Round Table. In the meantime, he admirably hid his abashedness, and said,

"Maybe we could all just sit in a circle for now."

~   ~   ~

CHAPTER 41
The Second Siege

Guinevere had no way of knowing it, but the spot where she was currently chained up in the middle of the castle courtyard was very close to the same spot that Lancelot had lost his arm. That ominous fact probably wouldn't have given her any pleasure on this day in which the sun climbed high in the sky and beat down mercilessly on her with its unceasing heat. Her wrists throbbed uncomfortably and her arms were painfully twisted behind her and forced around the tall wooden post that stood behind her. Her legs and feet ached from perching upon a large pile of wood that would soon make her day much hotter.

The only relief for Guinevere was that the post beside her was bare.

It was a small consolation, however, as Guinevere had been dragged out of the dungeon hours ago, shoved against this post, and left there. She now had no idea how long she would have to wait for her doom. As the hours had passed, the sun had climbed overhead, but there was still no sign of Vortigern. She wouldn't have put it past him to let her simply stew under the hot sun for days so that her torture could be drawn out a bit longer. The fact that the courtyard had remained mostly empty seemed to confirm her worries. Guinevere had assumed that her execution would be a large, public humiliation, but so far there had only been a few guards to keep her company. She was guessing that she'd be stuck here for a long while before the real show began.

Suddenly the doors on the king's balcony opened and two trumpeters strode out. They raised their brass instruments high and blew a heralding song. Apparently Guinevere was wrong, and she was bound to face the king sooner rather than later. She took a deep breath and braced herself for the worst.

In his finest, least stained robes, Vortigern emerged out onto the grand balcony, and he wasn't alone. Behind him were about a dozen men that Guinevere didn't recognize. Nonetheless, they were clearly the type of men that she wouldn't like to the run afoul of. One of them carried two curved scimitars. Another wore a cloak with a bear's head hanging off the back of it. Definitely not the kind of people to be taken lightly. And yet Vortigern led them all to the edge of the balcony with an air of importance.

He swept his arm in a wide gesture as he said to them, "My dear and distinguished friends." Several of them seemed to bristle at this address, but Vortigern continued as he pointed down at Guinevere, "This woman has been found guilty of the basest—"

"I'm still loyal to you!" cried Guinevere, cutting off the king's pronouncement.

Vortigern gritted his teeth, and tried to ignore her as he continued on, "—of the basest treason. She will be the first to perish on what will be—"

266

"Please, King Vortigern," cut in Guinevere again. "Please, you don't have to do this."

" —on what will be a glorious—" and he tried to press on.

"Show some mercy!" called Guinevere, breaking Vortigern's speech once again. Finally, it seemed to have been too much, and Vortigern spun to scream at her.

"Silence!" he shouted, and once again several of the men behind him seemed to bristle at his undignified outburst. "You have been condemned to die. You are not allowed to speak. I don't want to hear anymore from you!"

Guinevere ignored him as she looked to the empty post beside her and asked, "Have you at least chosen to spare my father?"

Vortigern laughed, clearly thinking he'd regained the upper hand as he said, "My dear, I wouldn't wish to deprive you of your last reward."

The king motioned to his guards below. Guinevere craned her head around to watch as they opened a small door along the courtyard. Two massive, ugly brutes trudged into the courtyard, and they dragged behind them a frail old man with wispy silver hair. Guinevere gasped at the sight of her father. He looked sickly thin and could barely walk as his captors pulled him toward the spare post beside Guinevere.

"No! Father!" Guinevere cried as she struggled uselessly against her shackles. Then she turned and shouted at Vortigern, "Show some mercy!"

"And what mercy did you show me when you BROKE MY HEART?!" screamed Vortigern.

Leodegrance was shoved against the bare post, and his skeletally thin arms were wrenched behind his back as heavy manacles were roughly clamped upon his wrists.

From the decadence of his over-looking balcony, Vortigern sneered and said, "I'm sorry, Guinevere, but I couldn't deny my friends here the pleasure of watching you both die, before—"

"A poor crowd for our execution," Guinevere cut in again, and to be honest, she was starting to enjoy it now. "Have your servants lost their taste for cruelty?"

"I wouldn't say that," Vortigern said through gritted teeth at her interruption. Then he yelled, "COME!"

This time a massive metal gate was opened, and finally the courtyard began to fill. The Saxons warriors that entered were all enormous, hulking, fierce, and terrible. Their massive chests were bare in order to expose garish displays of burns, brands and scars. As they entered by the dozen, many of them sneered and Guinevere saw yellowed teeth ground down to look like fangs. Vortigern's army looked like a nightmare ready to be unleashed.

Now Vortigern addressed them as he shouted, "My good men, this woman has betrayed us all. She dares to stand against your king and the great society I seek to establish under my rule. The fire that burns her must also burn in you. Take it out into the country and use it to incinerate any and all treachery. Light her!"

A black, hooded executioner with torch in hand entered the courtyard. He began walking toward Guinevere and as he did, she heard a small whisper, and she turned to see her father smiling weakly at her.

"My beautiful Guinevere, don't be scared," he said, nearly collapsing from the effort of it all. "We're together again. You found me. And now I will always be with you."

The executioner was getting very close.

"Don't worry, Father," said Guinevere. "We're going to be all right."

But from high on his balcony, Vortigern laughed.

"Guinevere, do you really want your final words to your father to be a lie?" jeered Vortigern from the safety of his overlook. "Or do you really think one of your heroic friends can still save you?"

"No," said Guinevere as she finally tossed her manacles aside just as the executioner drew within her reach. "I don't wait for a knight to save me."

She had actually picked the cuffs hours ago, but to keep up her ruse, she had had to hold the heavy, awkward manacles in place throughout her long captivity. Her hands and fingers ached from the long effort, but there was no time to dwell on it now. She had to make her move quickly. In a flash, Guinevere flipped her dress up and grabbed the dagger that she had concealed there so long ago. As she stabbed the executioner, she silently thanked Vortigern for being so besotted with her that none of his guards were brave enough to search her thoroughly. As the executioner fell, she grabbed his torch and the crossbow he had at his hip. Knowing that her long hours of training with the deadly weapon would now pay off, Guinevere ripped a piece of fabric from her dress, wound it around the arrow, lit it, and fired.

The flaming arrow arced high into the air, cleared the castle's wall and disappeared.

It all took Guinevere less than five seconds, and the stunned looks on the faces of all the men around her showed that she could've even taken a bit more time. Everyone looked even more confused, however, as they considered her actions. She could almost read the thoughts on their faces as they tried to figure out what she had just done and if she had really gone through all that trouble just to shoot an arrow into the air.

"I admit, I had expected more," said Vortigern.

"Just give it a moment..." Guinevere muttered to herself as she betrayed a hint of her own nervous impatience. It was taking longer than she had hoped.

"Seize her," ordered Vortigern. "Take pleasure in ripping her limb from limb."

The front row of Saxons leered as they began to take long steps toward her. Guinevere was getting nervous now. The Saxons were just a few feet away. Any moment. Guinevere gripped her dagger and prepared to fight the entire army herself when—

BOOM!

A massive explosion rocked the entire castle, and the stone wall that she had just fired over was blown to rubble. Huge hunks of rock and debris came raining down, much of it pelting the Saxon army, and Guinevere noticed that several of the warriors were rendered unconscious or even crushed. There was now a gaping hole left in the side of the castle, and just outside of it everyone could see the edge of the looming black lake.

With mouth agape, Vortigern watched the devastation from his balcony and cried, "HOW?!"

"You said so yourself, my king," said Guinevere. "It took me hours to get back here last night. Did you think I was idle?"

It was true that she had been busy in that short amount of time. After leaving Merlin's cottage, and after her brief encounter with Lancelot, Guinevere had raced back to the rebel camp and gathered up all of the explosives that were left. It was quite a considerable amount, almost enough to level a mountain. It hadn't been easy, but she managed to get it back to the castle and set it up against the quiet deserted corner that had been her preferred location for clandestine meetings due to the fact that it was rarely visited.

Vortigern still struggled to put it all together as he asked, "But why? Now you have nowhere to escape but into the lake!"

"You still don't understand do you, Vortigern?" she shouted. "I'm not trying to get out. I'm letting him back in."

"Who?" asked Vortigern, but his question barely had time to leave his lips when—

"ATTACK!" roared Arthur.

Everyone in the courtyard turned to see a small fleet of tiny boats gliding across the surface of the lake. Arthur and his men had arrived. They were dressed in beautiful suits of armor with their swords held high and ready for battle. The boats approached the large hole in the castle's defenses that was Guinevere's handiwork, and suddenly they were pouring in with Arthur at their head.

The second siege of Tintagel had begun.

The Saxon army spun to meet the invaders. It had been a stroke of luck that they had come into the courtyard without their armor on, but they never would've been caught without weapons at their sides. The towering, sneering warriors drew their long swords, clubs and axes and they charged at Arthur and his knights. They all met with a clash of steel that reverberated through the stone courtyard and into the history books.

"Cut them down, men!" Arthur ordered his loyal battle-ready men. "Today will be the day Vortigern falls!"

From the relative safety of his balcony, Vortigern shrieked, "Kill them! Slay Arthur! Slay the woman! Slay her father! Kill them all!"

The villains who had stood behind Vortigern were now headed for the door. The mad king spun and yelled at them, "Where are you going? This is just a minor skirmish! My men will conquer them and I'll emerge stronger than ever!"

Most of them didn't even pause their flight at his words. Only Yder stopped long enough to glare at Vortigern. "If you survive this, my blades will bathe in your blood."

Then the lord with two swords turned and swept away. Vortigern was alone. For a moment, he looked off of his balcony and surveyed the chaos of the battle below. He didn't like what he was seeing.

And so he too fled.

From her position down amongst the battle, Guinevere had seen Vortigern escaping into the castle. She knew there would be time for him later, but now her only thoughts were for her father. She turned toward his post and saw that Leodegrance was still painfully bound there. She also saw a particularly vicious-looking Saxon lumbering toward him.

"I've never killed a royal before," he grunted, but then was silenced as Guinevere rushed up behind him and buried her dagger in his back.

"And you never will," said Guinevere, and with a swell of pleasure she added, "No one will ever touch my father again."

The Saxon fell dead. Guinevere quickly rushed to the far side of her father's post and began to work at his cuffs.

"My God. Guinevere," sputtered Leodegrance. "You killed him."

"In these dark times, only the strong survive," said Guinevere, and her father's chains fell away.

"We can escape here together, my darling," the old man said. "I can help you. We can finally be free of this madness."

"Just finding you means I am free," said Guinevere, softly touching her father's face. It felt so good to finally be able to touch him again. "But we must get you away from this battle."

She realized it would be no easy task as Leodegrance stepped forward on frail, wobbly legs. They had barely moved when three more Saxons began to close in on them. They looked to be on the verge of attack, until Arthur himself arrived and the future king cut through the three barbarians as if they were nothing. As the Saxons fell, Arthur locked eyes with Guinevere and he smiled. Guinevere couldn't help but marvel at just how beautiful he was.

"Sir, I have three men whose only duty is to get you to safety," said Arthur, extending a hand to Leodegrance. "We better get you out of here."

"Yes. Yes, a good idea," said Leodegrance, then turning to his daughter he added with a wink, "I always liked this one."

Guinevere beamed at her father, and bade him good-bye with a soft squeeze of his hand. Three of Arthur's knights appeared, and created a small perimeter for her father. Guinevere watched them take hold of Leodegrance's arms and lead him toward safety. Guinevere longed to go with him, but she knew that her work was far from done today.

She leapt back into the battle and helped dispatch a Saxon as she fought alongside Arthur. It felt right to be at his side.

"You look good for a man who's been stabbed in the back," said Guinevere.

"Barely a scratch. I'm not going to say it didn't hurt, but no lasting damage. Your plan was perfect," said Arthur. "I'm just sorry it didn't work."

"It worked as well as I could've hoped, even if it didn't fool Merlin into trusting me. Vortigern was still angry enough to bring my father into reach, and now he's safe," said Guinevere, and then she added with a shrug, "And sleeping in the dungeon wasn't too bad."

Guinevere ducked and bobbed as she killed two more men almost just to prove that she still felt fresh, strong, and ready for battle.

"Nonetheless, I'd hoped this might cheer you up," said Arthur as he reached into his belt. "I promised to return it."

Arthur held out a familiar, slightly crumpled handkerchief. Guinevere tried to give him a witty reply, but suddenly her words were failing her. She did her best to blink back tears as she took the small piece of cloth from Arthur's outstretched hand.

"Thank you," she managed, and then she was thankful for the opportunity to kill a Saxon who had chosen that moment to attack her. It gave her a moment to wipe her eyes, and she was suddenly glad to have the handkerchief back for that very reason.

"Is Merlin here yet?" asked Arthur, pretending quite well that he didn't see her cry.

Guinevere and the man she hoped would be her future king looked up to the skies and saw that dark storm clouds were blowing in and starting to blot out the hot sun.

"Something tells me he's on his way," said Guinevere.

"We must get to Vortigern. Maybe we can stop them before they can raise the Red Dragon," said Arthur.

And the two of them, the king and his lady, turned and faced the battle together. Side by side their blades flashed and they slew any enemy that was foolish enough to try and stand between them and the terrible challenges that stood ahead. Yet without knowing it, they both silently vowed that no matter what stood in their way, they would face it together until the bitter end.

~ ~ ~

CHAPTER 42

The Wizard, the Dragon, and the King

Arthur and Guinevere burst into the throne room. Several guards had been stationed alongside the mighty doors, and though they sprang upon the united lovers, Arthur and Guinevere quickly and easily slew them as they strode onward toward their ultimate goal.

Vortigern stood beside the throne that he couldn't hope to hold much longer, and rummaged through his boxes of gifts as he tried to load up his arms with as much as he could carry. He seemed to have heard Arthur and Guinevere's noisy entrance, however, as he turned to face them. He dropped his armloads of treasure, and drew himself up to his full height, managing to strike an impressive figure despite the stains on his once regal robes. Arthur reminded himself that Vortigern may have gone a bit soft during his time on the throne, but he was once a powerful warrior and a gifted swordsman who had been able to go head-to-head with Uther Pendragon himself.

And now Arthur was really looking forward to cutting him down.

"Your time is at an end, Vortigern," said Arthur.

"I'd prefer to be called '*King*,'" Vortigern sneered.

"You won't be a king much longer."

"We shall see. I wouldn't count on your victory yet. For I still have many weapons at my disposal." And Vortigern's face twisted in anger as he shouted, "MERLIN!"

Suddenly the ceiling exploded above them. The stone cracked and was blasted apart as a bolt of lightning careened down into the center of the room and blasted the seal of the king that was deeply embedded in the floor beneath Arthur and Guinevere's feet. Arthur had realized at the last moment what was happening, and just as the lighting struck, he was able to shove Guinevere out of the way to safety. But it was at his own cost, and Arthur took the main brunt of the blast. It tore through him, and sent him flying across the room until he slammed roughly against the far wall.

Guinevere rushed to Arthur's side, and it was an indescribable comfort to him to have her there holding his hand. He focused on her, forced himself to breathe, to stay awake. Just for her. Just for her.

Across the room, the voice of the mad king and the wizard sounded as if they were coming from across an ocean, but Arthur made out the words.

"Merlin, it's time to end a long slumber," commanded Vortigern. "Raise the dragon."

The wizard's voice came next as it unnaturally floated through the air amongst the chaos outside.

"In cold, wet lake,
your power mires.
Now rise again,

278

to breathe your fires!"

Arthur struggled to keep his eyes open as he saw Merlin raise his crooked wooden staff into the air. There was a deafening crack of thunder that shook the air and caused even more of the ceiling to crumble in upon itself. As the thunder faded away, it was replaced by a new sound. A deep, resonant rumbling and Arthur knew they were too late. Vortigern and the wizard had won again, and all was soon to be lost.

~ ~ ~

The battle in the courtyard raged on, and Percival was beginning to feel like the hero that he had never felt himself to be before. Between Arthur and Uther Pendragon before him, Percival had been a good and loyal knight for nearly ten years now. He was smart and hard-working and had dutifully gone through years of training. But he had never felt like he had any particular skill with the sword. Until today. Suddenly it made sense, and the blade was flying wherever he bade it. He felt quicker, lighter, stronger, and more confident. He felt like a real knight.

Nevertheless, Percival knew that the odds were not good. Before they had set out for this dangerous mission, Arthur had clearly explained to Percival and the other knights that there would be hundreds of Saxons against their meager numbers. The Saxons were vicious and powerful and would kill with no mercy. But Percival didn't care today. His sword couldn't fail. And he was sure that he was going to emerge victorious.

"Hold strong, men!" yelled Percival, and he was surprised that he felt just as brave as his voice sounded. "Courage will win the day!"

"Percival, do you hear that?" asked one of his brother knights.

For a moment Percival paused in his fighting, and trained his ears to cut through the sound of a hundred swords clashing. There was clearly an unnatural rumbling sound that had followed the terrifying crack of thunder a few moments earlier. But now there was something more. Strangely enough, it sounded like a soft gurgling.

Percival turned and looked through the demolished castle wall, and saw that the surface of the black lake was beginning to bubble and break. After a few seconds more, the waters were churning, and white caps outlined the building waves that were crashing against the castle walls. And then Percival's heart jumped into his mouth as he saw it.

The first scales of the massive reptilian head broke through the surface of the water. Now the crown of its head was rising. Now the yellow eyes were visible, and the three-foot-long fangs, and the gigantic arching neck, and the huge leathery wings. The beast that had chased Percival through his nightmares for the last year had reawoken.

The Red Dragon was back.

The dragon arched its back and came up to its full height, towering into the sky, and stood at least fifty feet high. Percival, the other knights, and the Saxons were all hit by a spray of water, as the dragon spread its wings to their fullest span and shook off the water from the lake. Then the monster opened its terrible jaws, drew a breath, and unleashed a shriek that ripped through the air and froze Percival on the spot.

Then came the fire.

A tongue of flame shot out of the dragon's mouth straight up into the black sky above, and it was like a pillar of brimstone splitting the darkness overhead. The dragon beat its massive wings and soared upward, circling above them and driving all hope of victory from Percival's mind.

"Courage... will win..." said Percival once again.

But he didn't feel nearly as confident as before.

~ ~ ~

Guinevere held Arthur's hand and she felt the electricity flow through her. As she touched Arthur's skin, the hairs on her own arm raised.

"You took the blast for me," Guinevere said as she touched Arthur's side and found the spot where the lightning had hit him. Her hand came away covered in blood. "Why?"

"I remembered..." said Arthur, struggling with the words, struggling even to breathe, but locking his eyes with hers. "Through fire or storm, I will always come to your side."

The words from their childhood, from a life that they never got to live together, struck a deep chord within her. If they somehow got through this, Arthur would be a king, and lead the country and his people, and shoulder impossible burdens, and achieve amazing triumphs. But to her, he would always be the boy she had learned to ride horses with.

Guinevere leaned in and kissed him tenderly. A loving lady kissing her courageous king. And it felt right. It felt perfect.

"Poor, poor Guinevere," hissed Vortigern as he stepped nearer and shattered her moment of peace. "I will never understand why you chose to throw your lot in with him. I could've made you the most powerful woman in a century."

Vortigern and Merlin were slowly approaching where Guinevere sat cradling Arthur. Vortigern clicked his tongue at her as he drew nearer. But Guinevere looked to Arthur, and she noticed that his eyes flickered, just for an instant, to his right. And Guinevere saw it. Klærent the Stonebourne was still clutched tightly in Arthur's right hand, although he had no strength to lift it.

"An army. A dragon. A wizard. A kingdom," Vortigern said. "How could you hope to overcome all that I wield?"

"Well, you know…" she said as she spun with Arthur's legendary sword clutched in her hands, "one thing at a time!"

And with all her furious strength, Guinevere buried the Stonebourne into Merlin's stomach. It was hard to tell who was more shocked, the wizard or Vortigern. It was quickly clear, however, who was taking it harder, and Merlin crumbled to the ground from his wound.

"I feel like I should've seen that coming…" whispered Merlin, and the old man sighed a great breath and his eyes closed.

Guinevere rose to her feet and there was fire in her gaze. Vortigern stopped in his tracks, and even took a step back as he was stunned by her terrifying visage. The lady, however, wasn't moving back. Never again.

"You've kept me in fear," said Guinevere. "Made me do terrible things. Haunted my nightmares. Today we end it."

Her words carried so much power and fury Vortigern actually stumbled backward. Then in a moment of desperation, he buried his hand into the nearest box he could find.

And pulled out an old, rusty sword.

Vortigern looked at the meager weapon, then he looked at Guinevere.

And he decided to turn and run.

Guinevere was stunned. Kings weren't supposed to run away. She turned and looked to Arthur lying wounded on the floor. He was struggling, but he was able to force himself into a sitting position, and he nodded to her to go. That was all the encouragement Guinevere needed, and she sprinted off in pursuit of the king.

~ ~ ~

The skies had flooded with storm clouds, completely obscuring the once bright sun, and covering the courtyard in thick oppressive darkness. A heavy rain was beginning to fall, turning the ground to mud beneath Percival's feet. Yet he and the other knights continued to fight valiantly on.

But with each passing second, it looked more and more to be a losing battle.

"Hold strong, men!" shouted Percival. "Gather round and close ranks."

Percival had always been stronger with tactics than with an actual sword, and now he fell back on a simple battle maxim. There was strength in numbers. His fellow knights crowded around him and they all stood side by side, shoulder to shoulder, and back to back. For a fleeting instant, Percival had the image of a herd of cattle crowding together against the cold wetness of a storm. For the moment, however, it was a good move. They were still outnumbered by the oncoming hordes of Saxons, but now the brutish barbarians could only come at them one at a time, and each of the knights could help defend their brothers' flanks.

There was no doubt to Percival that they had managed to thin the numbers of Saxons. There was also no question, however, that he had lost several men of his own. And his small number of knights was far more precious against the overwhelming Saxon horde. With pangs of remorse, Percival glimpsed his fallen brethren sprawled out unceremoniously in the mud. Percival vowed to them that as long as he drew breath, their sacrifice wouldn't go unhonored.

I'm just not sure how much longer I'll be drawing breath, thought Percival ominously.

His fellow knights were standing strong, however, and their strategy of standing together seemed to be working for the moment.

Any Saxon that drew near quickly met his demise at the sure blade of one of the knights, or was easily defended away. As Percival struck down two oncoming barbarians in quick succession, he began to feel hopeful again.

Until the Red Dragon touched down in the courtyard.

The claws of its back legs sunk into the mud as it landed behind a group of Saxons. The Saxons might've been big and dumb, but they were at least smart enough to scatter when a dragon stood behind them. As the color drained from his face, Percival and his brave comrades found themselves facing off against a fully grown dragon. And although he wasn't sure if he was imagining it, the beast looked very hungry.

It sat back on its haunches and lifted its head as it drew in a long, rattling breath that could only mean one thing.

"Shields..." commanded Percival feebly.

He and his men lifted their trusty shields and placed them end to end, trying to form the best barrier that they could. And once again, Percival placed his desperate hope in the strength of numbers.

~ ~ ~

The battlements were slick with the fallen rain, but Guinevere's footing was sure as she emerged along the top of the castle walls. She had pursued Vortigern as closely as she could, but he had a huge head start. Even as she pushed herself to the limit, she had only been able to catch glimpses of the fleeing king's dark cloak as he whipped around corners, and several times she had to make her best guess as she followed his flight. Fortunately, she knew the castle at least as well as the Vortigern did. It was only in the last year that she had become acquainted with the lower depths of dungeons and hidden chambers. But she had spent her childhood with Arthur exploring the many halls and corridors of the upper levels. They had shared many happy afternoons seeking out the tallest vantage points so that they could glimpse the furthest corners of the kingdom they one day planned to rule. Now she had returned to the highest defenses of the castle, but with the same intention of claiming the kingdom as her own.

But she had lost Vortigern.

As the rain washed over Guinevere, she scanned the battlements that stretched across the top of the castle wall. Vortigern was nowhere in sight. There was no way that he could've crossed the wall already. For a moment Guinevere wondered if he had thrown himself off it, and she thought it would've been a fitting end to a cowardly king. She wasn't able to enjoy the thought for long.

As the oak door shut behind her, Vortigern leapt forward and seized her from behind.

He had been crouched and hiding behind the door, and Guinevere cursed herself for not checking there. Hadn't she known that Vortigern liked to lurk in dark places, and that he didn't mind lying down in the filth?

With a strength that she hadn't expected, Vortigern grabbed her by the shoulders, lifted her in the air, and then viciously slammed her to the ground. His entire weight pressed down upon her as she struggled to free herself.

"You dare challenge me here?" he yelled, looking as mad as she had ever seen him. "This is where I rose to the throne! This is where I killed Uther!"

"This is where kings go to die," she fired back.

Guinevere drew her dagger and stabbed at Vortigern. He was too quick, though, and he caught her wrist and forced it down to the hard stone floor beneath them. Then with his free right hand, Vortigern seized Guinevere by the throat and began to choke the life from her.

The rain was pouring down on them now, and Vortigern's hair and beard dripped from the deluge. Guinevere, too, was soaked, and her thick, tight braids had filled and were starting to come apart. Her always composed appearance was washing away under the relentless assault of the raging storm.

"I would've given you everything," said Vortigern as he squeezed the life out of her. "I could've showered you in gifts, power, and love."

Guinevere couldn't tell if it was just the rain streaming down Vortigern's enraged face, or if there were tears mingled in there as well. She could tell, however, that he was tightening the killing grip upon her throat.

~ ~ ~

In the ruins of the throne room, rain was streaming in through the hole in the mighty ceiling, and the piles of treasure beneath were becoming a sodden mess of stolen bounty. A peal of lightning illuminated the room as Arthur struggled to his feet. He pressed himself against the wall, and used it to force himself upright. Gingerly, he took an uneasy step and was pleased to find his strength returning. He took another step and another as he headed toward the mighty doors of the throne room, and back out to the battle which he meant to rejoin.

"Is the King already abandoning his throne?" came an ancient voice from behind Arthur.

The young king turned and saw Merlin also rising to his feet with Klærent still stuck in his belly. The wizard seemed to be taking his injury much easier than Arthur, however, as Merlin casually drew the sword out of his stomach and tossed it aside.

"You seem to have worked so hard to get here," said Merlin. "The throne stands unoccupied. The gold and riches are within your grasp. And yet you seem determined to leave it all behind. Interesting."

"No, you're right," said Arthur as he faced Merlin. "I think I'll stay. There seems to be work for me to do here."

Courage and anger flooded into Arthur, and it gave him strength. He stood tall and ignored the flashes of pain in his many wounds. It had been a tough few days for Arthur, but now, as he prepared to take on the wizard, the end was near at hand. One way or another, Arthur was finally going to see this through.

"You betrayed my father," said Arthur. "He trusted you, and you led him to his downfall. And you allowed a madman to plunge this kingdom into terror. I will fight you until my last breath."

"Strong words, my boy," mused Merlin. "However, your last breath may be sooner than you think."

Merlin raised his crooked wooden staff toward the hole in the ceiling, and there was a fresh strike of lightning and a new crash of thunder. Then the wizard's voice was carried by the storm:

"With wind and rain,
The land deforms.
No man is safe,
From my dark storms."

Suddenly the rain through the hole was a deluge, and massive winds came gushing in through the ceiling. It whipped through the throne room and instantly the piles of gold, jewels, paintings, gowns, and diamonds were lifted into the air and began to swirl. Arthur leapt and seized hold of Klærent as he rolled. He landed in the center of the room, and Arthur slammed the sword downward, plunging it deep into the floor atop the king's seal.

The winds were tearing at Arthur's skin, and he was being pelted mercilessly by flying treasure as a tornado formed within the throne room. Merlin stood near the throne itself, urging on the storm, but Arthur gripped his sword tightly as he braced himself against the storm. The Stonebourne held tight within the seal, as if it had returned to his home.

"How long do you think you can hold on, Arthur?!" cried Merlin, his magical voice riding upon the winds and seeming to come at Arthur from all sides.

"A king must never give up!" Arthur yelled back into the storm.

Arthur's feet left the ground as the winds pulled him upward, but Klærent remained his faithful anchor, and he summoned strength he wouldn't have believed he possessed. It was the strength of kings, and it flowed through his veins and swelled in his muscles and gave him ironclad belief that he would prevail.

"You truly believe you can be king?!" laughed Merlin. "You couldn't even keep your closest followers safe. Did not Sir Kay grow restless and die by your carelessness?"

With all of his might, Arthur wrenched his body and forced his feet back to the ground. He crouched low and braced himself against the terrible winds and the still buffeting treasure. Finally, he felt to be on solid ground, and he shouted defiantly back at Merlin.

"I failed to lead Kay, I admit it," he said. "A king must listen to his people."

Then with indefatigable determination, Arthur drew his sword out of the stone floor, and just as quickly he stabbed it back down again. This time, however, Arthur stabbed it two feet in front of him. He was now two feet closer to Merlin. Two feet closer to victory.

"You allied yourself with murderers," said Merlin. "How does that befit a king?"

Arthur raised his sword once more and stabbed it forward yet again. Another two feet closer.

"Guinevere and Lancelot are good people," said Arthur. "They may have lost their way, but their hearts were pure. A king can always find the best in his people."

Another stab. Another two feet.

"You let Gawain die for you," taunted Merlin.

"There will always be men willing to die for their king," said Arthur. "But a truly great king must be willing to die for his people."

Through the black winds of storm, Arthur was now close enough to see Merlin clearly. He wasn't close enough to strike at the wizard yet, but Arthur was close enough to lock eyes with the terrible magician, and Arthur glared at him as he declared,

"But I won't die today."

~ ~ ~

Flames danced around the edges of the united shields of the huddled mass of knights, but they held together bravely against the onslaught of fire that poured out of the Red Dragon's jaws. Many of the men had fallen already, and those who still stood seemed to be on the verge of collapse. But they only needed to wait a short while longer.

Lancelot was on his way.

He was the greatest knight in a thousand centuries, and he was flying to the rescue at incredible speeds. His short black hair bristled as he sped through the sky toward the Red Dragon and the battle of a lifetime. Lancelot's heart throbbed in his chest as he anticipated finally clashing with the terrible red beast, and finally getting his chance to slay a dragon.

Of course, it helped that he was currently riding a dragon of his own.

Lancelot clutched the pointed spine of a long, sleek White Dragon that streaked through the sky, racing toward Tintagel castle with its defiant purpose. The knight thrusted his sword arm forward, and urged the White Dragon on. Then Lancelot drew a deep breath and released a jubilant battle cry. The White Dragon caught his spirit, opened its mighty jaws to emit a majestic roar of its own, and together their cheer tore through the air.

The bellow of Lancelot and the White Dragon caught the attention of everyone in the courtyard of Tintagel Castle. Percival, the knights, and the Saxons all turned and looked to the skies to see Lancelot and his dragon streaking toward them. The Red Dragon also spotted them with its yellow eyes, and let out a shriek as it beat its wings and rose into the air. With a tremendous flap, the Red Dragon struck the air with its great leathery wings, and it surged forward in the direction of the White Dragon.

Lancelot felt electricity surge through his veins as his White Dragon charged at the red one, and all who looked on knew that an epic joust was about to ensue. The two dragons grew closer.

Closer.

Closer.

And suddenly they clashed.

Their battle raged high in the skies as they spit fire upon one another, and each tried to sink its fangs into the other's neck, and they clawed and slashed and ripped and tore with their razor-sharp talons. There was a symphony of bellowing roars and strangling shrieks as they each fought for supremacy. The two dragons raged and wrestled, and no one who watched from the ground could tell which held the upper hand.

And Lancelot was relishing every bit of it.

As the dragons battled, Lancelot clung to the back of the white one, and despite only having one arm, he never for a moment considered the possibility that he might let go, or that he might be bucked off. Amidst the flames and biting and scratching, Lancelot showed incredible strength and skill as he scaled the scales of his white beast. The greatest knight in the kingdom reached the top of the white head, then with a bellowing war cry of his own, he flung himself from one dragon onto the other.

"Who's the greatest knight now, Gawain?!" Lancelot shouted to the sky as he flew weightlessly toward the Red Dragon and landed with a crash atop its long snout.

The Red Dragon shook its terrible head and tried to dislodge the knight, but Lancelot would have none of it. He had gone to hell and back to bring the White Dragon here. And now Lancelot was exactly where he wanted to be: staring eye to massive yellow eye with the Red Dragon.

Lancelot braced himself against the ten-foot-tall horn that protruded from the Red Dragon's skull, and the knight drew back his sword arm.

"I couldn't have done this with two arms!" yelled Lancelot with a deep sense of satisfaction.

Then he plunged his sword arm all the way to his shoulder, deep into the Red Dragon's eye. The Red Dragon reared up into the air with a shriek of agony, its back arching in misery, and it came crashing down to the earth.

~ ~ ~

Vortigern lunged back in disbelief as he watched the Red Dragon tumbling lifelessly from the sky, and Guinevere finally saw her chance. The king's strangling grip slackened as the dragon crashed into the castle wall, and reduced it to rubble as it collapsed into the courtyard.

"NO!" screamed Vortigern in despair and rage.

Finally able to draw breath, Guinevere said to him with relish, "Your wizard's fallen. Your dragon's slain. Now it's your turn."

The mad king's black eyes glared at her in hate, but he was too blinded by anger to foresee her action. Guinevere reached up, and with savage pleasure she raked her fingernails down Vortigern's cheek and tore at the soft flesh. Vortigern dropped his jaw and screamed in pain.

In that instant, Guinevere spit.

A small wax capsule flew out of her mouth and landed in Vortigern's.

With a fierce upward jab of her hand, Guinevere cracked Vortigern's jaw shut. His teeth slammed together painfully, and he jolted backward, tumbling off of Guinevere. She was finally able to fill her lungs, and she watched Vortigern's eyes fill with terror as he brought his fingertips to his lips. The yellowing, filthy fingernails came back coated in a thick, black liquid.

"You—you... How?" the mad king sputtered.

"I simply had to wait for the perfect moment. And this was perfect," Guinevere said. "Good night, my king."

Vortigern collapsed against the short stone wall. His throat gurgled with the choking, black poison, and his breath became a weak death rattle.

"You were... supposed to be... mine," he said.

The pouring rain streamed down Vortigern's face and streaked his fine garments, but it was unable to wash away all of the stains and sins of his reign of villainy. Guinevere watched with a deep sense of triumph and relief as King Vortigern breathed no more.

~ ~ ~

Inside the throne room, Merlin urged the storm on. Its winds whipped and howled and beat mercilessly upon the young man who was crouched only a few feet away from the wizard. Merlin had to admit he was impressed by Arthur's resilience.

The boy may have what it takes to be the king after all, thought Merlin as he raised his staff high over his head once more. *Perhaps his father was right all along.*

Nonetheless, the wizard felt it was his duty to continue Arthur's trial by fire. Merlin twisted his staff and commanded the winds themselves, and behind him the grand throne was lifted up into the air. It rose high and floated just above Merlin's head as he asked, "Do you truly think you are prepared to take the throne?!"

Then with a wave of his staff, Merlin sent the massive, ornate golden chair flying toward Arthur. It sliced through the air like a golden blur headed straight for the boy who wanted so badly to be king.

But Arthur drew his sword out of the ground, and with a mighty swing he halved the flying throne and sent the pieces careening away, where they crashed unceremoniously against the walls.

"I'm not doing this for the throne!" shouted Arthur as he charged toward Merlin. "I'm not doing this for the crown! Or the castle! You can even take away the gold, and the title, and the glory, and I will still fight you with every bit of strength I have within me."

Arthur thrust the sword of legend forward, and pierced Merlin in the lower right abdomen.

"I do this for the people," said Arthur as the winds died away and the storm finally broke.

His power gone, Merlin slumped to the ground. Yet he looked up at the vision that was King Arthur's regal face, and the wizard thought,

Does everyone know about the appendix?

~ ~ ~

The rain had stopped. The black clouds were turning gray as the sun fought to break through the din. And the Red Dragon lay dead on the ground.

Percival could barely believe what he had seen. He glanced at the knights who stood beside him, and he saw that they all shared the same looks of amazement and disbelief. Then he turned his head the other way, and his momentary relief vanished.

There was still an army of massive, hulking, vicious Saxons. They still outnumbered Percival and his friends by at least four to one. And, more than ever, they looked thirsty for the blood of knights.

Percival, who had never been known for his bravery, raised his sword and said, "The job's not finished, men. Let us fight with every last breath we can muster."

His fellow knights raised their swords in unison, and together they prepared to face the terrible odds, when they heard a booming voice call to them,

"Ho! Percival!"

Knight and Saxon alike all turned to look at the carcass of the fallen Red Dragon, and they watched as a tall, bare-chested warrior slid down the nose of the dead beast and began to make his way toward them. Lancelot strode casually over to Percival, and it was as if he didn't even notice the army of gargantuan Saxons standing at the ready a few feet away.

"Percival?" said Lancelot again, seeming as though he couldn't believe his eyes. "You stayed? You fought?"

Not knowing what to say, Percival simply nodded.

"I am impressed," said Lancelot. Then the greatest warrior in all the land turned to take in the horde of brutes. Lancelot didn't seem worried as he said to Percival, "What say we live to fight another day? By killing them all instead."

Percival opened his mouth to respond, but he was quickly silenced by the jeering from the Saxon army.

"Nothing would make me happier than to cut them down, Lancelot," whispered Percival, "but we're still hopelessly outnumbered."

Lancelot laughed as he said without the least bit of concern, "But you've got the greatest knight in the kingdom. And this time —
"

Here Lancelot nodded upward just as the majestic, sleek form of the White Dragon landed and perched itself atop a nearby wall.

" — I've got the dragon."

The courage was coursing through Percival now. The sneering was gone from the Saxons. And Lancelot was pointing his sword arm defiantly.

"Men, let's raise hell! CHARGE!"

As Lancelot roared, so too did the dragon, and Arthur's knights pelted forward into battle. From that day until the end of time, Percival would be remembered as the courageous knight who stood beside the mighty Lancelot as they cast the Saxon hordes out of the lands of Briton. And no one, not even Lancelot, remembered that there once was a time when Percival wasn't considered among the bravest men in the kingdom.

~   ~   ~

His legs shuddered slightly from exhaustion as Arthur stood over the defeated wizard, and grasped the hilt of his sword which still protruded from Merlin's abdomen.

"Who told you?" gasped Merlin. "Gawain? Guinevere? How does everyone know about my weakness?"

"You're not as clever of a man as you think you are," said Arthur, as he pulled the sword out of Merlin and added, "And I also know how to defeat you once and for all."

The weak old man lay crumpled on the ground, looking up through his bushy eyebrows, and he caught Arthur's gaze. Merlin's eyes softened and twinkled, and Arthur finally saw the kindness that he had remembered in his childhood. Certainly Merlin had been strict at times, and he had a habit of forgetting Arthur's birthday, or he said he did anyway. However, Arthur couldn't forget that when he was a small child who was still discovering the world, Merlin would spend hours answering every question that could occur to a boy of four. Some of the questions were simple and some would've challenged the greatest philosopher, but Merlin always sat patiently and did his best to reward Arthur's curiosity. It was that man who Arthur saw now, despite knowing that the wizard had become an enemy who must be destroyed.

"You are ready..." said Merlin, and it seemed like his way of telling Arthur that everything would be all right, "to be King."

"I believe I am," said Arthur, although for the first time he understood the terrible weight of that destiny.

"I swore an oath long ago to your father that I would prepare you," said Merlin. "Today I have fulfilled that oath."

Unsure if this was a final trick from the crafty wizard, Arthur wavered as he raised his sword.

"You spoke to me through the sword and stone. You made me a killer," said Arthur.

"Yes, I did. I knew that you needed to act, but your good heart may have made you wait too long," explained Merlin. "And Vortigern was becoming too powerful."

"So you guided me to take out some of Vortigern's top men. But why would you send me after Guinevere?" asked Arthur.

"Hmm, an excellent query... Why would I send you to the one person who could heal you?" asked the old man, turning the question wisely. "So that you could be healed, of course. And, maybe, so that you could heal her too."

"No, you threw her and Lancelot at me," Arthur said, shaking his head.

"I had to bring the three of you together. I had to put you through fire in order to test you. In order to strengthen you," explained Merlin. "It won't be easy being the greatest king in the world."

"I can't trust you," said Arthur.

"I've understood what my role was for a long time," said Merlin. "Do what you must."

"You're too powerful to live."

"Ah yes, that is quite true," agreed Merlin, but then he added ominously, "but am I too powerful to die?"

Then Merlin closed his eyes, and laid his head down upon the floor. Arthur raised Klærent the Stonebourne high into the air and struck fast and true, and the wizard exploded in a burst of light.

Arthur knew it wasn't over, though. He slowly ascended the three steps where the throne once sat, and retrieved the crooked wooden staff that Merlin had dropped. Reverently, Arthur took it in both hands as he considered whether or not to banish the wizard forever.

Then, quickly and unsentimentally, Arthur cracked it over his knee and tossed the two old pieces of wood aside.

~ ~ ~

CHAPTER 43

The Rise of King Arthur

Just as the sun broke through the clouds, so too did Guinevere emerge into the courtyard of Tintagel castle. As she stepped around the boulders of demolished castle walls and past the fallen bodies of warriors from both sides, she couldn't help but feel a piercing remorse.

The castle has looked better, she thought. *But at least it's over.*

In her fist, she still clutched the long golden dagger. When she had first held it, the dagger had shocked her. Now it fit so well in her hands. With a flush of pleasure, she flung the weapon to the ground in revulsion, and hoped that it would be forever.

A ray of sunshine fell upon her face, and for a moment Guinevere stood there and basked in the light. She lifted her hand and touched the warm spot on her cheek, and as she did, she brushed aside a strand of hair that had come loose from her carefully woven braids. Almost without thinking, Guinevere's fingers climbed into her hair and she began to pull the perfect braids apart. Her long, beautiful brown hair tumbled down in a jumbled thicket of tangles. Some of it still held the shape of the braids, some of it went nearly straight, some was still smooth and rich, and some of it was an utter mess. There were bits that had been bleached blonde in the sun, there were bits that were still the color of the day she was born, and there were bits that had turned gray and would never be anything but. Guinevere shook her head, and her hair rustled in a soft breeze. And she felt free.

Across the courtyard, Guinevere saw the lifeless body of the Red Dragon, and beside its crooked, oddly peaceful head stood Lancelot.

"You finally got to slay the dragon," said Guinevere as she limped over to him.

"Finally," said Lancelot.

"Of course, you couldn't have done it without the book from Merlin's cottage, which I told you about," Guinevere teased him. "So really... I slayed the dragon."

Lancelot turned his back on the dragon, and Guinevere felt herself blush slightly as she saw Lancelot's eyes feasting upon her. He reached out his left hand and ran it through a strand of her now tumbling hair. Guinevere's cheeks went warm again, even though there was no ray of sun upon them now.

"I'm impressed that you were able to survive and make it back with the dragon," said Guinevere, by way of breaking what was quickly becoming an uncomfortable silence. "Tell me, what happened on your journey?"

"I'll tell you..." he said as he puffed up his chest, but then he sighed and added, "...another time. That's a great tale that deserves the proper time to tell it. Let's just say that it all ended well."

Guinevere nodded in agreement, then she tenderly touched Lancelot's sword arm.

"This seems to suit you now," she said.

"Maybe even better than my old arm," admitted Lancelot.

"So..." she dared to ask, "will you be able to rest now?"

"I don't know —"

He suddenly moved in close to her. Really close. And she felt his hot breath tickling her neck.

"Can we?" he whispered softly, longingly.

The warm, confused, befuddled feeling swept over Guinevere again, and her mind felt as if it was in a fog. Lancelot was coming nearer, and she wasn't stopping him. It felt wrong, but she wasn't stopping him. Their lips were so close now, but—

"Well, we certainly know how to make a mess, don't we?" came Arthur's voice.

Guinevere stumbled away from Lancelot and spun to see Arthur slowly navigating his way through a pile of rubble in the courtyard. His head was down, apparently doing his best to stubbornly avoid any unforeseen obstacles. His hand was at his side as he clutched his wounds, and Guinevere's heart went out to him. She dashed away from Lancelot without a backward glance, and she hurried to Arthur's side.

"So the wizard wasn't quite dead?" she asked as she propped herself under Arthur's shoulder.

"No," said Arthur. "I appreciate you leaving him for me. And thank you for softening him up."

"The wizard. The dragon. The mad king," Guinevere said with a half-smile. "I deserve a medal."

"The new king will see to it. For you and for Lancelot," said Arthur with a good-natured nod, then looking around he added, "Where is he?"

"He's just over there," Guinevere said, but as she turned to point, it quickly became clear that Lancelot was gone. Her eyes scanned throughout the courtyard, but he was nowhere to be found.

"I wish him well," said Arthur. "He wants to be the greatest knight of all time. And I believe he will be. But he has more dragons to fight. More damsels to save. More demons to wrestle."

As Arthur spoke the White Dragon rose up into the air. It had been on the other side of the wall, and from the water that dripped from its mouth, it seemed to have been quenching its thirst in the black lake. It stretched out its wings, let out a mighty roar, and then began to fly off into the distance.

Guinevere couldn't help but notice that, once again, the White Dragon had a knight riding upon its back as it soared off into the distance and disappeared.

"I'm guessing we'll see more of him," Arthur said to Guinevere with a knowing wink. "Whether we want to or not."

Guinevere nodded. She looked around at the demolished castle that was once her childhood home and then her adulthood prison, and she wondered what was to become of it under its new king.

"How will you rebuild all of this?" asked Guinevere.

"I won't," was his simple reply. "Let it lie in ruin."

Arthur hobbled forward to the hole in the castle wall, and Guinevere followed behind him. He stood at the edge of the lake and gestured out into the distance. Guinevere gazed out and saw a seemingly never-ending expanse of lake and field and forest and mountain. It stretched out beautifully before them, and was full of possibilities.

"I have a vision," Arthur began, "of a castle on a hill. The greatest, most beautiful kingdom the world has ever known."

"What will you call it?" Guinevere asked.

Arthur took a deep breath, full of importance and meaning, and then said, "I have no idea."

Guinevere smiled, and she looked into the face of her king. He turned to her, and took her hand in his.

"So what do you think?" he asked.

"About a new castle?"

"No. About a new beginning."

Then King Arthur leaned toward his Lady Guinevere and kissed her, and their great adventures began.

~ ~ ~

EPILOGUE
The Broken Staff

The once grand throne room lay in quiet ruin. Moonlight poured in through the broken ceiling and illuminated the fallen rubble and cracked regal seal. All manner of treasure was scattered about in a mess of stolen riches. Even the throne itself lay in scattered pieces after being crushed against the wall.

Suddenly a quiet shuffling of footsteps disturbed the stillness of the room, and an old woman with milky white eyes crept slowly through the piles of rubble. Carefully, so as not to fall, she wove a path through the mess until she finally reached the treasure that she sought.

The two broken halves of a wooden staff.

Her gnarled hands stretched out and grasped the twisted wood, and she lifted it up so that the two broken ends touched. Then she spoke, and though her voice was thin and tired, it floated magically on the air.

"Push back the years,
The days, the hours.
Restore my strength
With thy dark powers."

The two ends of the staff connected and shone blue, and as she raised the delicate light toward her face, her skin was bathed in the unnatural rays, and it slowly began to change. Her ancient face softened and stretched tight. Her wrinkles disappeared. The milky whites of her eyes gained new color. The gray wispy hair darkened and became thick. In moments, she had become decades younger, more beautiful and more terrible.

Newly restored, Morgana, Queen of the Feys, erupted into cold mirthless laughter, and as her emerald green eyes flashed, she plotted the destruction of the newly risen King Arthur.

~ ~ ~

THE END

~ ~ ~

For more of

THE LEGENDS OF KING ARTHUR

look for these installments:

Book 1 - THE FIRST ROUND TABLE

Book 2 - GAWAIN AND THE GREEN KNIGHT

Book 3 - LANCELOT OF THE LAKE

Book 4 - THE MIGHT OF EXCALIBUR

Book 5 - TRISTAM AND ISEULT

Book 6 - GALAHAD AND THE GRAIL

Book 7 - THE FALL OF CAMELOT

~ ~ ~

AUTHOR'S BIO

Ben Gillman is an L.A.-based novelist and screenwriter. He's been a fan of Arthurian legend ever since "First Knight" (starring Sean Connery as King Arthur) became the first movie he ever saw twice in the theatres. In college he studied English Literature and immersed himself in Arthurian legends as told by Thomas Malory and T.H. White. Now he's the writer of dozens of action-adventure novels and films, as well as many comedic sketches and plays. He lives with his wife, Vered, in Southern California.

Made in the USA
Monee, IL
22 July 2020